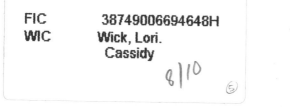

W9-AEB-175

LORI WICK

Cassidy

HARVEST HOUSE PUBLISHERS

EUGENE, OREGON

About the Author

LORI WICK is a
multifaceted author of Christian fiction.
As comfortable writing period stories
as she is penning contemporary works,
Lori's books (6 million in print)
vary widely in location and time period.
Lori's faithful fans consistently put her series
and standalone works on the bestseller lists.
Lori and her husband, Bob,
live with their swifly growing family
in the Midwest.

All Scripture quotations are taken from the King James Version of the Bible.

Cover photos © Panoramic Images / Getty Images; Stuart McClymont / Stone + / Getty Images;
Jane Nelson / Photodisc Green / Getty Images

Cover by Dugan Design Group, Bloomington, Minnesota

CASSIDY
Copyright © 2007 by Lori Wick
Published by Harvest House Publishers
Eugene, Oregon 97402

ISBN-13: 978-0-7394-8680-1

Printed in the United States of America

For A.J. and Emily—
How blessed we are to have you.
I love you both.

⇥ ACKNOWLEDGMENTS ⇤

To the special people who added to this book in so many ways...

- LaRae—What an amazing time we had with you on an amazing trip in an amazing state. As you said, it was like traveling with family, for you certainly are. Thank you so much, dear friend.

- Helen Ann—"I don't want to go to bed; I want to be in bed." Thanks for a delightful quote. I love you, Mom.

- Jack and Stella—It was wonderful to dine with you, Jack. You are a treasure. Thank you for the lovely hospitality, Stella. The story of the two of you and also of the moose are among my favorites.

- Todd—Those reminders about gasping and yawning are amazing to my heart. Thanks for being someone who gasps at God's holiness and goodness.

- Phil—Wonderful words on the life of Paul. Thanks for the encouragement to double our efforts. It gives us all hope.

- Bob—Oh, the places we've been. I didn't know what kind of ride it would be, but it's certainly been fun. I'll keep riding shotgun if you'll stay at the wheel. It doesn't matter where we go, as long as it's together.

Token Creek, Montana Territory
June 1880

CASSIDY NORTON, THE PROPRIETRESS of Token Creek Apparel, adjusted the shoulder of the brightly patterned dress she'd been working on and then stepped back a little.

"How is that, Mrs. Potts?" she asked the woman wearing the dress.

Mrs. Potts frowned into the full-length mirror and said, "It's still crooked."

Cassidy could not see what the woman was talking about, but she stepped forward to make another adjustment. She pinned and shifted and stepped back again, her brows raised in question.

"That's better," Mrs. Potts conceded. Cassidy smiled. She hadn't moved it much, but she had learned early on that pleasing the customer was paramount to her business.

"How is the waist?"

"It's good," the woman said, but she was still frowning into the mirror. Her face cleared enough to ask, "When will it be done?"

"In the morning."

"Not today?" she questioned, the frown returning.

"I thought you needed it Friday," Cassidy reminded her.

"I do. I just hoped to have it a few days early."

"Wednesday morning *is* a few days early," Cassidy said sweetly.

Mrs. Potts actually smiled. "It is, isn't it?"

Cassidy laughed a little, and the other woman shook her head.

"If all of your customers are like me, Cassie, I don't know how you keep from losing your mind."

"I love my customers," Cassidy said sincerely, helping Mrs. Potts out of the dress. "You included."

"I'm glad to hear it. God was smiling on Token Creek the day you came to town."

Cassidy thanked her with a laugh, made a few notes about some mending the woman wanted done, and then saw her out to the front of the shop. She wasted no time settling back at the sewing machine, finishing Mrs. Potts' dress in less than an hour. Cassidy was happy with the results and thought Mrs. Potts would be as well. She knew the other woman would return in the morning and pay in full. Mrs. Potts was one of her best customers.

That dress done, Cassidy was free to work on the other projects waiting for her attention.

⚜

"Hi, Brad," Cassidy said, greeting Brad Holden, the tall cowboy who had just stepped into her shop an hour after lunch.

"Hey, Cass," he said quietly, looking a little uncomfortable.

"Something I can do for you?"

"Maybe," he said cryptically, his eyes shifting around the rather feminine establishment with its small covered chairs, lacy curtains, and bolts of fabric.

Cassidy smiled and waited. Brad's eyes roamed the room a bit and then met hers. His own smile broke out when he saw the amusement in Cassidy's eyes.

"All right," he chuckled, his voice resigned. "I knew I would catch it if I came in here."

Cassidy laughed but repeated her offer.

"Yes," Brad said this time. "I want something for Meg—something pretty and comfortable."

"Is she already uncomfortable in that dress we remade?" Cassidy asked, frowning a little. She had just helped her friend, who seemed to increase in size daily, open the waistline on one of her calico dresses.

"No, I want something soft and lightweight that she can sleep in. She's not getting much rest right now."

"I think I have just the thing," Cassidy offered, not mentioning that she slept in the same fabric she brought from the shelf to hold out for his inspection. "You have your choice of colors."

Brad looked down at the sheer, lightweight fabrics in white, pale yellow, blue, and green. He fingered the very fine cotton, noting its near transparency. His gaze shifted to Cassidy's eyes.

"Perfect?" she asked.

"Yes. Can you make something for her? I think you must know her size."

"Certainly. If I have time, I'll bring it out tomorrow."

"You can do it that fast?"

"Unless something unexpected comes up, it shouldn't be a problem. Do you want to surprise her?"

Brad smiled before saying yes. "Leave it in your buggy, and I'll find it."

Cassidy laughed a little. He looked a bit like a small, mischievous boy just then. Brad didn't linger. Cassidy walked him to the door and then stood on the boardwalk in front of her shop and watched him put his hat back on and head in the direction of his aunt's house.

Brad's long legs covered the distance to Jeanette Fulbright's house.

Jeanette was his mother's sister and lived in one of Token Creek's finest homes. She was a widow with more energy than five women and one of the most generous people Brad knew.

Brad was in his aunt's yard when he realized his brother, Trace, was on the porch, meaning he'd just finished his own errands. Trace waited to go in until Brad joined him. Brad was older by twenty-one months, but they were often mistaken for twins. They were both tall, lean cowboys with dark hair, beautiful brown eyes, and mischievous smiles. They owned the Holden Ranch, a good-sized spread outside of town.

"You get done at the livery?" Brad asked.

"Yes. How's Cassie?"

"Fine."

"What did you need?" Trace asked.

"Something for Meg." Brad frowned a little. "She's not sleeping much."

Trace nodded, and the two men turned toward the door, not bothering to knock but slipping inside to greet Heather, one of the two women who worked for Jeanette.

"Well, boys," Heather said, smiling, a vase of flowers in her hands, "this is a nice surprise."

"Hello, Heather," Trace greeted. "Is our mother up?"

"She is. All settled on the porch. I'll tell your aunt you're here."

Brad thanked her and then followed his brother to the large sun-porch, technically a small conservatory but now "home" to Brad and Trace's mother.

Nine years earlier, Theta Holden had been severally beaten by her husband. Normally Brad and Trace's father was not a drinker, but one Saturday night Wes Holden came home very drunk and attacked his wife. The boys were still in their teens and woke to find their mother barely alive and their father hung over. It was obvious what had happened, and they had rushed her to town for help, leaving their father to fend for himself.

It turned out to be the last day they saw him. By the time their mother had been seen to and made comfortable at her sister's, their father was gone from the ranch. Had she died, he would have been wanted for murder, but Theta clung to life for almost two weeks before seeming to make a full recovery, at least physically. What no one expected was the change in her mental state, the one that could be seen in her glazed-over eyes. Theta never soiled her clothing and would eat when fed, but Heather dressed her and saw to nearly every need. She didn't speak or show any interest in books or songs. Unless urged to do so, she never moved from her chair. Few could break through the stare that had become normal. Some days having her sons visit seemed to agitate her, and they could not stay. This morning, she was completely unaware of them, but the boys still sat down and spoke to her.

"Meg was tired and decided not to come, but she'll probably see you next week," Brad told his mother, always talking as though she'd been a part of their life when in fact he'd met Meg after his mother's attack and she'd not been at the wedding. Brad added, "The baby is due in about two months, and Meg isn't feeling sick anymore."

The brothers looked at each other. They were used to this, and although it was not what they wanted, they were both glad to see their mother.

"We branded all day yesterday," Trace put in, his voice soft and deep. "The herd is growing strong, doing well."

For a moment it looked as though she would turn to Trace, but she kept staring out the window. Trace, the brothers had figured out one day, sounded the most like their father, and that was not always a good thing.

"Good morning." Jeanette appeared, hugging the nephews who were more like sons and bending to kiss her sister's cheek.

"How are you, Theta?" she asked as she always did. "It's a beautiful day."

"How are you, Jeanette?" Trace asked. "Not working today?"

"Since Cassie takes Wednesday afternoons off, and I'm at the shop all day, I take Tuesdays off."

"At that rate you'll be a woman of leisure in no time," Trace teased, and Jeanette laughed.

Jeanette's husband had been a very successful banker, and he'd left her in considerable comfort. Indeed, she still owned the bank. The part-time help she gave Cassidy with her sewing was not done for money but to get out more. For years she'd taken care of Theta on her own, but when it seemed obvious that her sister didn't know who was seeing to her needs, she hired Heather. It had been a good match.

"How's Meg?" Jeanette asked.

"Other than being a little tired, she's doing well."

"Why don't you come in for her birthday next week, and I'll put on a meal? Whom shall we invite?"

While Jeanette and Brad talked about this, Trace watched his mother. She didn't look bad—a little thin, but that wasn't the problem. It still hurt his heart that there was nothing left of the mother he had known. Her life had never been easy—his father had been a hard man to understand—but she had made a home for them. She had been constant, hardworking, and cheerful, and she'd loved her sons with every fiber of her being. She had taught them what the Bible said from Trace's earliest memory. Their father liked to go into town on Saturday night and not come home, so there wasn't always a wagon to get them to church. But that hadn't changed their mother's desire to teach them. And she didn't wait for Sunday. Any evening their father left them alone she would take out her Bible and share with them the way God had saved her and what He expected her to do with her life.

It was no surprise that both boys believed the Bible and what it said about salvation in God's Son. Their mother had not been a part of their daily lives for a long time, but they still felt her influence on them. Both men took their faith seriously, and when Brad met Meg, a woman who was serious about wanting a godly man in her life, it wasn't long before they fell in love.

"You ready to go?" Brad asked, surprising Trace.

"Sure," Trace agreed, dragging his mind back to the moment.

"Are you all right?" Jeanette asked.

"Just missing my mother," Trace admitted honestly, and Jeanette hugged him again.

The men took their leave a short time later.

***

"Is there a problem, Mrs. Ferguson?" Cassidy asked the woman who had the shop next to her. Cassidy had found that lady standing out front, frowning into the sky.

"A hornet's nest," Mrs. Ferguson answered, drawing Cassidy's eyes to the corner of the building.

"I'll get my broom," Cassidy said without delay, and the women went to work.

***

Back at the ranch, Brad saw to the wagon and team, which meant Trace was the first one into the kitchen. He greeted his sister-in-law, who sounded completely normal, but Trace could see that all was not well.

"You've been crying," he said quietly.

"You can tell?" Meg asked.

"Not at all," Trace swiftly denied, his brows rising. "Just a wild guess."

Meg laughed, but it was short-lived.

"If you can tell, Brad will notice."

"Why don't you want Brad to know?"

"He'll know I didn't take a nap."

Trace smiled. It was an ongoing battle between husband and wife, and in truth he found it endearing. His brother was trying to take care of Meg and baby her a little while Meg was insistent that she couldn't get everything done if she slept during the day.

It looked as though Meg was going to say something else just then, but they both heard the door. Giving her an amused but compassionate smile, Trace slipped away. Brad was in the kitchen a moment later.

"Hi," Brad greeted his wife before he kissed her. He looked into her eyes and saw just what Trace had seen.

"How did it go in town?" Meg asked.

"Fine. Did you nap?" Brad wasted no time in asking.

"No."

"Are your ankles swollen?"

Meg looked at him with a certain measure of exasperation and said, "Brad, I want to ask you about your mother and Jeanette."

"You can do that over supper," Brad said, having taken her hand. He led her to the living room and pointed to the sofa. "Sit down and put your feet up."

"I think I'll be all right."

Brad smiled and put his arms around her. The action was so tender that tears threatened, but Meg swallowed them back.

"Thank you for working so hard," he spoke softly in her ear, "and trying to make everything just right, but you have to take care of you."

Without warning Brad bent and lifted Meg in his arms, placing her carefully on the sofa. She wasn't lying completely back, but her feet were up, and if she put her head back, it would rest on one of the pillows she'd stitched by hand.

Meg tried one last tactic. "It's almost time to start supper."

"I'll be back for you in less than an hour. Even if you fall asleep, I won't let you stay out too long."

The look she gave him was slightly mutinous, and seeing it, Brad's gaze shifted to her legs. He lifted the hem of her dress enough to see her bare feet. There was little distinction between her calves and ankles. By the time he met his wife's gaze, his look had become stern.

"Don't you move," Brad said quietly. "I'll be back in an hour."

Meg didn't argue this time. She worried about things she wanted to get done until she fell asleep.

Cassidy closed and locked her shop door at the end of the workday and turned toward the Bank of Token Creek. It was her habit to close before the bank shut its doors for the night so she could make deposits she felt would be securer in the bank's safe.

Not even looking at the teller windows, she went to the manager's desk, smiling when the manager saw her and stood.

"Hello, Cassie," Chandler Di Fiore said, smiling in genuine pleasure at the sight of her.

"Hi, Chandler. How are you?"

"Fine. Were you busy today?"

"Steady all day. Just the way I like it. How about here?"

"A little quiet," Chandler said, counting the currency Cassidy had given him and writing the amount in her bankbook.

Cassidy took the book back when he handed it to her and studied the last total. She was doing fine with her expenses but tended to worry about the future. Having become lost in the facts and figures in her mind, it took a moment to realize that Chandler was watching her.

"I'm sorry," Cassidy said with a laugh.

"Did I make a mistake?" Chandler asked, a teasing glint in his eye.

"Not at all. I was just making sure I had figured right for the month."

"Are you going to be all right?" he asked, completely serious.

"Yes, Chandler, thank you."

"You're sure?" he asked, sincerely concerned.

"Yes," Cassidy smiled as she spoke and began to turn to the door.

"Wait a minute." Chandler stopped her. "Rylan had to cancel our men's study tonight," the banker said, speaking of their pastor. "Why don't we go for a walk?"

"What time?" Cassidy asked, liking the idea.

They decided when Chandler would come and get her, and Cassidy went on her way. For some reason Tuesday evenings tended to be lonely. Cassidy's steps were light because she knew that would not be the case tonight.

<hr />

Meg woke up with Brad's hands on her face and hair. He touched her gently, calling her name as she drifted back from deep sleep.

"Oh, Brad," she whispered. "Did I fall asleep?"

"You must have."

"I was cross with you," she said.

"I was cross right back," he admitted.

They looked at each other for a few minutes, and then Meg struggled to sit up. Brad helped her, and that was when she smelled supper cooking.

"How long did I sleep?"

"Only an hour, but Trace said he's starving."

Meg laughed a little, standing and stretching her back before starting toward the kitchen.

Meg and Brad had been married for only two years, so the men both knew their way around this kitchen. For that reason, the three of them fell to preparing the meal as naturally as breathing. Within twenty minutes, they were sitting down, Brad leading in prayer.

"Thank You, Father, for this food and the blessings we've enjoyed this day. Thank You for this family and this home. Please bless our efforts with the ranch and help us to remember that it's all from You. I ask that You take care of this baby inside Meg and that You take care of her in the weeks to come. Please provide a godly wife for Trace and help each of us to honor You in our lives. In Your Son's name I pray. Amen."

Both Meg and Trace echoed the amen, appreciating Brad's honest faith before the Lord. They passed bowls and began the meal. Not surprisingly, beef was on the menu, but so was a huge bowl of potatoes, early corn, baking powder biscuits with honey, and for dessert, a lavishly frosted spice cake.

"So how is your mother?" Meg asked the moment their plates were full.

"The same," Trace answered.

"Did that bother you today?" Brad asked, having remembered his brother's brief conversation with Jeanette.

"It did. I never just sit and look at her. We always try to talk to her, and today I realized how much I miss having her contribute to the conversation."

"But she wasn't agitated?" Meg checked. "You got to stay and speak with her?"

"Yes," Trace nodded. "It was nice in that way."

"She moved a little when Trace spoke," Brad remembered. "I still think she hears Pa. Oh," he continued, "Jeanette wants us in next week, Friday night, to celebrate your birthday. She wants to know whom you want to invite."

"Can I tell her on Sunday?" Meg asked.

"That's what I told her you would say," Brad said, smiling at his wife.

"I hate being predictable," Meg said, smiling back.

"I'll take predictable any time," Brad teased her dryly before the three began to discuss the guests Meg would want at the party.

⚜

The entrance to the apartment above Cassidy's shop was accessed from an outside stairway. Chandler climbed these outside stairs at about seven o'clock and knocked. Cassidy came right to the door, sweater in hand in case it cooled off before they got home.

"Ready?" Chandler asked politely; he was always polite.

"Yes. Is it very cold?"

"Not yet, but that sun is dropping."

The two started off, talking companionably about their jobs for the first block. Then Cassidy asked Chandler about his mother. She knew he'd heard from his family, who lived in the East, that her health had been in question.

"They think it's her heart," Chandler confided, having just gotten another letter from his sister. "She gets tired easily, but her spirits are good."

"That's good to hear. I can't remember, Chandler. Does your family share your faith in Christ?"

"Yes," Chandler answered, smiling at a memory. "I was seven and stole some money from my father's drawer. I came to Christ when my father talked to me about how serious my sin was, and how I would answer to God for all sins that were not covered in Him. I remember how familiar the words were, so I know I'd heard about salvation before, but I had never made that commitment myself."

"But you did that day?"

"Yes. My father had already punished me for stealing and then lying about it, but later, when the tears were dry, he told me he feared for me and explained salvation. Even as a little boy, I knew a peace after I'd prayed. I knew it was real that day."

Cassidy smiled at him as they continued to walk. It was wonderful to hear his story. She had not come from a home that was as settled as Chandler's. For reasons that were almost too hard to think about, she had had no contact with them since moving to Token Creek.

"That's a thoughtful face," Chandler mentioned.

"Just thinking about families. You must miss yours."

"I do miss them. It's been more than two years since I visited. I'm thinking about going back for a visit in the fall."

"Who does your job at the bank when you're away?" Cassidy asked, and the two talked about that for a while. Before it grew too dark to continue, they had covered myriad topics. At the end of the walk, Cassidy climbed the stairs feeling very content. It had been a very satisfying way to spend an evening and gave her much to write about.

Not many minutes later, she was ready for bed, her summer nightgown in place, her blonde hair hanging down her back, and her writing paper in hand.

Mrs. Ferguson found a hornets' nest outside her shop today, Cassidy wrote to her mother. *Remembering how you always handled them, I got the broom and then did my best not to get 'kissed.' It was in the front of the shop, and customers were scarce for a while, although entertained I'm sure, but no one was stung and the nest is gone.*

Cassidy went on to tell her mother about the customers of the day and her walk with Chandler. The *good-looking banker,* as Cassidy liked to call him. She didn't try to write too much, but as always her heart felt lighter just from sharing.

The letter done, she folded it carefully and reached for the carved wooden box that sat on her bedside table. This letter, along with all the others she'd written to her mother, went safely inside because it wasn't possible to send it. The task done and her heart prayerful, Cassidy settled down to sleep.

⚜

"You're drooping, love," Brad said to Meg, who sat next to him on the davenport.

"I'm tired."

"Go to bed."

"I don't want to *go* to bed; I want to *be* in bed."

Brad laughed at this but knew how true it was. Sometimes climbing the stairs and readying for bed was the hardest part of the day.

"I'm going," Meg said, pushing to her feet and telling the men goodnight.

Trace surfaced from the book he was reading long enough to tell his sister-in-law goodnight. Brad told his wife he'd be right behind her before looking down at the account book he had been poring over.

"What are you frowning about?" Trace asked, having noticed his face.

"Just thinking."

"Are we in trouble?"

"No," Brad said, but he didn't sound as convincing as Trace would have liked. "I'm for bed," the older Holden said as he closed the ledger and rose to follow his wife.

Trace went back to his book, but only for a moment. Brad had him curious. He soon set the novel aside to study the ranch accounts.

CHAPTER TWO

"Do you have time to sew a button on my shirt, Meg?" Trace asked in the morning, coming bare-chested into the room.

"Sure," Meg agreed, thinking nothing of his lack of attire. "Bring it here."

Meg and Brad were in the midst of breakfast, but Trace had slept in a bit.

"I went over the books last night," Trace said to Brad after he'd poured himself some coffee and reached for the eggs.

"Problems?" Brad asked.

"No, but it got me to thinking about last year's market. I didn't sleep too well."

Brad nodded. The men had driven their cattle to market in the fall and not received nearly the price they'd expected. It had been a huge disappointment and forced them to cut corners here and there.

"I'm headed out," Trace said, after a rather small breakfast. "Thanks for the shirt, Meg."

"You're welcome."

"Where are you going to be?" Brad asked.

"On the west side."

"I'll come with you." Brad finished his own breakfast in a hurry, kissed his wife, and went out the door.

Meg poured herself another cup of coffee, ignored the dishes, and reached for her Bible, very thankful and happy it was Wednesday, which meant Cassidy would be arriving after lunch.

*

"How does that look?" Jeanette asked Cassidy to check the hem on a man's shirt she'd been working on. The gentleman who ordered it was particular, and Jeanette wasn't sure he'd be satisfied.

"You might want to fix that one spot," Cassidy pointed out, "but I think the rest looks good. I'll know in the morning if he's pleased."

Jeanette looked at the younger woman for a moment, thinking, not for the first time, that she was special. Even when a customer was unhappy with the work, Cassidy never blamed Jeanette. As proprietress she took responsibility and never made excuses.

"Has Mrs. Potts been here yet?" Jeanette remembered to ask.

"Just before you came in."

"Was she pleased?"

"*Thrilled* was the word she used."

"If only they were all like that," Jeanette muttered.

"We'd be bored to tears," Cassidy said.

"Please, Lord," Jeanette joked, "give me some boredom."

Cassidy laughed before turning back to the sewing machine.

*

"Is something on your mind?" Trace asked his brother several hours later, not knowing what the look on his face meant.

"Just thinking," Brad said.

"About the accounts? Because I checked them over last night and worried for nothing. Things look good right now."

"No, it's nothing like that, and you're right, the books do look good."

But beyond that Brad did not elaborate. It was an odd time to remember, riding the range to look for stock in trouble, that he'd never asked Meg why she'd been crying. He was so intent on having her lie down. He tended to blame all her tears on fatigue. She often said her tears were because she was tired, so that wasn't completely his fault, but at the same time, he never had checked with her.

"Things look fine," Trace said, his eyes scanning the acres, bringing Brad back to the moment.

Brad nodded as he studied the same area. They'd grown up on this ranch, and even though they'd taken over at a young age, they were experienced in the ways of cattle ranching. Their father had been very good at it. They hadn't understood much about the expenses and pricing until after he left and they'd begun to study the account books, but since neither man had planned to do anything other than ranch, they naturally took over when Wes Holden was gone.

"I've got some work to do on that new saddle," Brad remembered.

"And I just remembered that I forgot to include those irons and that wagon hitch when I went to Stillwell's yesterday," Trace said, shaking his head a little, wondering where his mind had been the day before. "I'm headed in," he added, turning his horse. It was almost noon, and he'd not eaten much for breakfast. Brad turned his own horse, and the men started for home.

⚜

Pastor Rylan Jarvik, a large man by any standard, worked part-time at Stillwell's Livery. His church family was generous but also small, and he never wanted to be a financial burden to any of them. He didn't put in long hours at the livery, usually only twenty-five hours a week, and it was work he enjoyed, work he was suited to, and work that allowed him to stay in contact with the townsfolk he loved.

In fact, one of the perks of the job was seeing the church family, and on Wednesday afternoons, Cassidy Norton was a regular. Rylan had gotten into the habit of having a buggy and horse ready for her, and this day was no different. When she arrived the horse was hitched and waiting.

"Hi, Pastor Rylan." Cassidy greeted him with a smile.

"Hi, Cassie. How are you?"

"I'm fine. How are you doing?"

"I'm fine too," he said, smiling at her.

"Pastor," Cassidy forced herself to say before she could think herself out of it, "I have something I need to speak to you about sometime, but not today."

"That's fine. Maybe Jeanette will let us use her parlor."

Cassidy worried her lip over this statement, and Rylan wasn't long in catching on.

"Jeanette doesn't know?"

"Only Meg," Cassidy told him.

Rylan nodded. "We'll find a place where we can talk, Cassie, as soon as you'd like."

"Thank you," she told him, her relief visible to her pastor.

"Off to see Meg?" Rylan asked, deliberately changing the subject. "How's she doing?"

"I think she's well, but Brad did tell me she's not sleeping much."

"I've heard the last weeks can be hard," the pastor said compassionately.

"I've heard the same thing," Cassidy agreed.

"Maybe someday you'll know for yourself," he said quietly, a glint in his eye.

Cassidy tried not to smile, but he was a terrible tease, and sometimes he tried to play matchmaker, something that always made her laugh.

"I don't think I want to speculate on that at the moment," Cassidy told him.

"But, Cassie," Rylan began, "we've more than one fine, single young man."

"Is my buggy ready?" she asked pointedly, making the big man laugh.

"Right this way," he said, giving up for the moment.

"And anyway," Cassidy said after he'd assisted her into the seat and handed her the reins, "you can make a match for me as soon as you've made one for yourself."

"I'm working on it," Rylan replied. It was his standard reply, but Cassidy could see by his eyes that he wasn't sincere. Thanking him and smiling at him affectionately, Cassidy slapped the reins and started out of town.

⚜

"I need to ask you something," Brad said to Meg as he helped her clear the dishes from their dinner.

"What's that?"

"What had you cried about yesterday when I made you lie down?"

"Oh that," Meg said, not looking too happy about the question.

Brad watched her, not sure if he was in trouble or if the memory of it would make her cry again. "Did I do something?"

"No, but I'm still struggling."

It took Brad a moment and then he asked, "The fear?"

"Yes."

Brad nodded. Meg wrestled with fear about the actual birth of their child. She knew millions of women had gone before her, but she also knew she could die. The thought of leaving Brad alone to raise the baby by himself was very hard on her heart. It also plagued her to think of the baby not knowing its mother.

Brad put his arms around his wife and held her for a while, neither one speaking. After several minutes, he moved enough to see her face, his arms still holding her as close as her extended stomach would allow.

"First of all, God's view on this is that we trust Him for the future. God's design is for a mother and a father. Sometimes a child doesn't have both a mother and a father, but until *He* changes our situation, we will assume that God wants our baby to have both of us."

Meg nodded, her eyes not having left his, wanting very much to trust with him.

"Secondly, it took a long time to find you, and now that I have, I don't want you going anywhere. So don't even consider it."

Meg had to smile. Seeing it, Brad lowered his head. He kissed her and held her for a long time, knowing this would not be the end of it. Satan would tempt his wife again, but right now he prayed they would both trust. He then helped Meg with the dishes. Cassidy would be arriving soon.

⁂

It was not a long drive to the Holden Ranch, but even if it had been, the view of the Bitterroot Mountains, rising majestically around her, was not a sight Cassidy would ever grow weary of. The blue sky above her—almost cloudless today—seemed to stretch forever. She knew the Holdens were able to make this journey a few times a week, and a part of her heart envied them.

The horse was a gentle beast but able to move when urged, and Cassidy enjoyed moving fast in the buggy or on horseback. She was also a bit anxious to see Meg and hurried the animal on. It wasn't long before she was turning down the drive, not at all surprised to see Trace coming from the porch to meet her.

"How's Cassie?" Trace asked when the buggy stopped in the yard.

"Cassie's fine," that lady answered and asked, "How's Trace?"

"I'm doing well," Trace said, switching to the first person, holding his hand out to help her down.

"Thank you," Cassidy said before looking up at him and asking about his morning. Cassidy was always interested in others, and they answered because it was so obvious that her heart was genuine.

"We were on the range for a while, but both of us had work waiting for us in the barn."

"Doing what?"

"Brad is working on a saddle. I had a wagon part that needed fixing, and I forgot to get it to Stillwell's yesterday. So I'm stuck trying to work around it today."

"You don't have your own forge, do you?" Cassidy realized.

"No. We live close enough to town that we just use the livery."

"Is that the reason?"

"Yes. Bart Carlisle—he's another five miles out, and he does his own."

"Would you know how to do the work if you had your own forge?"

"Enough to get by," Trace said, starting to smile at her intense look. "But I'm no expert."

"Am I being mocked?" she asked lightly, having caught his eye, her head tipped in challenge.

"No," Trace denied with wide eyes, not the least believable.

Cassidy, working not to smile, started toward the house but stopped when Trace spoke.

"I think you forgot something," Trace said as he started to reach for the parcel on the seat.

Cassidy had seen Meg come to the porch and suddenly moved so Trace's body blocked Meg from seeing her face. Trace looked down at the small blonde in surprise.

"Leave it for Brad," she whispered. "It's a secret for Meg."

Trace smiled at her tone and the way she went instantly back to what she was doing.

"Thank you, Trace," she said in her normal voice, smiling at him in complete innocence and stepping around him to head to the house.

"You're welcome," Trace said, knowing he would have to stay put for a few minutes or Meg would want to know what he was chuckling about.

⁂

"This is my favorite fabric," Cassidy said, fingering the yellow-patterned calico in the baby quilt the women were making.

"I like that one too, but the green is my favorite."

"What is it this week?" Cassidy suddenly asked.

"A boy," Meg answered with a smile. "Mitchell James."

"Wasn't it Bethany Mayann last week?"

"It was, but that was seven entire days ago, Cass. A lot can run through your mind."

Cassidy laughed about this for a while, but when she looked at her friend, Meg's eyes were serious.

"Have you talked to anyone else about your secret?" the expectant woman asked.

"No," Cassidy replied quietly. "Rylan is next. I only just mentioned that I wanted to talk to him when I picked up the buggy. We'll have to find a place to make that possible."

"Did he ask you any questions?"

"No. It wasn't the place for that."

"I'll keep praying for you," Meg said, and Cassidy thanked her.

Cassidy had lived in Token Creek less than a year, but the women had become friends almost upon their first meeting. Something in each of the women reached out to the other, and little by little they talked about all aspects of their lives. It took a few months for Cassidy to tell all, but she eventually shared some painful facts about her family.

Meg was the soul of discretion, but Cassie's background wasn't a matter she could relate to—she hailed from a wonderful Christian home. She was a good listener, though, and believed with all her heart that God, with His own plan and in His own time, would take care of Cassidy and her family.

"Right there!" Meg exclaimed as she pointed, having watched Cassidy do an amazing number of even stitches at one time. "How did you do that?"

"Like this." Cassidy shifted so Meg could watch for a moment. Meg was a good seamstress, but Cassidy was excellent. And it seemed to come naturally for her.

"You try," Cassidy urged the older woman, and then watched Meg's needle move.

"How was that?" Meg asked, looking for approval.

"Much better. You're just one short of mine." Cassidy had done a swift count.

Meg looked very pleased about this and also relaxed about her ability. The conversation shifted to Jeanette and Brad's mother until it was time to make supper.

*

"How was the sewing?" Trace asked when he came in much later and found Cassidy setting the table.

"We're almost finished with the quilt."

"What will you work on next?" Trace asked, realizing how long Cassidy had been coming out on Wednesday afternoons.

Cassidy smiled and said, "Probably baby clothes."

Trace laughed a little. It should have been obvious to him but hadn't been until just that moment.

"Trace," Meg called from the kitchen, "is Brad coming in?"

"Not for a few minutes. Is there something I can do?"

Trace went that way without being asked, and Cassidy wondered if Meg knew how special that was. Both men were swift to help her, and she knew it wasn't only about the pregnancy.

Most of the men in the church family were unerringly polite. This was not true of all the men of Token Creek—some of them were downright rude, which probably explained why the men of the church family stood out to Cassidy.

"How's it going?" Brad asked as he entered the dining room, having come from the direction of the front door. Cassidy realized she'd been staring into space.

"Fine. Trace is in the kitchen. Meg needed something."

If Cassidy expected him to head that way, she was wrong. He hesitated, and his voice dropped.

"How did the nightgown turn out?"

"Very well," she answered with a smile. "Did you find it?"

Brad could only nod as Meg came from the kitchen.

"Oh, Brad, I didn't hear you."

"Hi," he said with a smile before bending to kiss her. "I came in from the front."

"Supper is almost on."

"I'll get washed up."

Meg watched her husband walk away, and Cassidy watched Meg.

"What's the matter?" the visitor asked.

"I don't know. I feel like he's not telling me something."

"From that short interchange?" Cassidy asked, hoping her face and voice would not give Brad away.

Meg shrugged. "I'm probably just imagining things."

The women went back to work on the meal and the table, and Cassidy was relieved. Brad was most certainly up to something, and Cassidy would rather bite her tongue than spoil the surprise.

⁕

For the first part of the journey back to town, Trace and Cassidy were quiet. On Wednesday nights Trace always tied his horse to the back of Cassidy's buggy and saw her back to town. Tonight was no different, except for the quiet. The four had talked nonstop over supper, but at the moment the couple headed back to town had nothing to share. Not until Cassidy sighed did Trace comment.

"Contented sigh or a tired sigh?"

"Did I sigh?" Cassidy asked with a frown.

"Yes, ma'am."

"Oh."

Trace waited, but Cassidy didn't share. He looked down at her profile and knew she was thinking. Not for several seconds did she look at him.

"Tired, I think," she answered, as though the question were brand new.

"You work hard," Trace said, wondering if that was all there was to it.

"Not today."

"Oh, I don't know about that. I think a break in routine can be just as tiring as work."

Cassidy thought about this. She always slept very well on Wednesday nights.

"I think you might be right," Cassidy said in wonder. "I *am* more tired on Wednesdays."

"Do you think you'll still come to the ranch?"

"What do you mean?"

"To sew with Meg—because it makes you so tired."

Cassidy turned her head, her mouth open in surprise, and caught the teasing glint in his eye. Not bothering to answer, she tried to hide her smile as she turned back to the front.

Trace did not keep at her. They were still a little quiet on the ride in, but it was comfortable. Once in town, Trace headed directly to the livery, and after helping Cassidy to the ground, took care of the buggy and horse. That done, his horse's reins in hand, they began the walk to Cassidy's store.

"How busy are you this week?" Cassidy remembered to ask.

"About normal, I think. Why do you ask?"

"I just wondered if you're coming back into town to study with Pastor Rylan and the other men."

"Actually I am planning on it. We're getting together Friday night. It's been a few weeks since we've been able to meet, and that's the first night we can fit it in."

They were at the side of Cassidy's shop now, at the outside stairway that led to her door. Cassidy stopped and looked up at him.

"Sounds great."

"You know, Cass," Trace said, his head tipped a little to study her. "You're always happy for others."

"Oh," Cassidy said, frowning a little. "I guess I am, but what made you say that?"

"I don't know. I just thought of it."

Cassidy smiled, remembering yet another thing she liked about Trace Holden. He was good at sharing his thoughts.

Trace only smiled back at the small blonde, urged her indoors, and told her he'd see her Sunday.

Cassidy wasted no time, knowing he had to ride all the way home, in slipping into her small upstairs apartment. She lit a lantern even though it was still light and thought about why she felt a mixture of weariness and restlessness.

Not only did Cassidy make and mend clothing, she also sewed quilts and displayed them in the window of her shop. They sold at a fairly fast rate, and she was nearly always working on one. Tonight would be a perfect time to get in some extra stitching, but for some reason her heart wasn't in it.

Opting to just sit by the window and watch the sun go down, Cassidy sat in her most comfortable chair and thought back on the day.

⁂

"What's this?" Meg stopped by the bed much later that night, her long-sleeved nightgown already in place.

Brad peeked out from the newspaper he'd been reading and tried not to look pleased.

"What does it look like?" he asked.

Meg picked up the thin garment and held it up for inspection. Knowing Cassidy's work by heart, she wasn't long in catching on.

"Did you have Cassidy make this?"

"Yes, ma'am."

Just about squealing in delight, Meg swiftly changed into the new nightgown and looked down at herself.

"It's so light and soft."

Brad only smiled at her expression and watched her closely. He caught it the moment she frowned.

"It's very sheer," Meg decided.

"Is that a problem?"

"I don't know."

"Meg," Brad spoke gently to his wife, "you're too warm at night, and you never leave the bedroom without your robe."

Looking down at herself, Meg studied the sleeveless design, V neck, and the way the garment stopped just below her knees. In truth she hadn't felt so cool all day.

Without speaking, she climbed into bed and put her arms around her husband. Kissing him softly, she said, "Thank you."

"You're welcome," Brad said, and kissed her right back.

Meg looked into his eyes. "I wondered what you were up to."

Brad smiled. "I can't get away with much these days."

"It all shows on your face."

"What's showing on my face right now?" Brad asked, pulling her a little closer.

Meg smiled without answering and kissed her husband again.

CHAPTER THREE

"Good morning, Jeanette," Rylan said quietly.

"Good morning, Rylan. Come in," Jeanette invited. The big man stepped inside her elegant home early Thursday morning. "Thanks for coming," the woman continued. "She's in a bad way."

Rylan only nodded, having been through this before, and followed Jeanette to the conservatory. At times, Theta Holden grew agitated. She didn't cry out or fight against Jeanette and Heather, but she shifted in her seat often and worried the padded arms of the chair. At times tears would roll down her face. The first time it happened, just two years earlier, Jeanette stood helpless and cried with her, but in time she learned to send for Rylan. His deep, calm voice had a settling effect on her sister, and if he was available, he was always willing to come.

"Good morning, Mrs. Holden. Your sister tells me you're not feeling the best this morning."

Jeanette, listening from the edge of the room, thanked God for her pastor. He did not make foolish or inane statements. It might have been tempting to tell Theta that he'd just happened to stop by, but instead told her he'd been sent for.

"I'd like to tell you what I read in my Bible this week," Rylan said, having taken a seat across from her and opened his Bible. "It's from the second chapter of Proverbs, and I love the promises I read here.

"Starting in verse three, it says, 'Yea, if thou criest after knowledge, and liftest up thy voice for understanding; if thou seekest her as silver, and searchest for her as for hidden treasures; then shalt thou understand the fear of the Lord, and find the knowledge of God. For the Lord giveth wisdom; out of his mouth cometh knowledge and understanding. He layeth up sound wisdom for the righteous; he is a buckler to them that walk uprightly. He keepeth the paths of judgment, and preserveth the way of his saints. Then shalt thou understand righteousness, and judgment, and equity; yea, every good path.'"

Rylan raised his head and saw that Theta was very still. She seemed to be listening. He didn't elaborate on what he'd read but began to sing softly, his voice a rich bass. He sang an old hymn about the love and faithfulness of God. He then prayed for Theta, asking God to bless her and keep her thoughts on Him. When he looked up, she was asleep. Rylan studied her pale skin and graying hair for a moment and then made his way quietly from the room.

"That's never happened before," he said to Jeanette when they were out of earshot.

"Her eyes closed right after you began to pray," Jeanette said, just as surprised as Rylan. "I was watching all the time, and I think she was ready to sleep right after your song."

Rylan smiled a little. "It's usually my sermons that put folks to sleep."

Jeanette laughed and saw him to the door.

"Thanks, Rylan," Jeanette spoke warmly. "I have to be at the shop, and I hated to leave her in that state."

"It's my pleasure, Jeanette," he said. "Let me know how she does the rest of the day." This said, Rylan took his leave. This was not a morning at the livery, and he had a sermon to finish.

❦

Chandler Di Fiore opened the bank with ten minutes to spare, knowing he had some work on his desk that needed attention.

His teller, Mr. Falcone, would be along shortly, and Chandler hoped to get a few things done before the streets grew noisy. The days were warmer now, and the door and windows were opened mid-morning and remained that way all day. Chandler did his best work when it was quiet.

"Good morning." Mr. Falcone, appearing suddenly, greeted his employer.

"Hello, Ed," Chandler said in return. "I think we're in for another warm one."

"I hope so. I'm still working to drive the memory of winter away."

Chandler smiled but didn't comment. His teller was a fine employee, but the cup was always half empty, never half full. Chandler, putting everything from his mind except the paperwork on his desk, managed to accomplish quite a bit before the first distraction. And that was a good thing because it was Abi Pfister, and she was not there on bank business.

"I've come, Mr. Di Fiore," she announced, stepping up to his desk, pencil and paper in hand. "I'm ready for your story."

Chandler welcomed the eccentric older woman, one of Token Creek's many characters, and sat down again once she'd taken a seat. It was common knowledge that Abi Pfister was writing a book, and not just any book, but a book on Token Creek and all its inhabitants, past and present. The book was to include details and events that she alone claimed to know. Few thought she would actually accomplish this because she interrupted most of her interviews with stories she had already recorded. She'd come to see Chandler twice about the details of his life, never quite getting them down.

"Now," Abi began, her work on her book very important to her. "Exactly how long have you been in Token Creek?"

"Four years."

"Exactly?" Abi pressed.

"It was four years in May."

Abi wrote and then looked at him again, her hat a bit askew but suiting her nonetheless.

"And you hail from where?"

"Boston."

"You were born there?"

"I was."

Abi speared him with a look just then, certain she was being laughed at, but Chandler's face gave nothing away. She bent back over her paper and continued with her questions.

"And your fiancée's name is Cassidy Norton, correct?"

"I'm not engaged to Miss Norton or anyone else," Chandler said, his voice not changing, even though he was surprised.

Abi looked up at him. "But Heller at the sawmill said that you and Cassidy were engaged."

"Were you getting Heller's story or mine?"

Again, Chandler's voice did not alter, but Abi knew she was being rebuked. Her eyes narrowed, and Chandler steeled himself for the moment she stood and stormed out of the bank. It surprised him when she sat back a little and her face changed to thoughtfulness.

"No fiancée?" she said quietly.

"No."

"A gal you consider your own?"

"No."

"What brought you to Token Creek?" Abi asked next, and the interview went on from there. And this time she got through. She finished with Chandler, seeming well-satisfied, and tried to work on Mr. Falcone's story, but he had customers to see to, and the regular interruptions frustrated her.

She left without warning, and Chandler was not sorry. He'd

learned from two past encounters that putting her off only brought her back another time. He hoped this would be the last.

※

"Thank you, Patience," Cassidy said to Meg's aunt, who had been looking for a certain color of thread. Cassidy had the very one, and Mrs. Patience Dorn had given her some fabric scraps she'd been collecting before she left the shop. Cassidy used them in her quilts.

Jeanette showed up just as Patience was leaving, and the two had a brief visit on the boardwalk out front. Jeanette came in laughing.

"What's up?" Cassidy wanted to know.

"Patience and I were reminiscing. We remember when Meg and Brad met. Meg was rather taken with him but couldn't tell what he was thinking. Patience said she knew Brad was perfect for Meg, and it was terribly hard to keep her mouth shut."

"Why was Meg in Token Creek?" Cassidy asked. "I can't remember that part."

"She visited every year, but that summer, Brad actually noticed her."

Cassidy smiled and went back to the sewing machine. Jeanette got to work on the jobs Cassidy had left for her, but her mind was still on her nephew and Meg. It had been a wonderful summer.

※

"Rylan!" A voice sounded at the pastor's front door. "You here?"

"Yeah!" Rylan shouted from the bedroom he used as an office. He came to the front room of his house to find Sheriff Kaderly waiting for him, having stepped inside.

"There's been a shooting. Can you come?"

"Certainly. Do I know the family?"

"I don't think so. Far side of town, somewhat reclusive."

"Children?"

"Two."

Rylan didn't ask any more questions but got his coat and left with the sheriff. He assumed this was a normal part of a pastor's life because it had always been this way. Sheriff Kaderly was not a member of his church family, but when there was a death, if the family looked in need of help, he always came for Rylan. Sometimes it led to a long relationship, and other times Rylan talked to folks he never saw again.

Praying as he climbed into the wagon the sheriff had come in, Rylan asked God to use him. The sheriff talked almost nonstop on the ride to the house, but that didn't hinder Rylan. He prayed for the family he was about to meet and for Token Creek's sheriff as well.

⚜

Meg took a loaf of bread from the oven and wiped her brow. It was awfully warm in the room, but the bread did not look done. She stared down at the loaf she thought she had burned, frowning in concentration. Behind her were cake pans, ready to go in next, but she wondered if something might be wrong with the oven compartment in the stove.

A pain, not intense, but making itself felt, knifed across her abdomen. Meg sat down at the kitchen table, her baking forgotten.

"It's too soon," she whispered to the Lord, knowing that if the baby came now, it would be about seven weeks too early. "Please don't let this start now. Please, Lord."

Meg sat for a time, waiting to see if anything else would happen. She felt her breathing relax as she continued to pray softly in the empty room.

"I want Your will more than my own. Well," she admitted, "I *want* to want Your will more than my own. Please change my heart, Lord. Please help me to accept what You have for me and this baby."

Meg tried to stop then. She tried to stop all speculation and prayer and just think about who God was. No more requests, no more thoughts of her own—just verses that told of His greatness, His lovingkindness, and His ability to provide.

When Meg laid her head on the table and fell asleep, she could not be sure. She also didn't know how long she'd slept, but when she woke she was still alone, and the bread was quite cool to the touch.

Moving a bit carefully, she went about her workday, no other pains troubling her. She thought that might have been the end of it but wasn't willing to take a chance. As soon as she'd fed the men lunch, she lay down on her bed. She thought her body might be in need of rest. It didn't matter that she didn't sleep, having taken that nap at the table. This small act might help the baby go full term, and that was worth getting behind in her work.

⸎

Chandler spotted Cassidy the moment she came through the door of the bank. She looked distracted to his eyes, and for a moment he thought about what Abi Pfister had said. He was not concerned with the wagging tongues of the townsfolk, but he would never want Cassidy hurt by someone's tongue, and in truth, he didn't know exactly how he felt about Token Creek's seamstress. She was a friend, certainly, one he cared for very much. But a hurt from his past made it difficult to say if he would ever let his guard down so he and Cassidy could be more than friends.

"Hi, Cassidy," Chandler greeted when she was close enough.

"Hello, Chandler." She smiled as she spoke, but there was strain in her eyes.

"Long day?"

"A bit, yes," she said, not elaborating as to how the day had ended. Abi Pfister had been in, trying to speak with her, and not happy when Cassidy did not have time. She was behind in some of her work and did not have the luxury of time for an interview. She had tried to explain to Abi that the next week would be better, but that woman had had an agenda, and when Cassidy had not fit herself into it, she'd been highly offended.

"Do you have a quiet evening planned?"

"Yes," Cassidy said gratefully, smiling as she thought about it. "Dinner at Jeanette's so I don't even need to think about what to make for supper."

"Sounds perfect," Chandler said, having taken care of her bankbook and handing it back. "Enjoy yourself and relax."

Cassidy thanked him and went on her way. Not until she was almost to Jeanette's did she stop to wonder why he'd known it was a long day. She tried not to think about how poorly she must look or how much it bothered her that Chandler noticed.

※

"Where's Heather tonight?" Cassidy asked as the two women sat down to eat and that woman's place remained empty.

"Theta had a pretty rough start to the day," Jeanette explained. "Heather's helping her into bed early tonight, and then she'll join us."

Cassidy nodded with compassion and bowed her head when her host did.

"Father in heaven," Jeanette began, "my life is so blessed because of Cassidy Norton. Thank You, Lord, for bringing her here to Token Creek, into our church family and into my life. I ask You to keep us mindful of You as we enjoy this meal. Help Theta settle in and sleep swiftly, and thank You for all of Heather's patient work. In Your holy name I ask these things. Amen."

"Amen," Cassidy echoed, thinking she was the blessed one. She had been forced to leave her home, with no promise of finding friend or family. She had found both.

In the midst of these thoughts, Jeanette passed the platter of roast her cook, Becky, had prepared and asked her how she thought business was going. It was the start of a great evening.

The end of the week neared, and Friday evening found Meg on the sofa, knitting needles in hand. Brad had joined her with the newspaper, but it wasn't long before his hand reached to massage her back.

"Oh, that feels nice."

"Laundry today?"

"Yes. It was on my list for yesterday, but so much went wrong with the stove that I got behind."

Brad had fixed the stove and all was well in the kitchen, but so much of Meg's day was centered in that room that it had been very disruptive. His hand continued to rub the muscles in the small of Meg's back until she shifted, her blouse moving and showing Brad a bit of skin. When he gently pulled the blouse and camisole free from her waist, allowing his hand to find the soft skin on her back, his wife turned to look at him.

"You're brother is still upstairs."

"It's not my fault," Brad said, moving his hand and looking innocent.

"It's my fault?" Meg clarified.

"Yes."

Meg set her knitting aside and said, "I can't wait to hear this explanation."

"It's your skin. It's so soft my hand can't help itself."

Meg laughed long and hard over this and eventually Brad joined her.

Fifteen minutes later, Trace came downstairs, cleaned up and headed for town.

"Have a good time," Meg said as he left.

"Thank you."

Brad had gone back to his newspaper, but only until he heard the sound of his brother's horse leaving the ranch property.

⁂

For more than a year Rylan had been meeting with Chandler, Philip Leffers, and Trace for personal Bible study. He was having the men work on various passages of Scripture. Each time they met, he assigned verses. When they met again, they would discuss what they'd learned.

Rylan's grasp of Scripture was great, and the men always learned from him, but the discussions they had were beneficial to each of them. Tonight they were in Ephesians, looking at the armor of God.

"It's good to be reminded of the battle we're in," Philip said when Rylan asked the men to comment. "I forget that too easily."

"I feel the same way," Chandler added. "I also don't think that I've looked at this the right way before. I mean, those verses come after a plain-worded reminder that the devil is the enemy."

"And he never grows tired," Trace put in quietly, having thought along the same lines. "But verse ten says it's in the power of the Lord's might. I was encouraged by that."

"Tell me," Rylan asked, "what sins are you men battling right now?"

It was a personal question, but they were used to this from Rylan and knew that he expected honest answers. They continued in the text but also talked about sexual temptations, greed, and worry about the future. They ended their time together with prayer—but not a swift closing prayer. It was a time when each man went to his knees and asked God for the help that only He could provide.

⁂

"Jeanette," Heather called softly to that woman in the wee hours Saturday night.

"What's the matter?"

"Theta seems to be crying in her sleep."

Jeanette slipped from her bed and followed Heather down the hall. Heather had turned on the gas lamps upstairs but lit a candle for Theta's room. Both women stood by the bed in their nightclothes, listening to Theta cry softly.

"Do you suppose they're happy tears or sad?" Heather asked.

Jeanette turned to stare at her. "I never thought about her having happy tears," the older woman admitted.

Heather looked at her in surprise. "But you're one of those people who cry when you're happy. Why wouldn't your sister?"

Jeanette had to smile at her. "Do you have any idea how good you are for me, Heather?"

Heather only chuckled, and both women realized that Theta had quieted.

"Maybe just hearing our voices helped," Jeanette guessed.

"I don't know," Heather said in wonder, often trying to guess what kept Mrs. Holden trapped in her body. "I do know this," she continued, "neither one of us will hear a thing in the service tomorrow morning if we don't get some sleep."

"You're right. Go to bed. I want to sit here for just a while."

"All right."

Heather disappeared across the hall, taking the candle with her. She left her door open—as she did each night—to hear if she was needed. The open door allowed her to know the exact moment Jeanette began to pray for her sister.

Sunday morning dawned warm and fine. The congregation gathered at the small church building, ready for teaching and worship. It was not a huge flock, but it was a serious one. Token Creek was not known for its upright ways, but this small group of believers took their faith seriously and met with regularity to pray, worship, and learn.

Walking the short distance to the church building, Cassidy entered the neat structure, saw the Holdens and Chandler in a pew and slipped in beside them. Jeanette and Heather came next and sat on Cassidy's other side. They visited until Rylan stepped into the pulpit. He smiled out at the group that gathered before opening his Bible.

"Proverbs 27:7 says, 'The full soul loatheth an honeycomb, but to the hungry soul every bitter thing is sweet.'" Rylan looked up from his Bible and smiled again. "I made eggs and toasted bread for myself for breakfast this morning, but I burned the bread when I wasn't paying attention. I ate the toast anyway because I was hungry. I didn't mean to burn anything, and I had planned to share this verse with you already. Don't you love the Lord's sense of humor?" Rylan asked as he smiled out at the congregation. "Burnt toast fits the description in the verse very well. I was hungry, and it tasted good to me."

Rylan looked back to his Bible and turned to another verse. "This one is Matthew 6:33. You've all heard it many times. Some of you probably have it memorized. 'But seek ye first the kingdom of God, and his righteousness; and all these things shall be added unto you.'

"A sated man doesn't seek. He's no longer hungry. He's satisfied and not willing to search. But a starved man will eat burnt toast. He's seeking, he's hungry. Have you ever noticed how fragile spiritual hunger is? One little delight and we're good for a while. We don't stay hungry for long.

"These verses are talking about real hunger—craving, pursuing, seeking. Empty-belly hunger. That's the kind of hunger God is looking for. Content in Him certainly. Content in who He is, and in the way He provides for our every need, but not satisfied. Not feeling so full that we no longer crave the knowledge and presence of God."

Trace listened intently to Rylan's words and knew that he'd not been so hungry lately. He was still in the Word, and missing fellowship with the church family would never occur to him, but he wasn't as thankful as he used to be. His heart was going too long without prayer.

"Are you still praying for Token Creek?" Rylan asked in closing.

"I was called to see a family this week that has been devastated by a death. The folks listened to what I had to say and want me to visit again. God can do great things in this town, this town that was in His heart as He hung on the cross. Never stop believing that. Never stop praying for the forgiveness and salvation of Token Creek, and praying not just for the townsfolk but for our church family as well." Rylan asked one of the elders to close the service in prayer and then added, "Lord willing, I'll see you all next week."

Some stood, and some turned in their seats to find conversation. Before Meg could do either, her Aunt Patience was there.

"How are you, dear?" she asked, giving her niece a hug.

"I'm feeling fine. I'm just too warm most of the time."

"Come for dinner," Patience invited. "Your uncle misses you, and you won't have to work over the stove."

"Let me check with Brad," Meg said, thinking this was just what she needed. Both Brad and Trace thought it a great idea. Everyone visited a bit longer, and it was nice to know that lunch was just minutes away and not all the way out to the ranch.

⚜

"Big plans for the day, Cass?" Chandler asked Cassidy as they exited the church house.

"As quiet as I can manage," Cassidy said, having realized near the end of the sermon just how fast her mind had been moving concerning business and every other aspect of her life. She'd been struggling with worry.

Chandler had been invited to Jeanette's and found himself hoping Cassidy would be there too. It didn't sound like it.

"Do you ever sew on Sundays?"

"Sometimes, but not for the shop. I just sew for myself if I think it will be relaxing."

The look on Chandler's face was comical. He looked surprised and then almost embarrassed.

"What's the matter?" Cassidy asked.

"Do I seem like an intelligent person to you, Cassidy?" Chandler's voice was quiet with his own chagrin and bafflement.

"Certainly."

"Well, I suppose in some ways I am, but I just now realized that you must sew everything you wear. I don't know why it never occurred to me before."

Cassidy laughed but then took compassion on him. "It's not that far-fetched, Chandler. You can order clothing, and Jessie carries plenty at the mercantile. I just like what I make better."

"How do you do this?" Chandler pointed to some intricate pleats near Cassidy's shoulder.

"You start with plenty of fabric—that helps. I actually ironed those in first. It was easier then."

"And I suppose the sewing machine makes all the difference."

"You have no idea. It's saved me hours of time, not to mention energy and money."

"Speaking of time," Chandler said, seeing that everyone had cleared out of the area. "I'm supposed to be at Jeanette's."

"Have fun," Cassidy offered, bidding him goodbye.

Chandler told her to enjoy her day and moved down the street. Jeanette's place was a little ways, but Chandler's long legs would eat the distance. Cassidy watched him for a while, but then realized she was hungry and took herself home to eat.

CHAPTER FOUR

"THAT WAS DELICIOUS," MEG SAID, settling into Jeb and Patience's parlor after lunch, feeling that she could sleep.

"Yes, it was," Trace agreed, looking over at Meg on the sofa, Brad next to her. The younger Holden began to smile.

"What are you staring at?" Brad asked, having just caught his brother's look.

Trace shook his head a little and said, "I was just remembering the weeks in this room when you wouldn't have sat next to Meg unless someone had been holding a gun to your head. It was a long summer."

Both Jeb and Patience agreed, and there was laughter all around. With little invitation, thoughts fell away to another time, two summers past when Brad Holden had spotted Meg—really seen her—for the first time.

"Brad, are you hearing a thing I'm saying?" Jeanette asked, trying to figure out what Brad was looking at over her shoulder.

"Who is that?" Brad finally asked, his eyes on the dark-haired young woman who'd come into the church building with Jeb Dorn.

"That's Meg," Jeanette said simply. "She's making her summer visit."

Jeanette would have gone right back to talking, but she could see she'd lost her nephew. He watched the kind way Meg Dorn smiled and talked to a child who came up to her, and then when Jeb had found a pew, that young lady sat with him, opened her Bible, and read.

And that had been the beginning for Brad. He didn't let his heart rush, but he became aware for the first time. Even Trace noticed his interest.

"So are you going to go see her?"

"Who?"

"Meg Dorn."

"No, why?"

"Why?" Trace asked with an exasperated roll of his eyes. "Because you're interested. Don't tell me you're not."

Brad didn't reply, but then Trace didn't need an answer. He noticed that the next Sunday Brad took a little extra time shaving, and the shirt he picked out was one of his nicest ones. And Brad caught Trace's eyes on him but didn't comment.

Trace wasn't the only one to notice. Patience Dorn had seen Brad looking Meg's way and did nothing to stop her heart from planning. She thought that either of the Holden men would be perfect for Meg and said as much to Jeb.

"Ask them to dinner," Jeb, a romantic in his own right, said, not minding his wife's thought at all. The Holden brothers were fine, believing men, and that would mean that their little Meg would be in Token Creek year 'round.

Patience was not going to waste any time. What she hadn't counted on was Meg's reaction.

"You can't do that," she told her aunt, her face showing her horror.

"Why not?" Patience asked in surprise, knowing that Meg had done some looking of her own.

"He hasn't given me any reason to think he's interested, Aunt Patience. I might have to spend the rest of the summer wishing the floor would swallow me."

"But he watches you," Patience argued.

"Be that as it may," Meg agreed, "he'll just have to find the courage to do more than that."

Brave words at the time. Before June ended Meg knew moments of despair. Brad was not a fast mover. It was clear to most folks that he had his eye on Meg, but he wasn't doing anything about it. She'd come in May, and it was the Fourth of July picnic before he found the courage to approach.

"How are you?" Brad had come near the Dorn table and was speaking to Jeb, his gaze managing to encompass them all.

"Doing well, Brad. How about yourself?"

"Fine, thank you."

"How's the ranch?"

"The spring was good. The herd is growing fast."

"So you'll head to market in the fall?"

"That's the plan."

Jeb didn't continue to question the younger man but gave him a moment to choose the next topic of conversation. Jeb was beginning to doubt if he could do it, but Brad surprised him.

"I was wondering if Meg might want to take a walk along the creek."

Jeb turned to his niece.

"I'd like that," she said quietly, and went with Brad when he turned away from the group and began a slow walk.

"Are you enjoying your summer?" Brad asked the first thing that came to mind.

"Yes. It's always great fun."

"A little hot at times?"

"At times, but I don't mind."

Brad glanced at her, wishing he could just go on staring. Her skin reminded him of fresh cream, and her eyes were a deep blue, almost turquoise. She wasn't smiling right now, but he knew her smile was one of the prettiest things he'd ever seen.

"I don't remember if I saw you last year," Brad said. "Did you visit?"

"All summer."

Brad stopped then and looked at her. Meg stopped with him. They were along the bank of Token Creek, the town picnic a little ways behind them.

"Did you change?" Brad asked, trying to place her in his mind.

"I don't know." Meg just held her smile. "Did you?"

Brad saw the amusement in her eyes and laughed. Meg couldn't believe how much she liked the sound, and she laughed with him.

It got easier after that. Brad headed into town at least three times a week and sat in the Dorns' parlor. He and Meg talked about everything under the sun, and if Jeb and Patience had been harboring any doubts, they soon disappeared as they got to know this young rancher with his subtle sense of humor, high values, and genuine faith.

As for Brad, he'd never been happier. Meg was his girl, and he knew they would have a future together. She was the one God had for him. He was sure of it. What he wasn't sure about was the timing, and that almost got him into trouble.

"Are you busy next Friday night?" Meg asked as August rushed away.

"No, what's up?"

"A party Jeb and Patience are giving me. Can you come?"

"Certainly, but didn't you tell me your birthday was in June?"

"It is," Meg said quietly, her eyes watchful. "It's a going-away party."

Brad felt as if the wind had been knocked from him. He'd managed to forget that Token Creek was not her home.

"Why are you leaving?" he asked, just managing to stay calm.

"My visit is over. My parents expect me home."

"New York is a long way away from Montana Territory."

"Yes, it is," Meg said, even as her heart begged Brad to say the words she longed to hear. She knew he loved her—he'd said it many times—but he'd never popped the question.

Brad was in shock. He had no idea how the days had moved so fast or how he could forget such a key ingredient to their relationship. He didn't say much of anything, however, and when Patience came looking for Meg, Brad excused himself and went home.

"So you're not sure about Meg?" Trace pressed his brother when Brad told him about the conversation. They were in the living room at the ranch.

"I'm very sure."

"Then why are you hesitating?"

"We don't have much extra right now, Trace. You know that. I wanted to offer Meg more."

"Brad," Trace responded in kindness and patience, "we never go hungry, and we both have plenty to wear." Trace's head went back so he could glance around the room. "This is a fine home. Meg won't find anything lacking."

Brad still looked doubtful and Trace, not even realizing it, delivered the final punch.

"What did Meg say when you explained why you wanted to wait?"

"I didn't tell her."

Trace had to laugh. "Well, prepare yourself, big brother, because she's either going to laugh at the absurdity of it all or be completely insulted."

"Why would she be insulted?"

"Meg isn't some spoiled little girl who would look at you and this home and ask for more. But that's what you're saying."

Brad thanked his brother, emotion making it almost impossible. He left for town just minutes later and asked Meg Dorn to marry him as soon as it could be arranged. Meg accepted in a heartbeat, and they were married that fall.

"Well, I for one am glad to see you on the sofa together," Jeb finally said, breaking into everyone's thoughts. "This courtship business takes it out of a man."

Both Meg and Patience laughed at him, but Brad had to agree—right up to the moment Jeb contradicted his own words. "So tell me, Trace, who have you got your eye on?"

Trace laughed but was saved from answering when Patience offered coffee. Everyone was too warm for that, but no one turned down the cake she offered as well.

The Holdens stayed for most of the afternoon, dozing and visiting the hours away, something they all needed. When it was time to go, both Dorns saw them off, Patience just remembering to mention the upcoming party.

"We'll see you Friday night at Jeanette's. I have your birthday present wrapped and ready."

"I can hardly wait," Meg said, hugging her aunt again.

The three left for home with the sun still high. It would be a warm ride, the memories of the afternoon even warmer.

⚜

"Hey, Jessie," Trace greeted the owner of Wheeler's Mercantile when he came into town on Tuesday.

"Hi, Trace. What can I do for you?"

"I've got a list here," Trace said, leaning against the counter and turning it so Jessie could read with him.

Jessie had almost all the supplies on hand but had to order the piece that Trace needed for the wagon. Trace thought his temporary fix would hold till it arrived. He knew Rylan or Pete Stillwell could make it for him at the livery, but he had remembered an item Jessie had showed him in the catalog and thought it might be better priced.

Thirty minutes later, Trace went down the street, the little blue dress shop on his mind. The last time he'd been in town, he'd not stopped to see Cassidy and regretted it. Between the mercantile and Cassidy's, however, was the bank. Trace decided to stop in and say hello to Chandler.

"Well, cowboy," Chandler greeted when he spotted Trace coming through the door.

"Hey, Chandler," Trace replied, the men shaking hands before Trace sat in the chair in front of the manager's desk, rocking back to get comfortable, hat going to his knee.

"What brings you to town?" Chandler asked.

"Supplies mostly. I'll throw in a visit to Cass and my mother as well."

"How is your mother?" Chandler asked, realizing he'd not inquired in a long time.

"The same. How is yours?"

"Doing all right. Taking things a little slower, but her letters are as sanguine as ever."

Trace had to smile.

"What?" Chandler had caught the look.

"Sanguine. That's an eastern-boy word if I've ever heard one."

Chandler had to laugh. It was true. No one in Token Creek talked the way he did, but that made him unique, and if someone had pressed him, he would have admitted to enjoying that.

"Oh, no," Chandler spoke under his breath, and Trace followed his gaze.

Abi Pfister had stepped inside the door. Chandler watched her, thinking she was back for another interview with him, but her eyes were on the tellers' windows and Mr. Falcone. When she saw that he was busy, she moved on her way.

"What's up with that?" Trace asked.

"She's writing a book on Token Creek and keeps trying to interview Mr. Falcone. She talked to me already, and I didn't appreciate some of the things she said."

"About the bank?"

"No, about Cassie and me."

Trace's brows rose. He knew Chandler could handle himself, but he was a little bit protective of Cassidy.

"Did Cassidy hear?"

"I don't know. I didn't want to ask her."

"Why was that?"

Chandler hesitated but then admitted, "Abi had heard that Cassidy and I were engaged."

Trace's frown was real when Chandler explained the whole story and realized Abi was just repeating what she'd heard. Cassidy's being engaged to Chandler, or even rumor of it, would not harm either of their reputations, but since it wasn't true, it would only cause awkwardness and possibly hard feelings.

"I'll be headed there." Trace was not one to beat about the bush. "I might ask her if Abi Pfister has been a problem, and I'll probably just tell her what you said."

Chandler nodded. He didn't know why he was willing to let Trace handle this but somehow thought it would be best.

"Well, I'd better keep moving."

"All right. I think we're on for Saturday night this time, aren't we?" Chandler asked, referring to the study with Rylan.

"Yes. I'll see you then, Chandler."

"All right, Trace. Thanks for stopping."

Trace didn't waste time but beat a path to Cassidy's. That lady was alone, bent over the sewing machine, and didn't hear him come in. He stood for moment watching her work and then threw his hat on the chair beside her. She didn't start like he thought she would but smiled and spoke without turning from her machine.

"Hello, Trace."

"How did you know that was my hat?" he asked, having been foiled in his joke.

"I'm an observant woman." Cassidy turned with a smile, inviting him to take a seat by moving his hat. "What are you doing in town?"

"Just errands and visiting," Trace said when he was comfortable.

"You sound like a man of leisure."

"I am when I can be," he said, and Cassidy knew he spoke the truth. During branding and cattle driving, all he did was work. "What are you working on?"

"A shirt for Merle North. It's a nice fabric, isn't it?"

"Very nice." Trace admired it but didn't let his mind lose track of his visit to the bank. "I need to ask you something."

"All right."

"Has Abi Pfister been in?"

"Last week. She was upset when I didn't have time for an interview."

Trace nodded, and Cassidy knew there was more.

"What's wrong?"

"She was spreading rumors she'd heard about you and Chandler. He set her straight, but when he told me, I wanted you to know."

"Why didn't Chandler tell me?"

"I think he was afraid of hurting you somehow."

Cassidy looked thoughtful, and Trace watched her.

"What bothers you more," he finally asked, "the rumor or that Chandler didn't tell you?"

"Both. I can understand Chandler was driven by compassion. I don't know what drives Abi Pfister. She's relentless with this book idea of hers. And just exactly what was said?"

"That you and Chandler are engaged."

Cassidy didn't know why the words pained her, but they did. She was glad Trace told her, but it wasn't easy to hear.

"Are you all right?"

Cassidy nodded. "Thanks for telling me."

"You're welcome. You'll be out at the house tomorrow?"

"That's the plan."

"All right. I'm headed to see my mother and then home."

"Thanks for stopping, Trace."

"Until tomorrow, Miss Norton," Trace said, tipping his hat and taking his leave, unaware of the way Cassidy sat thinking until a noise in the street interrupted her.

"I had a scare last week," Meg admitted to Cassidy the following afternoon.

"What happened?"

"Pain. It's not happened since, but for a moment I thought the baby was coming."

"How early would that be?"

"Right now, about six weeks."

"Are you taking things more slowly?"

"A little, but I feel good now and sometimes I forget."

"Well, I'll make dinner tonight, and you can just sit and talk to me."

"I don't think you need to do that," Meg began to argue, but Cassidy frowned at her and she stopped.

"You've got to take gifts when they're given to you, Meg," Cassidy said in quiet rebuke. "It might be your baby's life we're talking about here."

"You're right, Cass. I'm sorry."

"What are we having?" Cassidy asked, swift to put the incident behind.

"Steaks. The potatoes have to go in pretty soon, and then there's corn to boil."

"I think I can handle that."

"What can't you handle?" Meg teased.

"Abi Pfister," Cassidy surprised Meg by saying.

Meg pulled a face. "Has she been spreading rumors again?"

"How did you know?"

"Because that's her way. Did she say something about you?"

Cassidy told her the story, but Meg's reaction was much calmer.

"You're right. Chandler should have come to you, but as far as Abi is concerned, consider the source, Cass. Everyone knows she's a lot of talk."

"Yes, but evidently she heard it from someone else."

"Then Abi's passing it along is just what you need. No one takes her seriously, and the news will die all the faster."

Cassidy felt herself relax. Thinking about it again had been unsettling. She had wrestled with the gossip long after Trace had left. It had been almost bedtime before she remembered that she was not in control and that God had a handle on things.

"Were you serious about dinner?" Meg asked just then.

"Very."

"All right. Let's head out. You've got potatoes to wash."

Cassidy followed her pregnant hostess, thinking that cooking in the spacious ranch kitchen was going to be fun.

⁂

"Tell me something," Cassidy said to Trace on the ride home.

"What?"

"Why do you take me back to town when the days are long right now?"

"Because the male inhabitants of Token Creek just can't be trusted. It's pretty quiet on Wednesday night, and you're right, it's light at this time of the year, but if something were to go wrong with the wagon or the horse and it got dark out, you'd be in a pretty vulnerable spot."

"And all this time I thought it was my charming company," Cassidy teased him.

"Well, that too," Trace teased right back.

"Oh!" Cassidy remembered. "Don't let me forget to run up and get the fabric I forgot to take earlier. I told Meg I would send it with you."

"All right. What is Meg making now?"

"This is for a shirt for Brad. I cut a bit of that bolt I used on Merle North's shirt. I'm pretty sure she'll like it."

"But will Brad?" Trace asked.

"You tell me, since you're two of a kind."

"Brad and I? We're nothing alike."

Cassidy had a good laugh over this, but Trace wasn't done. "Actually we're less alike than you think."

"How so?"

"Lots of ways. He likes his eggs scrambled—I like mine fried."

"That's significant," Cassidy said with just the right amount of sarcasm.

"And I like my coffee black," Trace put in, clearly in his element. "Brad will drink it black, but he prefers his with milk or cream."

Cassidy had to laugh again.

"On top of that," Trace added, "his favorite book of the Bible is James. Mine is Luke."

"Anything else?" Cassidy asked.

"No," Trace said with outrageous calm. "That about sums it up. You see, we're very different."

Cassidy could not stop smiling at him. Trace looked over, not wanting to smile back but not able to help himself.

"Why is Luke your favorite book?" Cassidy asked.

"Because of the story of Christ's birth—that's my favorite account of it. I also think Doctor Luke just adds aspects that are special all through the book."

"Luke was a doctor?"

"Yes. Chapter four of Colossians talks about Luke the beloved physician."

"How did I miss that?"

"I don't know."

"I'm going to have to read Luke again with that in mind."

"I think you'll like knowing. You and Luke might have had some things in common."

"Like what?"

"His heart seemed compassionate in his writing. You're a compassionate person, Cass."

"That was a nice thing to say."

"It might have been, but it's also true."

Cassidy smiled at him and realized they were almost at the livery. Trace took care of the horse and buggy while Cassidy waited for him out front. It was light enough to walk on her own, but it was nice to be seen to her door.

"All set?" she asked.

"Yes, ma'am."

"Thanks for always doing that."

"You're welcome. Don't forget that fabric," Trace remembered to add.

Cassidy ran upstairs to get it as soon as they arrived, and when she handed it to Trace, he fingered it in his free hand.

"It is nice fabric."

Cassidy smiled at him and couldn't resist one more tease. "Let's hope Brad likes it too. We wouldn't want there to be yet *another* thing you're different about."

Trace tried to scowl at her, but his smile peeked through.

"Goodnight, Mr. Holden," Cassidy said with evident satisfaction.

"Goodnight, Miss Norton," Trace bid softly, still wanting to laugh.

Cassidy slipped up the stairs and didn't look back. Had she looked, she would have found Trace watching her all the way inside.

CHAPTER FIVE

CASSIDY LOOKED INTO THE FACE of the five-year-old in her lap and tried not to laugh. Heidi Vick was telling her a story about her new puppy, and some words came easier than others. Her brother, Franklin, caught part of the tale and, being two years older, sat at Cassidy's side to help out.

"He's supposed to sleep outside," Franklin elaborated, "but he cries, so Papa lets him in Heidi's room."

"That's nice for the puppy."

"Buster," Heidi corrected.

"I like that name," Cassidy told her, suddenly realizing how much she wanted children of her own.

"He's going to be big," Franklin added. "Papa says."

"Big as me," Heidi put in.

"That's big," Cassidy said and smiled gently at the little girl. Heidi smiled shyly in response, and Cassidy's heart melted.

"Cassie, did you have some supper?" the children's mother came over to ask.

"I'm getting there, thanks, Miranda. Maybe the kids and I will go together."

Miranda smiled at her children, who clearly liked this idea, and without further discussion the four of them headed toward the buffet supper that Jeanette, Heather, and Becky had prepared. Fourteen people had gathered to celebrate Meg Holden's twenty-fourth birthday, and once Brad had prayed for the meal, folks were left to visit or eat as they pleased. Cake and presents were planned for later.

"I'll sit by you, Miss Cassidy," Franklin said when they had their plates.

"Oh, Franklin, I'm glad."

"Me too," Heidi said, her mother carrying her plate.

And the children did sit near her, but they were busy with their food, and the women had a chance to talk.

"How are you feeling?" Cassidy asked Miranda, who was due about a month after Meg.

"I'm still sick in the morning, but that's normal for me."

"I thought that just lasted a few weeks or months."

"I think it does for most women. I know Meg felt fine fairly soon."

"And how about labor? Is it harder for you because of that, or doesn't it make a difference?"

"My labor goes pretty fast. I hadn't thought about whether that was tied into sickness or not. I'll have to think on that."

Cassidy nodded, quite taken with the topic, but Miranda looked up and laughed. Her husband, Chas, was trying to go through the buffet line. Parker, the youngest Vick, was perched on one arm, clearly not going anywhere, making it a bit hard.

"He's been so clingy lately," Miranda explained. "Chas gets home, and he's all Parker wants."

"We're having a girl," Heidi announced out of the blue.

"You are?" Cassidy asked.

"Then it's even," she said with complete logic, and Cassidy had to put her napkin to her mouth to cover her smile.

"It's very clear to her," Miranda said softly. "We keep explaining that God might have other ideas, but she sees it only one way."

"And then after the baby's born," Cassidy said, "it's a problem either way, isn't it?"

Miranda's eyes got a bit large. "I hadn't thought of that. If it's a boy, we'll have some explaining to do. If it's a girl, she'll assume that *even* is how God does things."

The women had a good laugh over this as Brad watched them from across the room. He'd been eating and talking to Heather, but Becky had needed her and he'd found himself on his own.

"All alone?" Meg asked, taking Heather's seat, lowering herself into the chair.

"Only just," he said, not sure how long he'd been watching Cassidy.

"You look thoughtful," Meg said, studying her husband's face.

"I am." He looked into her eyes. "I've got to be careful or it might get me into trouble."

Meg's brows rose before she said, "That was cryptic."

Brad grinned. Meg would have pressed him to explain that smile, but Rylan joined them, and the topic did not come up again.

Meg's second pain hit her after dinner on Saturday. She was working on the dishes. Brad had just thanked her for the meal and left for the barn when that familiar knifelike pain went through her. She was sitting at the kitchen table, panting for breath and praying when Trace came in.

"Meg?" He took one look at her flushed face and went to her side. "What is it?"

"Just a pain."

"Let me help you to the sofa."

Trace's idea of *help* was to lift her and take her that way. All the time he walked, Meg told him she was all right, but he didn't listen.

"I'm getting Brad."

"Trace!" Meg raised her voice, and her brother-in-law stopped and looked at her. Meg opened her mouth to tell him she was all right but decided against it. The pain had subsided, but she knew that Brad would only worry unless he could see her.

"Nothing," Meg ended up saying, and Trace placed her on the sofa and left the house.

Not surprisingly, he and Brad were back in just minutes, both a little breathless. They found Meg sitting up, not lying down as Trace had left her.

"Are you all right?" Brad asked, taking a seat beside her. Trace did not speak but sat in a chair and looked on.

"I am. It was one of those pains again. No worse than last time."

Brad stared at his wife and made himself say what he was thinking. "Have you considered the possibility of moving into town?"

Meg looked at him in surprise.

"No," she said slowly. "I must admit such a thing never occurred to me."

"What are you thinking, Brad?" Trace asked.

"Only that she might need to be at Jeanette's or the Dorns' so she would be closer to the doctor."

"I want the baby to be born here," Meg said.

"I want that too," Brad agreed, "but not at the risk of you or the baby."

The three sat for a time in silence. It was on the tip of Trace's tongue to ask Brad if he was being hasty, but with the lives of two people to consider, it wasn't that simple.

"Why don't you discuss it with Doc Ertz," Trace suggested. "See if he has any ideas or thinks that being closer will help?"

Both Brad and Meg liked the idea, but Meg wanted to wait until Monday.

"Are you sure?" Brad asked. "We can go right now."

"No, I'm tired, and last time it happened I was tired. I don't want to run the risk of a pain hitting on the way into town. I'd rather wait until Monday morning."

"All right," Brad agreed, and then turned to his brother. "When you get into town tonight, I want you to tell Rylan and then Cass that we have to cancel for tomorrow."

"No, Brad," Meg argued, touching his arm. "Cassie will help me, and I'll nap after the meal."

Brad looked at her. "You'll tell me in the morning if you suspect you're not up to this?"

"I will. Please, Brad. I've been looking forward to having them all week."

Brad bowed his head until his forehead lay against Meg's. He did not have the words to explain what this woman did to his heart. The desire to protect her and lay the world at her feet was amazingly strong.

"For the moment you're all right?" Brad questioned again, his voice soft, his mind barely aware of the way Trace left them on their own.

"Yes. I'm going to lie down for a while to make sure."

Brad put his arms around her. Meg held him right back. Brad did not want to rush this baby, but a part of him wondered if he would survive the waiting. He thought it might be almost more than a man's heart could take.

※

Trace rode away from Token Creek on Saturday night, his mind half on the town, half on the time he'd just spent with Rylan, Chandler, and Philip.

They'd been in the book of Mark, and the discussion had been very good. Rylan had shared some things that Trace had never thought of before. The authority of Jesus Christ in the Gospels was unmistakable, but for the first time, Trace really looked at the response of the people. Some were quietly skeptical, some openly doubted, and others wanted to put Christ to death.

It made Trace think about the kind of message a man had to have to rile folks that badly. He'd had his brother mad at him more than one time in his life, but Brad never wanted to kill him. There was no getting around the fact that Jesus did not garner a lukewarm response. And another thing was also clear: People had not changed all that much in all these years. They still wanted God on their own terms.

As Trace was recalling some of what the men had talked about and shared, some things he'd seen while riding through town came back to mind. He could not remember the last time he'd been in Token Creek on a Saturday night. It was not a safe place. Boisterous noise, both music and voices, poured from the saloons, and two women had tried to speak to him from the shadows of a building. Two drunks argued over a horse, and at one point Trace heard gunfire.

Rylan's words about praying for Token Creek came to mind. Rylan lived in town, not near a saloon but close enough to hear the noise each week. In some ways the ranch was insulated, and Trace realized how much he needed those reminders. He finished the ride home, praying for the folks of Token Creek and remembering the church family's role and need for prayer as well.

⁂

Cassidy came from her apartment Sunday morning, taking the stairs with practiced ease but coming up short when she noticed Trace waiting for her at the bottom.

"Well, good morning," Cassidy said, finishing the stairs and joining him at the bottom.

"Good morning. Can I walk you to church?"

"Certainly."

"Tell me something," Trace began as soon as they started down the boardwalk. "Do you go out on Saturday nights?"

"Rarely. It's not very safe."

Trace nodded. Amid all his thoughts the night before, it had taken some time to remember Cassidy, but as Trace prayed, her safety came flooding into his mind, and he'd not been able to think of anything else.

"Do you own a gun, Cass?"

"No."

"Do you know how to shoot one?"

"No." This time she frowned. "What is going on, Trace?"

"I was in town last night to meet with Ry and the other men."

"Oh." Cassidy was catching on.

"I had a quick refresher of how bad Token Creek gets on Saturday nights. I forgot how noisy and drunken it could be."

"It's pretty bad," Cassidy had to agree.

"Do you feel safe?"

"Most of the time. It's hard if someone starts a fight outside the store or I hear gunshots."

"How do you get to sleep?"

"If I'm very tired, it doesn't matter. If not, it takes a while."

They weren't far from the church then, so Trace stopped, knowing they had time. He looked down at Cassidy, wanting to change her situation but not knowing how. The thought of her not being safe bothered him no small amount.

"What are you thinking?" Cassidy asked.

"I'm just wanting you to be safe. Nothing has changed for you. You've lived here for months, dealing with Saturday nights as they come, but it's new for me."

"Well, thank you for your concern, but as I said, I make sure I'm inside, even before dark falls. And lost sleep is not the worst thing that can happen."

They had turned off Main Street now and moved on toward the church.

"Good morning," Chandler greeted.

66

"How are you?" Cassidy asked.

"Doing well. Yourself?"

"Fine, thank you."

"How are you, Trace?"

Trace said he was fine but then went ahead and explained to Chandler what he'd been discussing with Cassidy.

"It helps that she's upstairs," Chandler said. "And none of her apartment windows look down on the street."

Cassidy listened to this and felt just a bit amazed. It never occurred to her that these men had given this any thought. It was nice. She felt cared for, but it was also a surprise.

Music could be heard coming from inside the church now, and Cassidy moved toward the door. The men trailed her, and the three sat together. Rylan started the service just a few minutes later.

⊰❧⊱

"Are we set?" Brad asked Meg, looking around the laden table, seeing that she had put on another great meal.

"I think so," she told him with a smile and then said to the group, "If you want something you don't see, just ask."

Everyone sat down, and Brad prayed. "Father God, it's a privilege to have Rylan and Cassie join us. Thank You for their presence in our lives. Thank You for the fine meal, all the hands that worked on it, and Your great provision to us. Amen."

No other words were needed. Food and conversation were in abundant supply, and no one wanted to waste either. They spent more than an hour eating and talking, and then without further discussion, all ended up in the kitchen doing the dishes in record time.

"Meg is going to lie down for a while," Brad said when things wound down a bit and the group began to make their way back to the living room. "Don't feel like you have to rush away."

"If you don't mind," Rylan said, taking the opportunity, "Cassie and I are going to take a little walk down by your stream."

"Sounds good," Brad said encouragingly. "We'll have dessert when everyone is back."

Cassidy had not been expecting this, but she appreciated Rylan remembering that she wanted to talk. The pastor headed toward the door, and Cassidy followed.

"I hope this was all right," Rylan said as they left the porch.

"Thank you for remembering."

"How are things at the store?" Rylan asked.

"Much better than I ever dreamed. I'm not going to retire wealthy, but I have plenty to live on."

"What's your favorite part about the work?"

"Well, I love to sew, but the people are the best part. It's never the same twice."

"Token Creek is a special place."

"I didn't know that a year ago at this time, but it's very clear to me now."

"We've never talked about how you came here."

"I tell people I was looking for a business opportunity, and that's true, but it's not the whole story."

Walking along the stream, Cassidy told Rylan about her past, the painful details of her family, and her biggest burden of all: whether she'd been wrong to keep this information to herself.

"Whom do you think you should have told?" Rylan asked.

"I don't know. Meg doesn't seem to think it's everyone's business, but I wonder if I should be more open about it."

"I can't see a reason to broadcast your life, Cassie. Unless I've missed something you're not seeing any of the men in the church family. You would certainly have to share if that were the case."

"No, you haven't missed anything," Cassidy reported without bitterness. "There's no romance in my life."

Rylan watched her for a moment. She was so special. He could think of several young men who would do well to have her as a wife.

"Thank you, Pastor, for hearing me out," Cassidy said, "and not holding anything against me."

"There's nothing to hold against you, Cassie."

The two started back toward the ranch house, the conversation moving to the sermon and Rylan's reminders that morning about showing hospitality. Cassidy said she'd learned a lot about that from Meg.

By the time they got back to the house that lady had gotten up from her rest. The five of them enjoyed the pie Cassidy had brought and visited for the rest of the afternoon.

❦

"Is Rylan interested in Cassidy?" Brad asked Trace when the men were out Sunday evening feeding the stock.

"Are you referring to the walk they took this afternoon?"

"Yes. Is there something going on?"

"I don't think so," Trace said. "If Rylan planned to pursue Cass, he wouldn't wait until they were here to do it. They live four blocks apart."

Brad let the matter drop, but it stayed on his mind. Trace, on the other hand, had been completely up front with his feelings and didn't give it another thought. If Rylan's interest was suddenly turning toward Cassidy, he'd be very surprised indeed.

❦

Doctor Ertz was not overly concerned about Meg's pains. He was glad she'd checked with him, but he did not think there was anything to panic over. Getting closer to town might be a good idea, but he didn't think it was time for that just yet.

Meg and Brad were both glad for his opinion but realized it didn't answer their questions about when Meg should move to town, if at all.

"We'll figure it out," Brad said, walking Meg across the street so she could pick up some things at Wheeler's. "And you'll have to stay rested."

Meg's mind went to work on the changes she could make in her daily routine, not even seeing that Brad was holding the door for her once they'd reached the store.

"Oh, my, Meg," he said quietly, smiling at her.

"What?"

"You're plotting or thinking."

Meg bit her lip, her eyes brimming with a smile.

"Am I right?" Brad pressed.

"Yes," Meg forced herself to admit before slipping inside the store. She had a long list and wanted to get to it, but her concerns about finding ways to have more rest were real. Predictable and caught by her husband or not, it was something they would have to discuss.

⁂

"You'd better get to the livery," Jeanette told Cassidy on Wednesday afternoon. "Meg will wonder where you are."

Cassidy noticed the time and realized she was right. With a few last-minute instructions, Cassidy headed toward the livery and found Mr. Stillwell in attendance.

"Hello, Mr. Stillwell," Cassidy greeted the livery owner. "How are you?"

"I'm fine, Miss Norton. Here for your rig?"

"Yes," Cassidy answered, wondering where Rylan was and wishing she could ask.

"I'll have it for you in just a few minutes."

Cassidy thanked him and learned in a hurry that his idea of a few minutes was not hers. About thirty minutes later than her usual time—and wishing she had asked if she could ready the rig herself—Cassidy finally headed for the Holden Ranch.

Meg and Trace sat on the front porch, watching for Cassidy's buggy. She was running late today, and Trace felt disappointment fill him. He'd been planning this for two days, and Cassidy's not being on time had never occurred to him.

"Are you going to ask or tell?" Meg wanted to know.

Trace smiled and said, "How does 'strongly suggest' sound?"

Meg smiled at her brother-in-law, thinking he was almost as sweet as her husband.

"You don't mind, do you, Meg?" Trace asked.

"Not at all. We are talking about Cassidy's safety here. How could I object to that?"

Before Trace could reply, he spotted the buggy. He met her before she could climb down and helped her alight.

"Change in plans today," Trace said, glad that Meg had come off the porch to join them.

"What's up?" Cassidy asked.

"Shooting first, sewing later."

Cassidy looked at Trace, then Meg, and back to Trace. Finally she asked of Meg, "Is he serious?"

"He is."

"Why do I need to learn to shoot?" Cassidy asked Trace, feeling she needed to add, "I don't own a gun."

"We'll work on that detail later," Trace said with complete calm. "You need to know how to protect yourself."

Cassidy looked as though she wanted to say something, but no words came out.

"What's the hesitation?" Trace asked, not wanting to railroad her but convinced this was necessary.

"Guns are a little scary."

"I don't think you'll feel that way when you've learned to handle one."

Cassidy looked at him a moment. "Meg," she finally asked her friend, "do you know how to shoot?"

Meg nodded. "Brad taught me."

Cassidy's gaze dropped to Meg's stomach. "You'll be in the house, far away from all of this, right?"

"Yes," Meg said with a laugh, and Trace took that as agreement.

"Okay," he wasted no time in saying, "you take your things inside, Cassie. I'll see to your horse and come for you as soon as I'm done."

Cassidy felt as though she'd been swept up in a storm but could find no reason to object. She was waiting with a certain degree of fear when he showed up just ten minutes later.

❧ CHAPTER SIX ❧

Rylan had asked Pete Stillwell for the day off, feeling behind in several areas of study and ready to take some extra time to pray for the church family. His plan worked until just after lunch, when a knock on his door interrupted everything.

Abi Pfister was standing there, paper ready, requesting—almost demanding—an interview. Rylan was not thrilled, but neither did he have a good reason to say no, realizing this was better than her showing up at the livery. Rylan was sure his boss would not appreciate that, and someone who did not understand the workings of a smith could make it downright dangerous.

"When did you come to Token Creek, Pastor Jarvik?"

"Five years ago."

"Exactly?" Abi asked her standard question.

"Let me see." Rylan had to think. "It will be five years in August."

Rylan, standing on his front porch, watched the woman write, wondering what would come next.

"Why Token Creek?"

"I knew the pastor who was here. Pastor English was not in the best of health and knew he wouldn't be staying in the pulpit much longer. He wrote and asked me to come and meet the folks here. I did and I stayed."

"Where are you from?"

"Denver."

Abi, head bent, ready to write, stopped and looked up at him. "Denver? I didn't know that. It's a long way."

"Yes, it is. The trains make it shorter these days, but five years ago, when it was trains *and* the stage, it took a very long time."

"How long before you leave for another church?"

"I don't have plans to leave Token Creek."

"I thought all preachers moved around."

"Not all."

"Wallis told me they did."

Rylan had heard this about Abi Pfister. She liked to tell as much as she was told. He didn't want to get into a gossip session with her, but he thought this might be a good time for the conversation to get a bit personal.

"I think some do, but when I read my Bible I see great value in the local church family. The New Testament displays over and over again the importance of the local church, and as long as Token Creek needs a pastor, and I'm able and qualified for the job, I plan to stay."

"What qualifies you?" Abi asked, her paper dropping in spite of herself.

"The qualifications for an elder are laid out in First Timothy."

"An elder? I thought you were a pastor."

"I'm called pastor, but my job is that of elder."

"I never read the Bible," Abi said softly, still forgetting she was supposed to be interviewing Rylan.

"Is there a reason you don't?" Rylan asked kindly.

"It's an old book, and I like new ones."

"It is an old book, but not just any old book. The truths of the Bible are very relevant today."

"You have to say that; you're a preacher."

"I don't have to say that. I believe it with all my heart."

"Are you going to start preaching at me?"

"Is that part of the interview?"

Abi surprised him by giving a short crack of laughter. For a moment more she continued to be distracted but eventually went back to work.

"Where is your family?"

"Denver."

"Anyone going to join you here?"

"No."

"No wife, no children?"

"No to both."

Abi suddenly speared him with her eyes. "I don't know if I trust a preacher who isn't married."

"Why is that?" Rylan asked, not the least offended.

Abi was disarmed by this. She hadn't expected him to ask her why. "I don't know," she snapped a little. "I just don't."

"Well, if you figure it out," Rylan encouraged, his voice as calm as ever, "let me know."

Abi had no choice but to admire the man, although she did not let this show on her face. There was no artifice in him. She knew that Sheriff Kaderly thought very highly of him, as did everyone else she talked to. If rumor could be believed, Rylan Jarvik did not talk one way and act another.

"That's all for now," Abi said, putting her things into her bag, her lopsided hat bobbing in the process. "But I might be back."

"And I might be here," Rylan answered, a little tease in his voice.

"Well, I can always find you at the livery."

"I can't be interviewed if I'm working," Rylan took the opportunity to say. "It's not safe in a livery, and Pete Stillwell pays me to work."

Abi didn't like being reminded that she was in the habit of disturbing folks while they worked. Jessie Wheeler would never talk to her when the store was open, and if Abi had been thinking right, she would have realized that Jessie had customers who needed her more, and two daughters to look after as well. What folks didn't understand was that *she* had a book to write, and it was important.

"Was there anything else?" Rylan asked, and Abi realized she'd been standing there doing nothing.

"No," she said, her voice clipped. With that word, she turned and walked away. Rylan said goodbye, but she didn't answer, nor did she thank him. She never thanked anyone for their story. What she was doing was important. The folks of Token Creek should be thanking her!

❈

"It's heavier than it looks," Cassidy said after Trace showed her how to hold the revolver.

"Use two hands," he instructed, watching her closely.

"And you're sure it has no bullets yet?"

"Here, I'll show you," Trace took the weapon back, broke it open and showed her the empty chambers. "See," he said, holding it for her to examine. "All clear."

Cassidy looked into the gun and then up into the cowboy's face, shaded by his hat but still very clear.

"Trace," Cassidy said quietly, "what happened Saturday night that did this?"

Trace looked into her blue eyes, clear and trusting as a child's. He knew he had to leave Cassidy's life in God's hands, but if there was something he could do to prevent her being harmed, he had to do it.

"I've been naive about life in town," Trace admitted. "Jeanette is not on Main Street. She's away from the saloons. The other women I know live with their husbands or fathers. You're more alone on Saturday night than I ever realized. Teaching you to shoot does not make everything all right, but if there was ever a need to protect yourself, you would know how."

Cassidy nodded, not sure she could shoot this gun but not willing to admit that.

"Okay, take the revolver again, with both hands, and just point it at the target I set up."

Cassidy did as she was told, finding it a little easier with both hands, but also discovering that her arms tired easily.

"I think you might take for granted how strong your arms are, Trace."

"You sew for a living. You could probably crack nuts with those fingers of yours."

"That might be true, but I don't hold my sewing two feet in front of me, and my strength is not in my arms."

"Are you telling me you can't do this, Miss Norton?" Trace asked, a clear challenge in his voice.

Cassidy's chin came up. "I didn't say that."

"Then get that gun steadied and aimed."

Cassidy positioned the gun and then looked defiantly at her instructor.

"Anything else, Mr. Holden?"

Trace had to grin before saying, "Pull the trigger."

The weapon trembled a bit, but she did it, her face a mixture of fear and surprise even with that empty click.

"How was that?" Cassidy asked, a bit breathless, all defiance gone.

"Very good." Trace's praise was genuine. "Do it again. See if you can get things a little steadier this time."

Cassidy worked along strongly for the next thirty minutes. Not until Trace noticed the sweat trickling down her right temple did he realize she was without a bonnet or hat and the June sun was relentless above them.

"Let's take a break."

"A break?"

"I thought it might be time."

"I can do this," Cassidy said with certainty.

"Yes, you can," Trace encouraged, "but it's hot out here, and you're working hard."

Cassidy agreed and soon after their break learned that there would be no time for sewing that day. With the gun finally loaded, she would not stop working with the revolver until she got it right. Trace pressed her to knock *all* the cans from the fence, and that took some doing. Indeed it took until nearly suppertime, but she accomplished it.

⁂

"What are you looking at?" Meg asked Brad, catching him at the window when she thought he was working on some paperwork.

"Just the shooting lesson."

"How is she doing?"

"Good."

Hearing his distracted tone, Meg stared at her husband's profile. "What are you thinking about?"

Brad looked down at Meg, slipped an arm around her, and said, "Things I'm not ready to talk about. Can I tell you later?"

"Sure," Meg said, cuddling and working to keep her imagination calm.

Brad's free hand went to his wife's stomach, and he simply held her close. He was not willing to put thoughts into Meg's head when he wasn't even sure what to do with the ones in his own.

⁂

Cassidy was nowhere near as lively during supper as the Holden family was used to seeing. And when after the meal ended Trace suggested they head to town a little early, she did not argue. Trace didn't press her to talk but got her home without delay. He told her she'd done a great job, and she looked pleased, but there was no missing the fatigue that hung on her. It would not have surprised him to learn that Cassidy went to bed as soon she got home and slept hard all night.

⚜

Token Creek's seamstress was not the only person who took Rylan's words on hospitality to heart. Before she could invite the Holdens for a meal, the Vick family asked her to join them for Sunday dinner.

"This is Buster," Heidi told Cassidy with pride, taking her to see the dog the moment she arrived and looking very pleased when Cassidy went down on her knees to pet the puppy who had clearly just wakened. He yawned, and his little eyes began to close again as Cassidy stroked his downy-soft head.

"He's such a sweet dog, Heidi. No wonder you love him."

Heidi looked pleased and, as in the past, Cassidy's heart melted over her shy smile and shining brown eyes.

"Don't let that sleepy look fool you," Chas said, having watched the scene. "When he cries in the night or chews up my shoes, he's not so charming."

"Don't let Chas fool you either, Cassie," Miranda added, having to tease her husband. "This is also the man who lets that dog sleep on his lap after the kids are in bed."

Chas laughed at being caught. Miranda laughed with him and told everyone that dinner was ready. Parker had some rough moments because he wanted to sit in his father's lap and not his chair, but eventually his tears and attitude were dealt with and the meal began.

"Do you know Trace?" Franklin asked Cassidy while dishes were still being passed.

"I do know Trace."

"He talked to me today," Franklin offered, his little face showing pleasure without smiling.

"What did you talk about?"

"His ranch. I've been there. He has a horse."

"Yes, he does," Cassidy agreed. "I think his name is Quincy."

Franklin nodded in agreement, and Cassidy's eyes eventually swung to Miranda, who quietly filled her in.

"Franklin wants to own a ranch and have a horse someday. He thinks Trace and Brad are pretty special."

"Not a carpenter?" Cassidy asked, looking to Chas who had built several of Token Creek's houses and could turn his hand to anything involving wood.

"Not at seven," Chas said with a smile, not at all offended by his son's dreams. "He might change his mind when he sees how much cheaper a hammer is than a horse."

Cassidy was careful not to laugh out loud, never wanting Franklin to think she was making fun of him, but she was tempted. He was so sincere and sweet, and everything about the Vick children delighted her.

At the end of the meal, Parker even let her hold him, his three-year-old body warm and snug against her as they looked at a book, confirming yet again to Cassidy that she wanted children of her own. However, she never dreamed that Chas was already working to find her a husband.

❧

"Why have none of our men snatched up Cassidy Norton?" Chas asked Miranda much later that day.

Miranda looked at Chas, surprised to hear him say this. She wanted to tease him about matchmaking but stayed serious.

"Are you thinking of someone in particular?"

"Rylan and Trace are the first two who come to mind."

"Will you talk to either of them?"

Chas smiled. "Nope. If they're not bright enough to see that she's special, they don't deserve her."

The two shared a look and both laughed. Chas was done talking about it, having said all that was on his mind. Miranda, however, had a hard time getting to sleep, the future of Cassidy Norton filling her mind.

⁓

"And I need to have this fixed," Mrs. Hibbard said of the next thing on a long list, standing in Cassidy's shop on Saturday morning and pointing to a popped seam on a dress Cassidy and Jeanette had made. "I think if you had sewn this correctly the first time, it would have stayed sewn."

Cassidy did not argue but made note of the area, planning to fix the dress to Mrs. Hibbard's satisfaction. Jeanette, standing by to help, placed a pin in the spot so they would miss nothing.

"And here," Mrs. Hibbard displayed the last complaint. "The fabric doesn't look right here. I don't like it."

Cassidy looked at the skirt of the dress, not sure what she was supposed to be seeing.

"Could you show me exactly where, Mrs. Hibbard?" she asked.

"Right there!" that lady snapped. "See how the weave is off?"

Cassidy did not see and had no choice but to shake her head.

"Maybe if we go into better light," Jeanette suggested, full of admiration for her boss who did not answer back or try to defend their work.

"Right there!" Mrs. Hibbard pointed again, and Cassidy had to give up.

"I think what I want to do, Mrs. Hibbard, is simply return your money. I don't see what you need here, and I don't think I'm the best person to try to fix your dress. I can repair these other things, but I can't see what's wrong with the weave in the front here, so I'm just going to give you your money back."

"What about my dress?" Mrs. Hibbard demanded.

"Well, you'll have your money back," Cassidy said reasonably, "and maybe you can find someone else to fix the weave."

"Fine," the irate customer said tightly. "I'll be back for this on Monday."

Cassidy nodded. She would have to put off other work to get it done, but she wanted Mrs. Hibbard gone, and today could not be soon enough.

The door closed too hard when that lady exited, but Cassidy didn't say a word. Going directly to her sewing machine, she got to work on Mrs. Hibbard's dress. Jeanette's heart wrung with compassion over what she'd just seen, but she didn't comment or try to comfort her. She went back to her own work, hoping it would stay quiet for a time.

It didn't. The door opened not five minutes later, and both women looked up to see Chandler Di Fiore standing just inside the door. He did not look happy.

"May I speak with you, Cassidy?"

"Certainly."

"I was going over some accounts this morning, and I've made an error in yours."

Cassidy's heart sank a little, but she did not speak. Jeanette, owning the bank and having known Chandler for years, was not silent.

"Is it in Cassidy's favor, Chandler?" The older woman went right to the point.

"No. She actually has ninety dollars less than we thought."

Jeanette looked stunned by this, but Cassidy remained quiet, and her face did not give her thoughts away.

"I'm sorry, Cassidy," Chandler went on. "I assume the mistake is in your bankbook too."

"It's all right, Chandler. These things happen."

"Do you want to get your bankbook, Cass?" Jeanette asked. "You could send it with Chandler, and he could make sure it's corrected."

"Yes, I'll do that," Cassidy agreed, feeling a little numb. Ninety dollars was a lot of money. Her account had been nicely padded. She almost dreaded finding where the numbers would end up.

"I'm sorry, Cassidy," Chandler said again, his eyes searching her quiet face. He almost wished she would get upset with him. Her quiet response was harder to take than his own recriminations.

"It's all right, Chandler. I'll come after work, and you can tell me where things ended up."

"All right."

Cassidy went back to her sewing machine. Chandler stood for a moment, watching her, before looking at Jeanette with all the misery he felt. Her face was compassionate. Her husband had been a banker long enough for her to understand these kinds of mistakes, but that didn't make it any easier.

Chandler slipped back out the door into the warm day. He walked slowly back to the bank, the weight of this mistake resting heavily upon him. He hoped and prayed that when all was figured out and resettled that Cassidy would not be left in need.

※

Whom do you trust, Cassidy Norton? that woman asked herself as she sewed, her movements swift with agitation. *Where does your trust lie? Have you made your bankbook into a god?*

"Are you all right?" Jeanette had waited a little while to ask.

"I think so." Cassidy stayed bent over the machine. "I'm having a little talk with myself."

"Is it helping?"

For some reason this made Cassidy smile. She turned to Jeanette and laughed a little.

"Yes," the younger woman was able to say. "It's helping."

Jeanette laughed with her, and with both hearts still prayerful, the women went back to work.

Cassidy came back from the bank a little shocked. Her savings had been drastically depleted. At the same time, two folks had come in that day whom she'd never met. One ordered work, and the other was considering a project and even looking at one of the quilts.

Cassidy knew that God would not leave her alone in this. She had to make a living, and He was more aware of that fact than she was. Cassidy was talking to Him about that when she turned the corner to head up her stairs and found Trace Holden sitting on the bottom step.

"Oh, Trace!" Cassidy stopped short. "You startled me."

Trace came to his feet and removed his hat. "I'm sorry. I found your shop locked, and no one answered your door. I assumed you'd gone to the bank."

"Yes, I did. Are you meeting with Rylan tonight?"

"No, I came into town to deliver this."

Cassidy took the letter Trace was holding out to her. She looked at him a moment, but he just stood there. Cassidy eventually opened the letter and read.

Dear Cassie,

Sometimes it takes us a while. I'm only glad it didn't take longer. The three of us have talked, and we want you to stay with us on Saturday nights. Trace will come for you, or bring you later if he has study with Rylan. Your proximity to the saloons is not safe on Saturday night, and we won't take no for an answer. Gather what you need for tonight and in the morning,

and come with Trace. I know he won't leave
town without you.

Love, Meg

Cassidy read it, and read it again. She finally looked at Trace.

"Do you know what this says?"

"Sure. Brad and I were there when she wrote it."

"But the three of you are to come to dinner tomorrow after the service."

"Meg said you would bring that up. She said to remind you that we can help you with the meal, or we can make it another week when you've had more time to plan."

Cassidy opened her mouth to argue, but Trace had more.

"Your hospitality is appreciated, Cass. We were all looking forward to it, but it's not as important as your being safe."

"But I've been staying in my apartment for the eight, almost nine, months I've lived here."

"But things are different now," Trace said.

"How so?"

"I've been reminded as to what town is like on Saturday nights, and that's just not going to work for us anymore."

He had sounded almost arrogant, and Cassidy's chin came up. Trace recognized the signs from their shooting lesson the previous week. Without warning, he put his hat back on his head, sat down on the step, and talked out loud to himself.

"It's going to be a long night on this step with no dinner and no breakfast. And I'm not going to be very fresh or even shaved for church in the morning. It's a sad thing."

Cassidy's hand came up to cover her smile. Trace didn't look at her, or he would not have managed to keep his own smile hidden.

"You're pathetic, do you know that?" Cassidy asked.

Trace heard the acquiescence in her voice and stood. With one hand the cowboy indicated the stairs. "If you'll gather your things, Miss Norton, I'll wait for you right here."

With unconscious grace, Cassidy swept up the stairs. She knew some moments of panic about what to take and how to make it work in the morning. She didn't actually believe she would do this every week, but for the moment, she gathered her things and went back downstairs.

Trace assisted her into the wagon, and almost before she could gather her thoughts, they'd pulled under the wooden arch where the Holden Ranch sign hung. Meg must have been watching because both she and Brad were in the yard waiting for her.

Without warning, the events of the day came flooding back to Cassidy. The sight of her friend, standing there in warm welcome, put tears in her eyes. Meg saw them but didn't comment. She put her arms around Cassidy and hugged her close.

"This is where you belong on Saturday nights, Cass," Meg said quietly. "We'll take care of you now."

Cassidy, who had been ready to argue about this plan, could only thank Meg and the men. She had been so confident that God would take care of her, and wasn't He doing that right now?

CHAPTER SEVEN

"How did it go at the bank yesterday?" Jeanette asked Cassidy as soon as she arrived at the church.

Cassidy looked into her eyes for a moment before saying, "Let's just say I'm glad I have steady work."

Jeanette nodded and gave her a swift hug. She was so proud of the younger woman that she could barely speak. Cassidy was not panicked or angry but was facing this setback with calmness and humility.

"Something you want to share with me, Cass?" Trace was suddenly saying into her ear.

Cassidy turned slowly, not aware of how close he'd been when Jeanette questioned her. "Why do you ask that?"

"It just sounded like something was a little bit wrong."

Cassidy didn't realize her chin had come up until Trace reached with one finger and pushed it back into place.

"What's up?" he pressed, and Cassidy thought fast.

"Jeanette was asking me about work."

"At the bank?"

Cassidy mentally scolded Jeanette for checking on her in a public place but was rescued from answering when the music started.

"We'd better sit down," Cassidy said, and Trace had to smile at the relief in her voice. Whatever was going on, she did not want to talk about it. He would certainly not press her, at least not right then, but the eyes he had trained on her were not missing much.

"We've talked off and on about the fear of the Lord for more than a year now," Rylan said near the end of his sermon. "I've had varying responses concerning that topic, but the one that strikes me the most is about time lost, time wasted. What does a person do who's started to fear the Lord too late? I don't mean too late in the sense that there's no hope, but too late as in time lost.

"My best answer is to look at the life of Paul, who as an adult had his life completely turned around by God. Once Paul understood who Christ was and what He'd done for him on the cross, there was no stopping him. He doubled his efforts. He worked all the harder for the start he had. In the same way we need to double our own efforts. Double our humility, our zeal, wisdom, and devotion.

"Don't be discouraged. Paul wasn't. You talk about wasted time, Paul was born late, but he made up for that, and we can learn from his example. When you read Paul's letters, keep that in mind. Remember that he doubled his efforts.

"Let's pray together. Father God, we thank You for Your Word and the example of men like Paul. Thank You for being the God who lets us start the race late but still win. Help us to go from this place with You on our mind and hearts. Bless each one here and in Your will and time bring us back together next week. In the name of Jesus I pray these things. Amen."

The congregation dispersed, but Brad looked thoughtful. Meg noticed his face and took his hand.

"Are you all right?"

"Yes. I was encouraged by those last words."

"I was remembering my father with his milking," Meg said. "When the cows didn't give as much milk as he'd counted on, he used to say there was nothing more he could do. I always felt my mother's helplessness in those times. I don't know what made it come to mind, but not being helpless in this is so freeing."

"Yes, it certainly is," Brad agreed, giving Meg's hand a squeeze. Almost before he was done saying this, Trace came to stand beside them.

"Are we going to Cassie's now?" the younger brother asked.

"Did she already head out?" Meg asked.

"She must have because I don't see her."

"Let's go," Brad said as he stood. They had decided to eat at Cassidy's, but Brad knew she would want to do more than she needed. She was like Meg in that way, very caring and a bit too hard on herself.

The three went to Cassidy's and found her working hard. She had pulled her small kitchen table away from the wall so everyone would fit around it and was heating a pot of something on the stove. The contents smelled wonderful, and it became obvious that Cassidy had already planned ahead. While they watched, Cassidy finished mixing cake batter, and poured it into pans that went into the oven of the cookstove.

"I think things are ready," Cassidy said with a smile, wondering why she hadn't done this months ago. "Please sit down."

"We were all ready to help you," Meg said, smiling at her friend as she began to put food on the small table.

"I had things in pretty good shape, and I left right after the service so I could get started on that cake."

"Is it the recipe you gave me?" Meg asked when Cassidy sat down with them.

"Yes, it's my favorite."

"It's our favorite too," Brad said dryly, knowing that when Meg made it, he and Trace tried to eat it all. Meg, thinking the same thing, laughed at him.

The table fell silent then, and for some reason Cassidy felt awkward.

She wanted to ask one of the men to pray but suddenly felt herself blushing. Trace caught her look and came to the rescue.

"Do you want me to pray?"

"Please," Cassidy answered, glad to have an excuse to close her eyes and gather her thoughts. She wasn't sure she caught any of Trace's prayer, but she had managed to pray and calm down before he said amen.

"How's business?" Brad asked Cassidy as they began to eat.

Cassidy didn't answer, and Brad found her looking at his brother.

"I didn't put him up to that," Trace said, preferring things to be out in the open.

Cassidy looked apologetic and turned to Brad. "It has its ups and downs, but I make it every month."

"I'm glad," Brad said, wanting to ask what had just gone on but forcing himself not to.

"Any interesting customers this week?" Meg asked, also wondering if something was wrong but opting to change the subject.

"I had an interesting order," Cassidy said, not wanting to talk about Mrs. Hillard even if she didn't mention her by name. "One woman wants a rather elaborate tablecloth. It's a very creative design—just not very practical."

"Why is that?"

"She wants some quilting and piecework. It would be nice if she was going to use it for a bedspread, but I don't know that I would want people eating off of it."

The men ate quietly while the women discussed this tablecloth. The food was very good, so it wasn't hard work, but when Meg suddenly noticed how empty their plates were, she laughed.

"Not interested in tablecloths, Brad?" she teased.

"I'm interested in ones that are holding food I can eat."

Husband and wife shared a smile. Trace was reaching for more bread, and Cassidy pushed the butter a little closer to him before checking on her cake pans. She brought the cakes out to cool, and then the conversation shifted to the sermon.

"I had never seen Paul in that light before," Trace shared. "It's motivating."

"And challenging," Brad put in. "There are no excuses."

"And I appreciated his reminder of how much we have to be humble about," Meg added.

"When was that?" Trace asked.

"At the beginning of the sermon. He was talking about how much we need saving, and then mentioned the last verse in Second Corinthians and the way Paul ended his letter with God's grace being upon us."

The conversation roamed to other sermons until they had finished their food. Cassidy cleared the table and started on a frosting for the cake. She didn't get far, however, because Meg settled in the living room, her feet up, eyes heavy, wanting to know what sewing project Cassidy was working on.

"The same quilt. It's not going that swiftly."

Cassidy brought out the full-size quilt in an amazing array of colors. It was technically a rag quilt, but Cassidy had matched the fabrics so well that she still managed to create a beautiful design.

"Go to sleep," Cassidy said, finally noticing Meg's face. The men had settled in the room, Brad with a newspaper and Trace looking at the bookshelf. Cassidy went back to the small kitchen and kept going on the frosting. It wasn't long before Trace followed her.

"What flavor?"

"What do you think?" Cassidy asked with a smile.

"Chocolate," Trace said with satisfaction, having sprawled at the kitchen table. "So tell me," he went on, "are you sure you're all right?"

Cassidy turned from the bowl to answer. "I am, Trace. Thanks for asking."

"All right," Trace nodded, watching her. "I'll expect you to say so if you're not."

"I will." Cassidy smiled at him, thinking that his caring was very sweet.

Trace nodded and got slowly to his feet. "I'll get out of your way."

"All right. I'll have this ready in a bit."

Trace went back to the living room to find his brother and sister-in-law dozing. He got comfortable in the chair and continued to think about what he'd heard Jeanette say that morning.

In the kitchen, Cassidy thought about it as well, glad that Trace had not pressed her but almost wishing she could discuss it with him. She dismissed the idea as fanciful, finished the cake, and made coffee. As soon as Meg woke, dessert would be ready.

⁂

Jeanette spent a long time thinking about Cassidy and her finances early Monday morning. She wanted to give her some money but not have Cassidy know whom it was from. At the same time, she and Chandler were the only ones who knew about the bank mistake, and Cassidy was sure to figure it out.

Jeanette looked down at the table, her Bible open to Proverbs. She had been reading when she remembered Cassidy, and without much encouragement her brain had been off and running.

Going back to Proverbs, Jeanette told herself that she had to have her own level of trust for Cassidy's life. She also realized she didn't have to dwell on helping her. If she was supposed to do that, something would come to mind.

⁂

"How are you?" Chandler asked Cassidy, having come to see her on Tuesday at lunchtime. The two had not talked since Saturday.

"I'm fine, Chandler. How are you?"

Chandler looked at her, not sure if she'd misunderstood him or not. He'd been tortured by the mistake and figured she must be in the same state.

"I meant," Chandler tried again, "how are you in reference to my news last Saturday?"

"Most of the time, I'm all right. Sometimes I worry."

"I feel as though I didn't express to you how bad I feel. I don't think I said enough."

"I appreciate that, Chandler, but it's not your fault. It could have happened to anyone."

Chandler nodded, but it was hard to accept Cassidy's forgiveness. He knew her finances. She worked hard for what she had and trusted his bank to take care of it. He felt they'd let her down. It wasn't as though they'd taken money from her. It was money she didn't have in the first place, but she'd thought she had it, and that made it a miserable situation.

"Tell me something," Chandler asked, truly wanting to know. "Why are you all right with this?"

Cassidy had to think about that. Some of the answer tied in to her past, and she wasn't going to talk to Chandler about that, but she still wanted to answer his question.

"I try not to be too impressed by money," Cassidy began. "You might wonder what that has to do with anything, but it is part of the answer. I have no guarantees that I'll have business next week. Folks might decide not to order anything, or they might not need to have anything fixed, and then it will be a lean week.

"That's what I counted on the money for. It's not there so I can feel good about myself. I've known people who had money, but you would never know that by talking to them. Jeanette is that way. There are others who have money and make sure everyone knows it. I also know folks who don't have any money but talk about nothing else. I don't appreciate any of that. It's not important enough to talk about.

"I would not mind having some surplus so I can give more

generously to the church family and others, but outside of my needs, I don't want a lot of money."

Cassidy could feel herself babbling and stopped. She wondered if she'd offended Chandler. After all, he worked with money all the time. She felt her face grow warm and made herself look him in the eye.

"Did any of that make sense?"

"Yes, Cassidy. Thank you for telling me."

Cassidy heard the thoughtfulness in Chandler's voice and wondered what he was really thinking. She wanted to ask him—it was important to her to know—but Mrs. Hibbard chose that moment to come in.

"I'll see you later," Chandler said, and after greeting Mrs. Hibbard went on his way.

"Hello," Cassidy said cautiously to the lady in her shop, not sure if she was up to seeing her.

"Hello, Cassidy. I wish to order a dress."

Cassidy had all she could do not to gawk at her. She kept her features schooled, however, and her voice even. "I'm not sure if that's a good idea, Mrs. Hibbard. I wasn't able to help you before, and nothing has changed in the way I do things."

"Are you saying you don't want my business?" that lady asked in shock.

"I'm saying the way I sew doesn't please you."

"Well." Mrs. Hibbard seemed flustered but did not leave. "I guess I thought you would at least be willing to try again."

Cassidy stared at her and knew what she had to do.

"I'll make another dress for you, Mrs. Hibbard, but there will be conditions. I won't return your money next time. I'll make repairs that are clearly my fault, but I can't afford to make dresses I don't get paid for."

The look on the other woman's face told Cassidy she had hoped for that very thing. Her eyes darted around the room a bit before coming back to Cassidy.

"I'll think on it," Mrs. Hibbard said after a moment.

Cassidy nodded and was not given time to say anything more. Mrs. Hibbard turned and left without a word.

"Shame on you, Mrs. Hibbard," Cassidy spoke softly into the empty shop. "You're old enough to know better."

Only just remembering to pray for that lady, Cassidy went back to her sewing machine. She was very thankful when the next customer was Mrs. Potts. Not only was she kind and fun to work for, the order she left with Cassidy was a large one.

<hr />

"This looks great," Cassidy said sincerely to Meg on Wednesday afternoon, studying the careful handwork on the shirt she was making for Brad. "He's going to be pleased."

"I want to ask you a favor."

"Okay."

"Can you put the collar and cuffs on?"

"I can, Meg, but you don't need me."

"Oh, Cassie," Meg said with a laugh, trying to persuade her friend. Cassidy was not falling for it, seeing that Meg was doing a fine job. But then Meg sealed the deal.

"I'm going to have this baby anytime now, and I don't have a sewing machine."

Cassidy had to bite her lip to keep from laughing. "That was pathetic. You know that, don't you?" she asked.

"Yes, but did it work?"

Cassidy couldn't deny her. She agreed to finish the shirt if Meg didn't need it before next week. The women gave up on sewing and went to the kitchen.

"Do you think you still remember how to shoot?" Trace asked Cassidy on the way back to town. Both were on horseback. The livery had rented the buggy Cassidy usually took, so this time she simply requested a horse.

"I think so," she spoke on a laugh. "My arms ached for days, I hope you realize."

"You worked hard."

"I didn't have a choice. My teacher was impossible, very demanding and strict."

Trace turned to look at her, but Cassidy kept her eyes to the front and fought a smile.

"It's terrible," she went on conversationally. "I have to make a living with my hands and arms, and then on my day off I'm expected to work like that."

"Is that right?" Trace spoke up.

"Um hm."

"That's not the way I remember it."

"Well, of course not. You're older than I am. Your memory is failing."

Trace could not hold his laughter, and Cassidy joined him, looking very pleased to have momentarily gotten the upper hand.

"Oh!" Cassidy exclaimed, "your aunt's birthday is coming up. Do you know of anything special I could get her?"

"You're asking me? I think Meg might be your best bet on that."

"You must have some idea," Cassidy pressed him. "I could make her something, but that seems rather obvious."

"How so?"

"I don't know. I thought it would be more fun to come up with something original."

Trace's face was fully turned to her now.

"And you think *I'm* the one to come up with an idea like that?"

Cassidy bit her lip but still ended up laughing. His face was so horrified she couldn't help herself.

"All right," Cassidy said, trying a new tack. "What did you give her last year?"

"The same thing I give her every year, a hug and a kiss."

"What did Meg give her? Do you remember?"

"No."

"Oh, that's right, your age and memory are going."

Trace smiled before he could catch himself. "You're rather impertinent, Miss Norton. I hope you know that."

Cassidy only laughed and continued to tease him about his aunt's birthday gift. They laughed all the way back to town. Not until Trace had seen her back to her apartment did Cassidy realize she still didn't have an idea for Jeanette's birthday.

❦

The following Sunday the Token Creek church family celebrated the Fourth of July with the townsfolk. This year it was on a Sunday, so they were all running a bit late after the service but were no less welcome. Tables had been put along the creek where it was cooler for the potluck.

Cassidy came with her basket of goods to share, set her dishes on the table with all the other offerings, and turned to find Jessie Wheeler at a table. Her daughters were with her. Cassidy joined them and was most welcome.

"How are you, Jessie?" Cassidy asked.

"I'm doing well. Yourself?"

"Most weeks it's going well. I appreciate the folks you send my way."

Jessie smiled. "You heard about that, did you?"

"Yes. More than one woman has told me that you redirected her when you didn't have what she needed. So once again, thank you."

"You're welcome," Jessie said, smiling in a way that made her look just like her two blonde daughters.

"Hi, girls," Cassidy called in greeting.

"Miss Cassie," Clancy, the youngest, wasted no time in saying, "we brought beans."

"That sounds good. I made a cake."

"What kind?"

"Chocolate."

Cassidy smiled when Clancy licked her lips.

"You got her attention," Jessie said, laughing at her younger daughter. "Oh, here comes Rylan," she said next, and Cassidy turned to see Rylan and Chandler headed their way.

The two men greeted the ladies, and all fell to talking. Not until Mayor Lake, who had been in office for almost six months, welcomed the folks and thanked everyone for coming did people start toward the food tables. Food was plentiful and delicious, and folks did not need to be asked twice. The festivities had officially begun.

"How are you?" Brad asked his wife, having taken her to Jeb and Patience's house to lie down. They were on the way to the picnic when a pain had hit her. She had fallen asleep, and Brad had stayed close by.

"I'm sorry," she began.

"There's nothing to apologize about, Meg. You can't control this."

She sighed and tried to sit up. Brad helped her before sitting down beside her, an arm around her.

"On top of that," Brad went on, "it's going to be warm out there, so a little time indoors is not all bad."

"Did Patience and Jeb go?"

"Um hm."

Meg smiled. Brad sounded sleepy, and she could tell he was comfortable beside her.

"You should have slept when I did."

"You were only out for about ten minutes."

"Do you want your own ten minutes?"

Brad smiled at the temptation but said no. The two left for the picnic a little while later.

⚜

"It's the Fourth of July, Mama," Trace said quietly, wanting to be near his mother right now. "The picnic is going on by the creek. I don't remember if we ever went to one of those when I was younger."

Trace stopped, not letting his mother's silence bother him. He looked around the porch at the plants and nice furniture. His aunt had done a fine job making it cozy and comfortable.

"Brad and Meg went to the picnic. I'll join them later. Jeanette is there too. I think Becky is going to stay with you for a while so Heather can go."

This said, Trace allowed a good deal of silence to fall. He looked at his mother, just enjoying being with her for this time and telling her different stories and things from his heart before Becky came with something for her to drink.

"Thanks, Becky," Trace said thickly, all of a sudden feeling emotional.

"You're welcome," Jeanette's cook said, smiling with all the kindness she felt, wishing as Heather always did that Mrs. Holden could snap out of her trance and enjoy her fine sons.

CHAPTER EIGHT

"How did she do?" Brad asked Trace about their mother as they made their way home. The picnic by the creek was winding down, and Meg was flagging.

"Very well."

"Maybe it helped to be there alone," Meg suggested.

"Maybe," Trace said, thinking about the possibility. He usually went with Brad, and perhaps visiting his mother alone was worth more consideration.

"Who won that last footrace?" Brad suddenly asked, remembering some of the games that had been played.

"I think it was Adam Stillwell," Meg said.

"You should have raced, Brad," Trace put in.

"I don't know," Meg said doubtfully and without malice. "I'm usually faster."

"That's true," Brad agreed immediately, and Trace looked at his brother for a moment.

The three fell quiet after that. It was still very warm out, and Meg, less than three weeks from the baby's due date, was warm and uncomfortable. Brad got her inside as soon as they arrived home and then went out to help Trace put the horses away and feed the stock. They'd been working for fewer than ten minutes when Trace remembered what Meg had said.

"Is Meg a faster runner than you are?" he asked his brother, standing by the stall watching Brad put feed into a bucket.

The smile that came over Brad's face was slow and a bit mischievous. He was still smiling when he said, "What Meg doesn't realize is that chasing her is as fun as catching her. It's not something I ever rush."

Trace had to laugh as he went back to work, glad he hadn't asked about it in the house. Meg would have wanted to know what was going on, and the younger Holden had no plans to give his brother's secret away.

※

"Here you go," Cassidy said as she offered Meg a cup of water and a piece of spice cake. The expectant woman sat at the kitchen table, her face flushed from the heat, watching Cassidy work on dinner. From the doorway Brad watched the scene. He was early coming in, Meg on his mind, almost wishing the baby would come now and not wait until next week.

They hadn't moved Meg into town, although both Jeanette and the Dorns were more than willing to have her. Meg had been feeling well, and it seemed that even if her pains came on her, the timing was good. Brad knew he would still send Trace for the doctor, but a peace had come over his wife lately, and between the two of them, they thought being at home was best.

Cassidy had continued to come each Wednesday, and each time the women did less sewing as Cassidy worked to make Meg comfortable, doing small jobs for her so she could relax and always making supper that evening.

Right after the Fourth, Cassidy had come with a meal already prepared. Patience Dorn had sent everything with her for that evening's meal and then some. They had enjoyed the food for days.

"Hey, Brad," Cassidy called, suddenly spotting him.

"Hello," he said quietly as Meg had dropped off, nearly sitting upright. "How's she doing?"

"She says she's just too warm."

Brad looked down on his wife, remembering the speech he'd given himself many times. Babies were born all the time. Women did this all the time. That didn't change the facts, however. This was new for them—every bit of it. Meg's growing stomach, her pains, the movement of the baby—all of it. Not to mention the days and weeks that would follow. They would be parents. A wonderful thing, certainly, but serious too.

"Are you all right?" Cassidy asked.

"Yes, thanks, Cass. And thanks for taking care of so many little things."

Cassidy only smiled at him as it seemed very small to her. Meg was her friend, the sister she'd never had, and there was nothing she wouldn't do for her.

Knowing that Cassidy would be there for Meg until he came into supper, Brad went back to the barn door he and Trace were working on. It was time to admit to himself that he was ready for this baby to come. At the moment he didn't think he'd ever been readier for anything in his life.

"Some folks gave me some money for you, Cassidy," Rylan told that woman when he came into her shop the next day. Cassidy had turned from her sewing machine. Now both she and Jeanette stood and stared at their pastor.

"Money for me?" Cassidy clarified.

"Yes."

Cassidy looked at Jeanette, who shook her head no, able to honestly do so. She had not been able to think of a way to give anonymously and had never pursued it.

"Why?" Cassidy asked next.

"They didn't say. They only said you had been heavy on their hearts, and they wanted you to have twenty dollars."

"Was it Chandler?" Cassidy asked next, a bit suspicious.

"As a matter of fact, no. It was one of our church families, and that's all the more I can tell you."

While Cassidy stared at the big man in their presence, he grinned and looked around. "This is a very feminine place, isn't it?"

Both women smiled and learned in a hurry that Rylan was just getting warmed up.

"I know you must have men customers, Cassie, but you haven't decorated for them at all." Rylan shook his head, wandering around a bit and taking everything in. "I know! What about some boots—dusty ones? You could put them right by this little velvet chair. That would make a man feel at home.

"Or!" Rylan exclaimed, still prowling around, the women laughing together. "Instead of these little silk ties on the curtains, you could go with leather straps. Maybe something from an old horse's bridle."

Rylan looked expectantly at the women now, his eyes innocent, while they tried to control themselves.

"Well?" he questioned. "Are my ideas welcome or not? I'm sure I could come up with more."

"I don't know if we can take more," Jeanette said, gasping for air.

"Here you go, Cassie," Rylan approached, holding out the money to her.

Cassidy looked at it and then up at him.

"Please tell this family how much this means right now. I—" Cassidy began, but couldn't find the words.

"I'll tell them," Rylan spoke gently, his kind smile making Cassidy want to cry.

Jeanette walked the pastor outside, and when she came back, Cassidy was standing right where she left her.

"That was wonderful," the older woman said.

"Yes, it was. I asked God to send me more work. I asked Him to give me the strength to work harder if He sent more work. My imagination didn't include anything like this."

"'Him who is able to do exceedingly abundantly above all that we ask or think,'" Jeanette quoted from Ephesians.

Cassidy could only nod. Her heart was so blessed, and the reminder that God was watching her was sweet indeed. She went back to work, praying for the family who had shared with her and asking God to bless them in every possible way.

Meg had made it through another day, her due date just a week down the road. She tired easily, her back hurting all the time, but she got done what she could. And if the evening meals were a little less varied than usual and her part in the conversation a little lacking, the men she lived with never uttered a word of complaint.

On Thursday Brad and Trace had been working fairly close to home and were indoors a bit early that evening. They helped put the food on the table, and then all three sat down to eat. Both Trace and Meg bowed their heads so Brad could pray, but the room stayed silent. Not until they both looked up did Brad speak, and it was to Trace alone.

"I'm not going to ask God to provide a wife for you any longer."

Trace looked at his brother but didn't reply.

"I can't do that when I think He's already provided one."

Trace nodded a bit before saying, "I assume you're talking about Cass?"

"Yes. You need to marry that girl."

"I think she has feelings for Chandler."

Brad had not expected this. He stared at Trace, thinking that it wasn't supposed to be like that. In his mind all Trace needed was a push from him. All he needed was his older brother to point out to him that Token Creek's seamstress was the perfect wife for him. Before he could find words, Meg spoke.

"She hasn't said anything to me about having feelings for Chandler."

Trace did not look convinced. Little things he'd witnessed in the past—at church, and even as recently as the Fourth of July picnic—lingered in his mind.

"I can't take that chance," he said at last. "If I throw my hat into the ring and she's in love with Chandler, I lose my friendship with Cassidy Norton."

Neither Brad nor Meg needed to ask Trace if he wanted their help. His answer would have been a resounding no. The three sat in silence for a few more minutes before Brad bowed his head to pray. Trace found out during the prayer that Brad had changed his mind: He asked God again for a wife for his brother.

※

Trace ran some errands in town before picking up Cassidy on Saturday evening. He hit the bank, Wheeler's, and the livery, and even managed a stop at the Dorns'. Meg was looking for something she thought her Aunt Patience might have. Trace did all of this in record time, and he thought he might have time to stop and ask Rylan a question. Abi Pfister had other ideas. She caught him just as he was leaving the Dorn house, paper in hand.

"Mr. Holden," she said in a commanding voice. "If I may have a moment of your time."

Trace wondered what would happen if he said he didn't want to be in her book but saw no reason to be antagonistic.

"Good evening, Miss Pfister."

"Were you born in Token Creek?"

"No, I was born in Pennsylvania."

"What city?"

"Allentown."

"What brought you here?"

"My parents bought the ranch."

"What year was that?"

"I can't remember."

"Your father. Where is he now?"

"I don't know," Trace said, and something in his voice actually got through to Abi. With a swift glance at his face, she changed the direction of her questions to Brad and Meg.

"Has the baby been born?"

"No, ma'am," Trace answered, wondering how long this would go on.

"What about—" Abi began, but stopped short. She had spotted someone come from inside the house across the street who was evidently more interesting than Trace. Without so much as a by-your-leave, Abi was away, paper in hand, to assail some other hapless victim. Relieved he'd lost her attention, Trace went on to Cassidy's, the timing just right.

⁂

"I can tell you had a good night's sleep," Trace said to Cassidy as soon as he arrived in the kitchen early Sunday morning. That lady was at the table with coffee.

"Why is that?" Cassidy asked, sending Trace's brows up.

"You were not yourself last night. The longer the evening went, the slower your speech got, and when you blinked it looked like your lids were weighted."

Cassidy's mouth opened, and Trace laughed at her.

"I was tired," she tried to argue, "but it wasn't that bad."

The look Trace gave her before pouring himself some coffee was clearly skeptical. Cassidy shook her head at him, and the cowboy smiled.

"How's the work going in the barn?" Cassidy asked.

"Very well. We're almost done."

"And then you leave for your cattle drive in August?"

"September, mid to late."

"How long are you usually gone?"

"At least two weeks."

Cassidy nodded. Meg had told her some of this. She would move into town. She hadn't done that in the past, but with the baby being so young, Brad wanted Meg with her aunt or his own.

"How about some eggs?" Trace offered.

"You're going to cook?"

"Yes, ma'am," he said, readying the pan.

"Should I be afraid?"

Trace just held a smile and said, "I'll have you know I was cooking in this kitchen long before little Meg Dorn came into Brad's life."

"And you survived?"

Trace turned from the stove and put his hands on his hips. "Are you hungry or not?"

"I'm hungry." Cassidy's tone and face had become very meek. Trace was not the least bit fooled but turned back to the pan before she could see him smile.

⁂

"Why don't you stay home?" Brad suggested to Meg when she groaned a little just getting out of bed.

"It's tempting, but I think I need to get moving. I also hate missing Sunday mornings, and that might be forced upon me after the baby's born." Meg sat for a moment on the side of the bed and suddenly smiled. "And besides, Patience said my cousin came into the world on account of a buggy ride. I'm sure the wagon could be just as effective."

Brad laughed and went to heat water for shaving. Meg told herself that the longer she sat, the worse it would be. With that little reminder to herself, she forced her body to move.

"Before you leave…" Chas Vick stood and spoke the moment Rylan finished the prayer that dismissed the congregation. Even Rylan stared as Chas made his way to the front.

"I have an announcement to make," Chas continued when he faced the congregation. "In three weeks, on Sunday, August eighth, we'll be giving our pastor a day off. That day is Rylan's five-year anniversary with our church family. We'll be having testimonies, a time of prayer, and a recounting of our church family history, and we'll end it all with a potluck lunch." Chas angled a bit so he could look at Rylan's surprised face. "And no sermon."

Everyone laughed at the look on Rylan's face, and Rylan had no choice but to laugh over his own surprise.

"So please don't miss that time with us," Chas finished. "If you have a testimony to share or a song you would like us to sing that day, see any elder except Rylan by the first Sunday in August. There will be more details in the weeks ahead. Thank you."

There was a good deal of talking when Chas stepped down. Clearly folks were excited, and some still laughed at the way Rylan shook his head in mock pity.

"Five years," Cassidy said to Meg, who was next to her. "It would be wonderful to be here so long."

"I think so too. I mean," Meg clarified, "I was certainly around for part of that time, but not the full five years. I do remember my aunt and uncle being excited about Rylan's coming but sad too because they loved Pastor English and he was dying."

"I didn't know that."

"He didn't die here. He went to be with his family in Denver, but he lived only another year after he left."

"So Rylan came just in time."

"Pastor English brought Rylan here. He was the reason Rylan came."

Cassidy had never heard any of this. It made her very excited for the second Sunday in August.

⁂

"Are you headed out?" Jeanette asked Cassidy the following Wednesday.

"Yes. I was hoping to hear news on Meg by now, but that didn't happen."

"So was I," Jeanette said almost wistfully. This was going to be the grandchild she would never have. She thought about Theta, and her heart clenched a little. Jeanette would have adopted grandchildren, and Theta would have grandchildren she wouldn't even know.

"Are you all right to stay?" Cassidy asked, having misunderstood her look.

"Yes, I was just thinking about this baby. Give Meg my love and tell her to get going."

"Yes, ma'am."

And Cassidy did give Meg the message, but all Meg did was laugh. In fact, it wasn't until Cassidy went to spend the night there on Saturday that Meg took Jeanette's words to heart. Just after midnight Meg's pains began. Trace was dead asleep when his brother came to his room and asked him to ride for the doctor. Cassidy heard the voices in the upstairs hall and peeked open her door to find Brad holding a lantern.

"Has it started?" she asked from around her door, coming awake in a hurry when she saw Trace rushing for the stairs, his shirt only half on.

"It has," Brad said before slipping back into the bedroom, trying to remain calm even as he questioned their decision to be so far from town and Doctor Ertz.

Praying for her friend, Cassidy put a robe on and made her way down to the kitchen, lit another lantern, and put the coffeepot on. She sat at the kitchen table, not as awake as she thought, and waited for the coffee to boil. She heard Trace come back with Doctor Ertz but stayed where she was. Trace eventually wandered in.

"Hey," he said, his voice still rough from sleep.

"Hi," Cassidy said in return, thanking him when he went to the pot and poured mugs for each of them.

"Let's move to the living room," Trace suggested. "It's more comfortable in there."

Cassidy trailed after him as he led with the lantern and made herself comfortable in one corner of the sofa. Exactly when she dropped off to sleep, she didn't know. Neither was she aware of Trace and the blanket he spread gently over her.

***

"That was bad!" Meg gasped, relieved that Doctor Ertz was there but a little afraid of how much harder things might get.

"You're doing all right," the doctor said, checking her again. "Do you feel like you need to push?" he asked.

"Yes," Meg said, still breathing heavily.

The doctor turned to Brad and asked, "How long ago did things get going?"

"She woke me with her first pain at midnight."

The doctor shook his head, knowing it was only about two o'clock.

"It's almost unheard of in a first baby. Things don't usually go this fast, but I think you should go ahead and push, Meg."

Meg nodded, tired but a little excited too. When the next pain hit, she pushed for all she was worth.

***

Trace stood frozen at the bottom of the stairs and listened to the tiny cries of a newborn baby. His heart pounded with the intensity of what he was feeling. All he could do was stare when Brad came down the stairs.

"A girl," he said quietly.

"Meg?"

"She's good."

It was then that Brad caught the shimmer in his brother's eyes and felt tears thick at the back of his own throat. Wordlessly the men embraced.

"Kiss Meg for me," Trace managed when they broke apart.

"You can come up in a few minutes."

"Okay."

"Where's Cass?"

Trace laughed a little. "She fell asleep in the living room."

"She'll be sorry she missed it."

"It was fast," Trace said, just now realizing it.

"That's what the doctor said."

The doctor was coming down the stairs just moments later, telling Brad that all was well with both Meg and the baby.

Brad thanked him and walked him to the door, but Doctor Ertz only clapped him on the shoulder and laughed a little.

"If I'd known it was going to go that fast, I might have advised she stay with Jeb and Patience."

Brad had to laugh to. He'd steeled himself for hours of misery, but as with everything else in the pregnancy, it hadn't been the way he figured.

It took a moment for Brad to realize the doctor had left. He'd been standing there staring into the dark yard, letting the weight of the night's events sink in. He was a father.

When Cassidy awoke, the living room was light and she was alone. Struggling into a sitting position and pushing the hair from her face, she tried to remember why she was in the living room. Her heart felt as though it stopped and then started again when she remembered Meg and the baby that was coming.

"Good morning," Brad called, coming from the direction of the kitchen, a tiny person in his arms.

"Oh, Brad," Cassidy whispered. "I fell asleep. I was going to pray Meg through the whole thing, and then I fell asleep."

"It's all right," Brad said with a smile, taking a seat next to her. "Would you like to hold my daughter?"

Cassidy couldn't speak. Brad put the baby in her arms, and all she could do was stare in wonder at the perfect little person God had sent.

"It went fast," Brad was saying, but Cassidy barely heard him.

A girl. Her friend Meg had had a girl, and she was the loveliest thing Cassidy had ever seen, all pink and rosy, her tiny brows and lashes very dark like her mother's.

"How's Meg?" Cassidy suddenly remembered to ask, looking anxiously at Brad.

"She's sound asleep. I brought Savanna down so she could rest."

"Savanna? You named her Savanna? That was Meg's favorite name."

"Mine too," Brad said.

Cassidy smiled hugely. When she spoke again, she was looking at the baby but still made Brad laugh.

"I believe I'm going to sell my shop. I'm quite certain I should move here to the ranch to be a full-time nursemaid."

CHAPTER NINE

CASSIDY ENDED UP GOING WITH TRACE TO CHURCH. She was not going to leave the ranch without seeing Meg, but that lady woke up with an hour to spare. As Cassidy sat on Meg and Brad's bed, the two friends were able to visit, hold the baby, and share in the miracle that had happened in the night.

"I'm selling my business," Cassidy said, making Meg smile. "I already told Brad. I'm going to be moving out here full time and taking care of this baby."

Meg laughed but still said, "She's wonderful, isn't she?"

"Amazing," Cassidy agreed. "I don't know if I'll make it all the way until Wednesday."

"Come back with Trace after the service," Meg invited.

"Your family will want to visit," Cassidy said, making herself step aside. "Just as soon as they hear, they'll be on their way."

"I'm glad you were here," Meg said.

"Then you didn't hear the news," Cassidy returned dryly, frowning at herself. "I wasn't here. I fell asleep in the living room and slept through the whole thing."

It hurt Meg to laugh, but she couldn't help herself. Holding her stomach and trying not to laugh too hard, Meg took in Cassidy's disgruntled face, her own slowly turning red with laughter.

Thinking back on it now, sitting by Trace in the wagon on the way to town, Cassidy had to smile. Trace spotted it.

"Thinking about the baby?"

"And Meg. She was very understanding about my sleeping through the birth."

Trace's own shoulders shook.

"She laughed too," Cassidy admitted, the disgruntled look back on her face.

"You meant well," Trace said, but the words came out on laughter, and she knew she was not going to be allowed to forget this.

Cassidy might have said more, but they both spotted the buggy coming toward them. Jeb and Patience Dorn were headed for the ranch. Trace stopped when they came abreast of the wagon.

"You must have seen Doc Ertz," Trace guessed.

"We did," Patience said, "but he wouldn't tell us anything—only that everyone was doing fine."

Trace smiled slowly.

"Trace Holden," Patience spoke, sounding like the protective aunt she was. "I'm sure Meg had her baby. You've got to tell me what she had."

Trace only smiled at her, and Jeb laughed. Patience gave up on him.

"Cassie," she began, but everyone had to laugh when Trace's arm went swiftly around that lady so his hand could cover her mouth.

"We've got to get going," Trace said, managing to sound regretful, all the time holding Cassidy's mouth under his fingers. "Otherwise we'll be late for the service."

Again Jeb could only laugh, and Patience had to join him. Trace put the wagon into motion, and Jeb did the same. Cassidy turned to look at the man next to her.

"I wasn't going to tell," she defended herself.

"I couldn't take that chance," Trace returned without apology.

"So tell me," she said. She was not going to let it drop. "Will I be allowed to speak to anyone this morning? Or are we keeping this a secret from the entire church family?"

"I wouldn't torture you in that way." Trace managed to sound repentant. "It would be cruel not to allow a woman to talk for that many hours."

Cassidy's mouth dropped open, and Trace shouted with laughter. That he was more than pleased with himself was quite clear.

"You can stop laughing any time now," Cassidy said, but he chuckled his way into town.

As soon as they were spotted coming alone to the church, the congregation made swift deductions. And Cassidy ended up with plenty to tease Trace over. *He* was the one who could not stop talking about his newborn niece.

⚜

Jeanette walked home swiftly from church. She would head out to see Meg and Brad in a few hours, but in the meantime she had someone else to talk to. Asking Heather not to disturb her, Jeanette went to the porch, shut the door behind her, and sat down to speak with her sister.

"She's here, Theta," Jeanette whispered past a suddenly tight throat. "Your granddaughter was born in the night. Brad has a baby girl."

For long moments Jeanette could not say anything. Tears poured down her face, her eyes desperate to have her sister focus on her and the news she was sharing.

"Oh, Theta, I don't know if I can stand this. You would be so proud of Brad and Trace. They're both so special. And Meg. She's amazing, and she's made Brad a father. You're a grandmother, Theta."

Jeanette's heart couldn't take any more. She sobbed into her handkerchief, fresh grief pouring over her. She cried loudly enough that both Heather and Becky heard her. They would not have disturbed her for anything short of a fire, but it hurt their hearts to hear Jeanette cry.

An hour passed before Jeanette emerged from the room. She did nothing to hide the tears she'd shed, and at Becky's insistence, allowed herself to be fussed over, sitting down to have some dinner. Heather requested the small buggy and horse from Timothy, who did odd jobs and had kept the grounds and stables for Jeanette as long as anyone could remember. As soon as Jeanette was done eating, both women saw her on her way, convinced that a visit to see baby Savanna was just what she needed.

⚜

"I didn't know feet came in this size," Trace said, Savanna lying on his arm. Brad chuckled from his place next to him on the sofa, both men just wanting to look at her. "Look at those toes," Trace said next, and Brad could only stare.

For a moment he looked at the way Trace dwarfed his daughter and knew that when he held her it must have looked the same way. Savanna fit on Trace's forearm, and her pale skin and tiny hands were almost startling next to Trace's huge tanned paw.

As they watched, Savanna decided to peek her eyes open. There had been very little of this in the fourteen hours she'd been with them, and both men responded.

"Hey, Savanna," Trace said.

"Can you wake up?" Brad coaxed. "Your mother wants to get a better look at your eyes."

In the midst of this, the front door opened, and both men heard Jeanette's greeting. Almost at the same moment, Meg came from upstairs, a bit wobbly, but doing well. The family gathered in the living room. With more than a little laughter and even some tears, they told Jeanette the story of Savanna's arrival.

⚜

There is no way to describe how I feel about Meg's baby, Cassidy wrote in a letter to her mother that night. *I didn't know anything could be so tiny and perfect. The envy I feel that Meg has a husband and*

baby is not the vicious type, but it's still there. I can't help but wonder
if God's plans for me will ever include anything so wondrous.

Cassidy could not keep writing. She kept picturing the baby in
her mind, her heart in awe over God's work. Closing the letter and
folding it for the box, she lay quietly for a long time before she slept,
thoughts of Savanna Holden filling her mind.

Thinking back on Rylan's sermon, Trace sat up in bed on Sunday
night and read the notes he'd taken. Rylan had been talking about
God knowing people's every thought and feeling, and how foolish they
were to think that they could hide any fears or sins from Him.

Rylan shared many verses, and Trace began to turn to some of
them, starting with Proverbs 15:11: "Hell and destruction are before
the Lord; how much more then the hearts of the children of men?"
And then 2 Chronicles 6:30 and 31: "Then hear thou from heaven thy
dwelling place, and forgive, and render unto every man according
unto all his ways, whose heart thou knowest; (for thou only knowest
the hearts of the children of men;) that they may fear thee, to walk
in thy ways."

Trace read these verses over a few times before going to the first
chapter of Acts where he read, "They prayed, and said, Thou, Lord,
which knowest the hearts of all men." The last verse Trace had written
down was the one he decided to memorize, Psalm 44:21: "Shall not
God search this out? For he knoweth the secrets of the heart."

I think You don't know me sometimes, Lord. I try to hide the fears
I have and my doubts about the future, thinking all the time that no
one knows. But You do. Please help me to trust You with all of me
and all of my life.

Trace lay quietly then, thinking about the full day it had been. He
was ready for the life Brad had, at least he believed he was, but clearly
God had other ideas, or it would have happened for him too.

I really do struggle to trust You at all times, Lord. In those hard

times, when Meg is in labor or finances are slim for the ranch, I turn
to You and trust, but for my whole future, it doesn't come so easily.

Trace went on to confess his lack of faith and trust, and to ask
God to help him to see his faults right away, take responsibility for
them, and commit to change. It had been a long day. Trace was weary,
but he didn't let himself fall asleep until all was right between him
and his God.

Meg sat in the rocking chair Brad had moved into their bedroom,
her daughter in her arms. Brad was asleep. With a heart so full of
amazement she could barely form thoughts, she held her daughter
close, rocking her and kissing her small head. She had nursed her
for a while, not sure Savanna had taken much in, but the baby had
fallen to sleep again and Meg found herself wide awake.

These first few weeks would probably be draining. Her schedule
would be off with a baby to take care of. Savanna's needs would take
a little getting used to, but at least she felt well. Savanna had been
born in less than three hours. Meg was barely even sore.

"Meg."

That lady heard a soft murmur from the bed but knew that Brad
wasn't really awake. She stayed quiet, not wanting to wake him,
and sure enough, the room fell quiet again. It was then that Meg
knew she had to try to sleep. She would be worth nothing the next
day if she sat up half the night holding a baby who wanted only to
sleep. Surrendering Savanna back to her cradle, Meg climbed into
bed and tried not to think about how weary she was going to be in
the morning.

"Good morning, Trace," Jessie Wheeler greeted the moment she
opened her door on Monday. "You're in town early."

"Yeah," Trace agreed, suddenly doubting his intentions.

"Something specific I can show you?"

"Boots," the cowboy said, glad she offered.

"For yourself?" Jessie asked, already moving that way.

"No." Trace found it easier to respond when she wasn't looking at him. "I need to see the smallest pair you have."

Jessie stopped and stared at him. After a moment, she smiled very gently.

"Did Meg have her baby?"

Trace nodded, unable to hide his pleasure.

"Boy or girl?"

"A girl. Savanna."

"That's pretty. And of course she needs boots."

"That's what I was thinking."

Jessie laughed a little, but there was nothing mean-spirited about it. She took Trace to a shelf and produced the smallest pair of boots he'd ever seen. They were all black with just a tiny bit of detail. Trace picked them up, unable to stop his smile.

"They were actually a special order, and then the customer changed her mind," Jessie explained. "And because they're rather pricey, they've never sold."

"How much?"

Jessie gave him a number that would call for a bit of extravagance, but his heart was set on Savanna having boots. She was a rancher's daughter and nothing else would do.

"I'll take 'em," Trace said.

Jessie wrapped the boots neatly, handed them off with a smile, and spoke some final words. "Be sure and bring her in once they fit."

Trace had to laugh. Small as the boots were, Savanna's feet would take a good deal of growing to fit into them. The cowboy thanked the mercantile owner and went on his way.

"Well, Trace," Chandler called with pleasure when that man stepped into the bank. "What brings you to town on a Monday morning?"

"Just a quick trip to Jessie's." Trace grinned and then admitted, "I've been spending my hard-earned cash."

"Come to get more?"

"As a matter of fact, yes."

"How are Meg and the baby?" Chandler asked as he got the money Trace requested.

"I'm not sure how well the night went. Meg was tired this morning, but I guess that's to be expected."

Chandler nodded before asking, "When do we meet with Rylan again?"

"I don't know. I think I heard Philip say his schedule is busy right now."

"At the telegraph office?" Chandler asked with surprise.

"Yes."

"When do you leave for Burton?" Chandler asked next, checking on the cattle drive.

"We're planning on September thirteenth."

"Is there much to do before then?"

"Not as much for me as for Brad. He's going to move Meg and Savanna in here to Patience and Jeb's, so he's got more to do on his list."

The men talked about nothing in particular for the next few minutes, and then Trace left the bank. He was going to head straight out of town but decided to make a swift stop to see Rylan. That man wasn't home. Trace left for the ranch still not knowing when the men would meet again to study.

"I didn't think this day would ever come," Cassidy said to Meg on Wednesday afternoon. "I've been dying to hold this little girl again."

"I find that I don't want to do much else," Meg admitted, looking at her daughter in Cassidy's arms.

"Just say the word," Cassidy said in a singsong voice, "and I'll move out to take care of her."

"But how does that allow *me* to play with her all the time?" Meg asked.

"Oh!" Cassidy said in surprise, realizing she'd gotten it all wrong.

The friends looked at each other and laughed. The noise startled Savanna, which just gave Cassidy a reason to hold her closer, rubbing her nose into the baby's soft cheek.

"I saw your Aunt Patience on Monday," Cassidy remembered. "She said she was coming out again."

"She came for the whole morning yesterday," Meg said. "We had such fun and got so much done. Savanna slept a lot, and that was helpful."

"I would be torn," Cassidy said. "I would know I had things to get done, but if Savanna was awake, I would want to hold her."

"I even hold her when she's asleep," Meg admitted softly.

"How do the men like having her around?"

Meg smiled. "Brad was just complaining that he hadn't held her that much. If Trace so much as hears a sound out of her, he's got her in his arms."

Cassidy smiled. This was not a side of Trace she had seen. It wasn't impossible to imagine—he was a caring man—but it still gave Cassidy pause.

"Oh!" Meg suddenly said. "I just remembered something."

Cassidy watched the new mother as she rose from the sofa and moved toward the kitchen. She returned carrying the smallest pair of boots Cassidy had ever seen.

"Where did you get those?"

"Trace came home with them. Aren't they amazing?"

"They're so little!" Cassidy exclaimed, taking one in her hand.

"They are, but Savanna won't wear them for ages. Her feet are tiny."

Before Cassidy could answer, the women heard the back door open. Brad came in long enough to tell Meg that their neighbor was in need of some help. Bart Carlisle, who owned the next ranch up the road was short two men, and both Brad and Trace were headed out to give him a hand. They planned to be back for supper, and in a very short time the women went back to talking to and about Savanna. They never did get to that day's sewing project.

***

The second Sunday in August finally arrived. Rylan was awake early, feeling a little odd not to have a sermon on his mind. Could five years really have passed so swiftly? Rylan lay in bed, the day already feeling warm, letting his mind drift back. He'd been just twenty-one the summer he'd come to Token Creek. There had been no guarantees that the congregation would want him to stay. Larry English had asked him to come, confident that he was the man for the Token Creek church. Rylan had trusted him and come. Without warning, five years had slipped by.

***

"In preparing for today," Chas Vick shared, standing at the front of the church, "I talked to a lot of people. It's probably more customary to allow the man who's being honored to say the closing words, but I wanted to do things in chronological order, which means you've got to hear Rylan's story about coming to Token Creek. Trust me when I tell you it's the best place to start."

Chas took a seat, and Rylan moved to the front. He caused his congregation to roar with laughter when he suddenly produced his

Bible and said, "Now if you'll turn with me to the book of—" Rylan stopped, having pulled off the joke, and then began his story.

"I actually arrived in town on a Thursday. I had ridden trains and stagecoaches for days, and when the coach stopped here, I was dusty, hot, and tired. I also had no money to make the return journey.

"I was standing on the boardwalk, looking around and getting my bearings, when a man approached me and asked if I was looking for work." Rylan smiled a little at the memory. "I was broke enough that I didn't say no, at least not until I found out that he wanted me to keep the peace in his saloon."

The congregation loved this, and Rylan did not continue until the laugher died down.

"The next person to speak to me was Pete Stillwell. I still thank God that he spotted me as I was headed past the livery. He asked me if I'd ever done any smithing." Rylan paused, looking confused. "I can't imagine why he would ask that. I've always had the impression that I looked like a banker."

Even as the congregation laughed, Rylan continued. He explained the way he'd found the parsonage and how Larry English took him in. The congregation was expecting him, and after a month of spending time with them, preaching each week and answering as well as asking questions, Rylan was asked to stay. Pastor English took his leave by the fall, and Rylan had been with them ever since.

"I can't believe five years have passed," Rylan said as he wrapped up his part. "It's been the most amazing time of my life, and I thank you for everything you've been and done. I'm looking forward to today, and to the next five years."

Many other people shared stories when Rylan sat down. Some were light and fun, and some were tear-filled as the congregation recalled the way God had worked through Rylan and God's Word, and how their lives were changed. They sang songs and shared testimonies for three hours before Chas wrapped things up and said it was time for dinner.

The group exited to the area at the back of the building. Tables had been set up between the church and the parsonage, and the celebration continued there.

❧

"The first time I met Rylan," Chandler shared with Cassidy and some others as they ate lunch, "I did a lot of staring."

"Why was that?"

"His size. I loved his comment about looking like a banker. I've always thought that he couldn't look less like a preacher."

"He is a big man," Cassidy had to agree. Chandler, Brad, and Trace were all very tall, but Rylan topped each of them and was large to boot.

"The pastor I grew up with could not have been more different," Chandler continued. "He was barely five feet tall and as slim as a reed."

Everyone at the table fell to talking about their past church families, but Cassidy didn't share. She had come to Christ as a teenager, and some of her memories from that time were painful. Talking about anything relating to the past made her uncomfortable. And when she spotted Meg holding Savanna, she went to steal the baby away, needing a little time alone with her thoughts.

❧

"That was amazing," Cassidy said. She and Jeanette were the last to leave the potluck and were speaking to Rylan.

"Yes, it was," Rylan agreed. "What an encouragement. What a testimony to our saving God."

"Thank you, Rylan," Jeanette said, a hand to his arm. "We would not be who we are without you."

"Thank you, Jeanette. Thank you both for coming."

The women said their goodbyes and started off. Jeanette stopped long enough at Cassidy's door to tell her she would see her in the morning, but the older woman was long gone by the time Cassidy took her Bible indoors and came back down the stairs.

At the moment Cassidy felt restless and a little lonely. The day had been wonderful, but she didn't have family to go home to, and right now she missed that.

Moving slowly down streets she normally didn't visit, Cassidy took herself on a walk so she could pray for folks in Token Creek. She studied different homes as she went, and even stopped outside the Brickel mansion. It was the largest home in town, even larger than Jeanette's, and if the inside of the three-story mansion was as magnificent as the outside, Cassidy knew it must be a sight to see.

She enjoyed the view for a while but felt the cool night air coming in fast. Not wanting to get caught out after dark, she found her way back to Main Street. Once she'd turned toward home, she did not waste any time but was soon climbing the stairs at the side of her building.

The walk was just what she had needed. Her apartment no longer felt lonely but cozy and comfortable with its familiar surroundings. Cassidy settled in with a book and then did some quilting. The rest of the evening flew, and before she knew, it was time for bed.

*

"Where has the time gone?" Patience asked of Meg near the end of August, even as she looked down at the baby in her arms. Savanna was already a month old. Meg had come to town with her shopping list and planned to leave the baby with her aunt for a few hours, but the two had started talking.

"Isn't she big?" Meg commented, drawing a smile from her daughter.

"When she smiles," Patience said softly, her eyes drinking in the baby girl, "my heart melts like butter."

"You'll have to write and tell my mother all about it."

"Don't you already do that?" Patience asked.

"Every week, but I write from a mother's viewpoint, not a grandma's."

"When are they coming?" Patience asked.

"In the spring. They wanted to come for this cattle drive, but time and funds won't allow it."

"The spring will be a great time to visit," Patience said, thinking that her brother and sister-in-law were never going to want to be separated from this baby once they'd seen her.

"Oh," Patience suddenly said. "When you get to Jessie's, tell your uncle that I do need the brown sugar."

"All right. How long is he helping out at the store this time?"

"Didn't you hear?" Patience asked. "Abel, the boy who works for Jessie, broke his leg. He won't be back for weeks."

"Oh, no."

"He's so active, he'll probably drive his mother out of her wits."

Savanna chose that moment to smile at her Aunt Patience, and all talk of the townsfolk stopped. Meg, knowing her daughter was in good hands, took her leave. Her first stop: Cassidy's shop.

CHAPTER TEN

"TELL ME ALL THE PLACES YOU'VE BEEN," Jeanette requested when Meg came to the shop. Cassidy was out at the moment.

"You are my first stop."

"I thought you were planning to come in early," Jeanette said with a frown, trying to remember what Cassidy had told her when she said Meg was sure to be by.

Meg's look was comical. "Let me tell you about planning when you have a baby. There is no point. I was headed out the door at least an hour before I actually left. Savanna decided to spit up all over me, so I had to change my clothing and hers. Then your older nephew had to check with me forty times to make sure I was going to drive slowly, since I was on my own.

"Somewhere in there, I put my reticule down and couldn't find it. It had my list for Jessie's store and my money. Trace kept remembering things he wanted me to pick up, and just as I was headed out the door, Savanna soaked through her clothing and had to be changed again."

Jeanette enjoyed this account immensely. She knew Meg was deeply thankful for her daughter, and all the dry tones and eye rolling were an act.

"Well, sit down a moment and rest yourself," Jeanette invited, some handwork in her lap.

"Where is Cass?" Meg asked when she got comfortable, realizing she'd expected the younger woman to join them any moment.

"She's making a delivery."

"I didn't know she ever did that."

"This is a special case," Jeanette said with a smile. She began to explain, even as she wondered how Cassidy was faring.

~❦~

"Please come in, Miss Norton," Halston, the butler, invited. Halston had visited her shop early one morning and given her measurements and an order for five shirts. The shirts were for Hiram Brickel, who—if rumor could be believed—never set foot out of doors.

Cassidy stepped into a large foyer from which an ornately carved stairway rose to the second floor. Wide hallways flanked by pillars led in two directions, and Halston began to walk down one of them, saying over his shoulder, "Mr. Brickel is waiting for you."

He took Cassidy to a double doorway, opened it, and stood aside for her to enter. Cassidy didn't hesitate but stepped into a large parlor, beautifully furnished but dim, even on this sunny morning.

Standing by the fireplace was a man Cassidy judged to be at least thirty years her senior. His hair was liberally sprinkled with gray, but his frame was upright and his eyes were keen.

"Do you have the shirts?" the man asked her with a surprising amount of force.

"I have one shirt, Mr. Brickel," Cassidy said, moving a little closer. "I wanted to make sure you were pleased before I made the rest."

She received little more than a grunt in reply and stood still while the older man came toward her, took the shirt from her hands, and began to inspect the seams, even going so far as to tug roughly here and there. She wanted to ask this rather refined gentleman if he planned to mine or dig ditches while wearing the shirt but kept her mouth shut.

"I'll have to try it on," he finally said.

"Would you like me to leave?" Cassidy offered.

"I do not change my clothing in the parlor," he informed Cassidy coldly, and she had all she could do not to laugh. "You may wait here until I return."

Cassidy nodded and stood looking around the elegant room. She didn't do more than turn in a circle, but from every direction, the parlor was impressive. A large ornate fireplace with turquoise blue stone and a carved oak mantel was the focal point of one wall and took up a great deal of space.

The rest of the room was just as beautiful. The trim around the windows was dark oak, as was the upholstered furniture, which was covered in dark blue velvet. Cassidy was studying a side table with a marble top when she realized Mr. Brickel had been gone a long time. When he did return, he began barking orders the moment he stepped through the door.

"You could have taken a seat!" were the first words Cassidy heard.

"Thank you," Cassidy said, unsure how to reply. Then she noticed the shirt. "Oh, Mr. Brickel, it looks very nice on you. How do you like the fit?"

"It's fine," he said, his voice was cold again. But his eyes had warmed some and were watchful. "When will the rest be done?"

"In a week," Cassidy improvised, hoping she could do it.

"You'll bring them yourself?"

"Yes, I can plan on that."

"Good. We'll have coffee now. Halston!"

"I'm sorry." Cassidy was not going to allow that. "I have to get back to the shop."

The coldness came back to Mr. Brickel's eyes, but Cassidy was not intimidated.

"Do you still want the other four shirts?" she felt a need to ask.

"Of course."

"Then I'll see you next week."

"And you'll stay for coffee then," Mr. Brickel announced.

"No, sir, I can't. But I thank you for the offer."

This said, Cassidy began to move toward the door.

"Why not?"

The force was back in his voice, so Cassidy stopped and turned to him.

"There are several reasons, Mr. Brickel," Cassidy began, wondering if having his business was going to be worth it. "I won't go into any of them right now, but each one makes it impossible for me to stay."

His eyes were even colder now, and she thought he would cancel the rest of his order, but he stayed quiet. Only when Cassidy said that she would see him next week did he nod. She had to be satisfied with that, and this time when she turned for the door she did not stop or look back.

❧

Jessie Wheeler was Jeb Dorn's cousin. A younger cousin certainly, but still a cousin. For that reason Jeb was the first person Jessie called when she needed help in the store. And because Jeb made furniture from out of the workshop he had built behind his home, he was usually able to come with little or no notice.

It was for this reason that Meg made her last stop at the store. She was in no hurry to get done, and it gave her some time with her uncle.

"Hi, Meg," Jessie greeted when she arrived. "How's that baby?"

"She's wonderful."

"Did she like her boots?"

Meg had to laugh. "I don't know about Savanna, but Brad could not stop smiling."

"Trace was pretty excited," Jessie said, watching Meg reach into her bag. "Big list today?" the shop owner asked.

"Not huge, but enough to keep Jeb busy."

Both women laughed when Jeb called from the back, "Did someone say my name?"

Meg went that way, passing and greeting both of Jessie's girls. She found her uncle in the stockroom and joined him.

"How are things going?"

"Just fine. Jessie was having Abel organize some of this stockroom. She said she couldn't find a thing."

Jeb looked like a kid in a candy store. He was an orderly, organized person, and being set loose on the stockroom was right up his street.

"Oh," Jeb went on, "I almost forgot. Miranda had her baby last night."

"Oh, that's good news! What did she have?"

"A girl. Nellie."

"Heidi will be thrilled," Meg said, causing them to both laugh. The church family knew that Heidi wanted things "even."

"What can I find for you?" Jeb offered finally, now walking with Meg in the aisles.

The two set to work, not in a hurry and doing as much talking as shopping. Other customers had needs from time to time, Saturdays being busy, but for the most part Meg was able to take her time and finish her list. She also settled her account with Jessie and was on the way to get the baby and head for home a solid hour before she had expected.

⁂

"How did it go?" Jeanette asked.

Cassidy stood speechless for a few minutes. Her mind still working to process what had happened with Hiram Brickel.

"Cassidy?" Jeanette's voice had changed from curiosity to concern.

"He wanted me to stay for coffee. He nearly insisted."

"What did you say?"

"That I couldn't. I even offered to cancel the order, but he didn't want that."

It was now Jeanette's turn to be speechless. She stared at her boss, taking in the flushed cheeks and thoughtful eyes and wondered if she should feel concerned.

"Do you have to deliver the rest of the shirts?"

"Yes, next Saturday."

"I'll go with you."

"Who will watch the store?"

Jeanette's brain raced for another solution, but Cassidy was ahead of her.

"I'm not afraid to go back there," Cassidy spoke with confidence, setting her bag down and putting on an apron. "I was surprised by it, but I'm not afraid."

"Tell me exactly what happened," Jeanette said. And Cassidy would have, but Chandler came in.

"Hi, Chandler," Cassidy greeted, her eyes quickly telling Jeanette that she wanted the other subject dropped. "What can we do for you?"

"Just some mending," he said, showing them the two shirts he'd torn and lost buttons from.

Cassidy offered to fix the shirts while he waited, but Chandler said he wasn't in a hurry. The three stood and talked business until Chandler remembered he had an appointment and needed to get back to the bank.

Jeanette was ready to have Cassidy finish her story, but there wasn't a moment to breathe for the rest of the day, not that the women complained about having more business.

❧

"How was your day?" Trace asked Cassidy as they started out of town that evening.

"It was interesting," Cassidy said, not sure how much she should share.

"In what way?"

"I got a big order and delivered part of it. I've never done that, and it just turned out to be a bit of a surprise."

"That's unusual, isn't it?" Trace commented.

"What do you mean?"

"Oh, I don't know. I would assume it's a woman who can't get out, and I didn't think Token Creek had too many folks like that."

"It wasn't a woman," Cassidy admitted quietly, and even though she wasn't looking at Trace, she was aware of the way his head swiveled rather swiftly to stare at her.

"You went to this man's house?" he asked quietly.

"Yes."

"Was his wife there?"

"I don't think he's married, but the man who works for him was there."

Trace's gaze went back to the road as he tried to compute this. That she didn't want to spell this out for him was obvious, but it didn't change Trace's concern for her.

Trace did not continue to press her, and Cassidy thought she'd heard the end of it. She was wrong. Much later that night, when Meg took the baby upstairs for the night and she found herself alone in the living room with Trace, that man stared intently at her for a time.

"So it's like this," Trace said without warning. "I didn't think I needed to hear the whole story, but I do. I appreciate the fact that you don't want to gossip to me about a customer, and if we were just talking about business, I would stay out of it. But we're talking about your safety, and that changes everything."

Cassidy stared at him, her mouth opened a bit. It was very clear he had been thinking about this, and that surprised her completely.

"Go ahead," Trace said when she didn't begin. His voice was calm, but his eyes were intent. "Tell me everything."

"And if I don't want to?" Cassidy asked out of curiosity.

Trace smiled and said, "I'll tattle."

The word was so funny coming from this full-grown man that Cassidy had to put her hand over her mouth to keep from laughing. When she could control herself, she had another question.

"To whom will you tattle?"

"Everyone," he began with great satisfaction. "Brad, Meg. I assume

Jeanette knows, but I'll tell Heather, Jeb, Patience, Chandler, Rylan, Chas, and Miranda, just to name a few."

"But you don't know anything!"

"I know enough to raise their concerns. You'll have more people checking with you than you have hours in the day."

"You're a horrible person. Do you know that, Trace Holden?"

"Not at all." He was looking very pleased with himself. "I'm just looking out for a friend."

Cassidy was opening her mouth to say more when Brad came from upstairs. He joined them in the living room, and Cassidy took full advantage.

"How's the baby?"

"She woke up, so Meg is rocking her a bit."

"She's growing so fast," Cassidy said, even as she saw Trace rise.

"As much as we want to visit," Trace said to his brother, "Cass and I have some business on the porch." Trace had come, taken Cassidy by the hand, and pulled her to her feet. Cassidy wanted to laugh again but simply walked to the porch. When her eyes met Trace's, he read the indulgence there and put both hands up.

"Humor me, Cassidy. You might be just fine, but I'd like to know the details."

Cassidy told him what had happened at the Brickel house, and Trace did not look pleased.

"Why didn't you want to tell me?" was the first question Trace asked.

"I thought you might do just what you're doing, making a bigger deal out of this than it is."

Trace was not offended that she wasn't taking it as seriously as he was, but that didn't mean his opinion would change.

"Why are you going back?" Trace wanted to know next.

"I told him I would."

"Couldn't you send word that the shirts need to be picked up?"

"I said I would bring them, and I will."

Trace's head tipped a little in thought. "Why aren't you afraid?"

Cassidy shrugged a little, and said, "Mr. Brickel's interest was a surprise, but he wasn't threatening."

Trace contemplated this for a while, knowing that Saturday would be busy. He would have preferred to be in town when she made this delivery, but he couldn't make that work.

"I want you to do me a favor."

"What's that?"

"Tell Rylan."

"What will that accomplish?"

"I just want him to know that you're going. I want someone other than Jeanette to be aware of the situation—a man, by the way."

Cassidy stared at her friend. She was very touched by his concern but wasn't sure it was necessary. The whole episode had not upset her—it had only surprised her.

"Cass?" Trace said, having watched her the whole time.

"Hm?"

"Do you have a problem with Rylan knowing?"

"No, I just don't think it's needed. It seems to be a bit much. I'm going to finish the shirts and drop them off. That's all."

"What if he presses you to stay? What if he does something unexpected, like touches you or won't let you go?"

"If I don't come back, Jeanette will go for help."

Trace had to smile before saying, "Put like that, it does sound like I'm overreacting. But I won't feel that way if this man turns out to be threatening."

"I'll tell you what," Cassidy said, making a decision. "I'll let you speak to Rylan if you want to. I'm staying out of it. And if you do talk to him, please make it clear that I don't want or need any company that day. I'm not worried that something will go wrong." Cassidy rose to go back inside but said one more thing. "Not that I don't appreciate your concern."

Trace didn't try to detain her but simply followed her back into the living room. He would talk to Rylan without stirring things up unnecessarily. He was not in a panic, but he didn't know enough about Hiram Brickel. To simply do nothing wasn't an option.

⁂

"What am I doing?" Rylan asked the congregation on Sunday morning as he opened his mouth and then covered his mouth with his hand. The group gathered looked at him, most people smiling even if they were a little confused.

"Any guesses?" Rylan moved his hand and asked. "Chas?" Rylan called on that man.

"Are you yawning?"

"Maybe," Rylan said cryptically. "What else?"

"Getting sick?" someone called from the back.

"That's possible," Rylan joked.

"Surprised about something," Brad suggested.

"Gasping," Philip guessed.

"Okay," Rylan said with pleasure. "We're getting somewhere. Watch me again and ask yourself this time if I'm yawning or gasping."

Rylan put his hand back over his mouth and looked out over the group. A few seconds later, he moved his hand and began his sermon.

"Isn't it interesting how the same action can look like two very different things? If I'm yawning, you're going to rightly assume that I'm tired or bored. Watching me might even make you feel tired. It's contagious.

"However, if I'm gasping you're going to get a little excited yourself and want to know what's going on. You won't be the least bit bored or tired. You're going to want to know what I'm excited about. It will be just as contagious.

"What was your latest response to God's Word? A gasp or a yawn? Have you begun to yawn when I mention the fear of the Lord? Is that subject getting old for you, or are you still gasping?

"I want us to take some time this morning and work to grasp the greatness and holiness of our saving God. We'll start in the book of Exodus, chapter fifteen. Follow along as I start reading in verse eleven. I'm going to read through to verse eighteen. Don't miss the powerful words here.

"'Who is like unto thee, O LORD, among the gods? Who is like thee, glorious in holiness, fearful in praises, doing wonders? Thou stretchedst out thy right hand, the earth swallowed them. Thou in thy mercy hast led forth the people which thou hast redeemed: thou hast guided them in thy strength unto thy holy habitation. The people shall hear, and be afraid: sorrow shall take hold on the inhabitants of Palestina. Then the dukes of Edom shall be amazed; the mighty men of Moab, trembling shall take hold upon them; all the inhabitants of Canaan shall melt away. Fear and dread shall fall upon them; by the greatness of thine arm they shall be as still as a stone; till thy people pass over, O LORD, till the people pass over, which thou hast purchased. Thou shalt bring them in, and plant them in the mountain of thine inheritance, in the place, O LORD, which thou hast made for thee to dwell in, in the sanctuary, O Lord, which thy hands have established. The LORD shall reign forever and ever.'

"Did you grasp those words, my friends? This is an awesome, powerful God we serve. Turn next to the last book of the Bible. I'm going to read from Revelation 15:4: 'Who shall not fear thee, O Lord, and glorify thy name? For thou only art holy: for all nations shall come and worship before thee; for thy judgments are made manifest.' This verse reminds us that our God is holy and is to be feared.

"Are you grasping that yet? Are you getting it?" For emphasis, Rylan put his hand over his mouth for just a moment more. "A gasp or a yawn. We choose, don't we? We serve a great and awesome God, and that's what we need to grasp. There is nothing to be yawned at here. It's too big to waste our time yawning.

"Before I pray, I just want to send you off with one final thought. Ask God to help you grasp His greatness and holiness. Remember this one thing: A proper *grasp* leads to an appropriate *gasp*."

Rylan prayed and dismissed the flock a few moments later. Cassidy and Chandler had been sitting with the Vick family, and conversation wasn't long in coming.

"I needed that," Chandler admitted to the others. "I can't remember the last time I needed a sermon more."

"It was excellent, wasn't it?" Chas agreed. The women nodded in agreement.

"I won't look at yawning the same ever again," Cassidy put in.

"Can you both come for lunch?" Chas suddenly asked.

"I can," Chandler agreed.

"Thank you," Cassidy said, "but Jeanette asked me to join her today."

"Another time," Miranda said warmly, wondering if her husband had been doing a bit of matchmaking. She caught his eye as they said their goodbyes and found a smile lurking there. She knew in an instant that she'd guessed correctly.

⁙

"And she plans to go back this Saturday?" Rylan made sure he had the facts.

"Yes," Trace said. "She's not afraid, and I'm proud of her for that, but I just wanted you to know."

"I'll check with her on Saturday morning," Rylan said.

"Thank you."

"Does she know you're telling me?"

"Yes. She didn't think it was necessary but didn't object to my mentioning it."

Rylan nodded, his eyes studying Trace for a moment. He wanted to ask if the relationship was changing from friendship to something more, but other people were visiting close by. He didn't think anyone would hear, but he wasn't willing to take a chance.

Trace broke into Rylan's thoughts when he thanked him for the sermon and went on his way. Franklin Vick was waiting to talk to him, and as Rylan hunkered down to the little boy's level, he did his best to concentrate on Franklin alone.

❧

"Have I told you," Brad began, catching Meg in the kitchen alone after Sunday dinner, "how fun it is to hug you?"

Meg smiled as his arms went around her and looked up into his eyes. "You might have missed yesterday," she teased.

Brad cuddled her close and said, "Much as I love my daughter, I certainly enjoy holding just my wife."

"You won't hear any complaints out of me," Meg said just before they kissed.

In the living room, oblivious to everyone but the little person in his arms, Trace smiled when Savanna let out a huge yawn.

"That was a big one," he said. "You must be getting sleepy."

She smiled up at him, and Trace felt the familiar sensation in his chest. He didn't know anyone could affect another person's heart the way this baby had. He loved her in a way he couldn't explain and thought he might do anything for her.

She yawned again, and Trace was suddenly back in the sermon. He'd needed the words this morning just as much as the others had. And even though they hadn't talked about it, he felt just the way Cassidy did: He would never look at yawning the same again.

CHAPTER ELEVEN

JEANETTE HAD BEEN WORKING STEADILY along on Wednesday afternoon, getting plenty done in Cassidy's absence, when a man stopped outside the shop. The sky was full of bright sunshine, making it hard to see through from outside, but indoors Jeanette noticed his presence and watched him for a moment. She thought he was ready to move on his way when he reached for the door handle.

"Can I help you?" Jeanette offered when he came fully inside.

"I'm looking for Cassidy."

"She's not here right now. Is there something I can do?"

"When do you expect her back?"

Jeanette did not like the question and suddenly realized she didn't like the man. His eyes never stayed in one place, and neither did his hands. Not caring if she lost business or not, Jeanette's chin came up a bit as she answered.

"I'm in charge right now. If you want to order something, you'll have to tell me."

"I'm still thinking about it," the man said, smiling a smile that Jeanette did not trust. "Do you make men's shirts?"

"Yes," Jeanette answered, the coldest response she'd ever given to a customer.

"I may be back," the man said, nodding a bit, putting on his hat, and turning toward the door.

Jeanette said goodbye when he glanced back at her, but she had held her place in the shop. She only moved once the door shut so she could look out the window and see where he went. Jeanette watched him walk deeper into town, not liking or trusting anything about him.

⁂

Chandler arrived on Thursday morning for his shirts. Cassidy had had them done for a few days but kept forgetting to take them to the bank when she made her end-of-the-day trip. He came as she opened the store. Jeanette was not there yet.

"How are you?" Chandler asked warmly, his heart suddenly realizing how much he enjoyed being with this woman and wishing he knew how she felt about him.

"I'm fine. How are you?"

"I want to hear more than 'fine,'" Chandler said. "How are you really?"

Cassidy looked at him. "Do I not seem fine?"

"That's not it. I ask it that way because of me, not you. I have a tendency to ask that question and not really listen to the way people answer."

"Well, that's kind of you, Chandler, but I think the answer is still fine."

"How about financially? How are things there?"

"I've been busy and had lots of orders, and someone did give me some money."

"That was kind. Who was it?"

"It was done through Rylan. He was asked not to say. It came at a time I really needed it—not so much for my bank account but for my heart."

Chandler stared at her for a moment, his mind taking in that special statement.

"What did I say?" Cassidy asked, not sure what his look meant.

"Your heart and bank account—I liked the way you put that."

"I have to think that way or I would be prone to worry all the time," Cassidy admitted.

Chandler nodded, understanding completely. As a bank manager, he found there was no end of things he could worry about. He was telling Cassidy this when Jeanette arrived.

"Good morning!" she greeted them. "I'm sorry I'm late. My sister was having a rough time."

"Is she all right?" Cassidy and Chandler asked at almost the same time.

"She is, but I'm going to head home in a few hours to check on her."

"And I'd better get to the bank," Chandler said. "It was good talking to you, Cass. Bye, Jeanette."

The women saw him to the door, took a moment to figure out what needed to be done that day, and went to work.

***

"Oh, no, you don't." Meg spoke under her breath as she looked out her kitchen window. A full-grown bull moose had come into the yard and was eating off the Juneberry bush. Meg, remembering the baby was asleep, grabbed the broom and headed out.

"Go on!" she shouted as she neared. "Get away from there!"

Meg brandished the broom in the moose's direction, but he didn't seem overly fazed. He looked in her direction but went right on chewing. She was about to get closer, even hit him if she had to, when the report of a rifle sounded behind her. It startled her into dropping the broom, and the moose certainly got the point. He jerked violently before running for the hills.

"You scared me!" Meg scolded Brad, who was coming toward her.

"Meg." Brad's voice was patient, but his eyes were a little stern. "What have I told you about coming after moose with a broom? That's why we keep the rifle in the kitchen."

"Savanna is sleeping," Meg argued. Brad's mouth opened in surprise, causing Meg to bite her lip.

"Better Savanna awake than you hurt or worse," Brad said, trying not to smile at her guilty face.

"Was that shot from here?" Trace asked, having just come in on his horse. The answer was obvious from the weapon in Brad's hand.

"Yes," Brad answered before Meg could. "Meg was using a broom to scare a moose away."

Trace's face was too much like Brad's. He looked as though he was ready to scold her as well. Picking up the broom, Meg made her exit with the excuse that she needed to check on the baby.

⚜

Not once had Cassidy let her mind drift. With Theta on her mind, Jeanette had not remembered to tell her about the man who had been asking for her until well after lunch. Cassidy's heart had sunk a little with what Jeanette described, but it was already Thursday and she still had two shirts to make. She had not had time to give way to speculation and fear—until now.

Now she was alone in her apartment, the day over and the business closed. Not even bothering to start dinner, Cassidy sat at her small kitchen table and tried not to think about what the visit might mean. But it didn't work. She had run out of time, and she knew that.

Cassidy began to pray. She hadn't had many choices before coming to Token Creek. She had done what she'd been asked to do. If that was all coming to an end, then she would have to trust that God had a plan for her future. This, however, did not stop the grief that filled her heart. If she had to leave this church family and this town, she thought it just might break her heart.

※

"How are you, ladies?" Rylan asked of Cassidy and Jeanette first thing Saturday morning. Indeed, they had barely gotten the door unlocked when he appeared.

"We're fine," Jeanette said, wondering at his smile. She wondered even more when she saw Cassidy smiling in return.

"I completely forgot that he was going to talk to you," Cassidy said, causing Jeanette to frown in confusion and Rylan to laugh.

"When do you go?"

"As soon as I pack the shirts in my bag."

"I'll be at home," Rylan said to Jeanette, "unless of course Cassidy would allow me to accompany her."

Cassidy was shaking her head no when Jeanette asked what was going on.

"Your nephew was concerned about my interaction with Hiram Brickel. He spoke to Rylan because he can't be in town today."

"I'd almost forgotten about that," Jeanette said as it all came rushing back.

"I'll see you shortly," Cassidy said, starting toward the door. Just before exiting, she thanked Rylan for checking on her but left without hesitation.

※

"Good day, Miss Norton," Halston greeted Cassidy as he let her in the mansion.

Cassidy stepped across the threshold but did not move so he could shut the door. She held the neatly folded shirts out to him. Without thought, he took them.

"I hope Mr. Brickel will be pleased."

"He would like to see you," Halston said, thinking fast when he realized she was going to get away.

"All right," Cassidy said, but she didn't move.

Halston admired her mettle. He gave a slight nod of the head and moved down the hallway toward the doors of the large parlor she remembered from her first visit. Cassidy watched Halston disappear inside. She heard an angry voice from within but could not make out the words. A few minutes passed before a very agitated Hiram Brickel came from the room.

"Why is the front door hanging open?" he barked.

"Because as soon as I'm paid, I'm leaving," Cassidy stated quietly.

"I told you we would have coffee. It's all ready!"

"Thank you." A note of steel had entered Cassidy's voice, but her look was kind. "If you recall, Mr. Brickel, I told you I could not stay."

Cassidy's face was calm, but Mr. Brickel looked as though his heart was ready to stop.

"Pay her!" he finally spat at Halston as he turned and slammed back into the large parlor.

Cassidy told herself that he was not worth the money, but it wasn't often that anyone ordered five shirts. Further orders would have been nice.

She thanked Halston when he'd paid her, noting that he looked completely unperturbed about the whole episode and even thanked her kindly for coming. Cassidy was on her way a short time later, her heart a little uncertain about Mr. Brickel's response but thankful that she had very little to report.

❧

Trace forced himself to put Cassidy into God's hands. For that reason, when he arrived very early in town, he went directly to see his mother—that, along with the fact that he was leaving in ten days' time and would probably not have a chance to see her again.

"Hello, Becky," Trace greeted when she checked to see who had come in the front door.

"Oh, Trace, I'm glad you're here. She's had a rough day."

Trace nodded, wondering if his presence and voice might not make it worse, but he still went in the direction of the porch. Heather was there, and he found his mother asleep.

"How is she?" Trace asked quietly, seeing that his mother's nurse did not look as cheerful as she usually did.

"Horrible." Heather wasted no words, although her voice was as compassionate as always. "I'm not surprised she's asleep. It's the second time this week she's fretted and cried off and on all day. And she won't eat."

"Why don't you go rest for a while, Heather. I'll find you if she needs something."

Heather's sigh was audible. "I believe I'll take you up on that, Trace. Thank you."

Trace lowered himself into a chair, pleased that he'd come here first. He was actually looking forward to telling his mother all about Savanna's latest smiles and obvious signs of brilliance, but it was nice to sit quietly too. He did not sleep and his mother did not wake. Heather was gone for about an hour, and Trace took nearly all of that time to pray.

⚜

"Well, Trace," Cassidy said with soft surprise. He was at least an hour earlier than she'd expected.

"Hello," the cowboy said calmly, but his eyes took in every detail of Cassidy's face. Her hair was coming down, but other than that, she looked completely normal. "How was your day?"

"My day was busy. How was yours?"

"Not too bad. How did it go with your delivery?"

Cassidy smiled a little and just kept from shaking her head. Jeanette had wanted every detail, and Rylan had stopped later to check on her, wondering about the details as well. And her day *had* been a busy one.

"Can I tell you on the way to the ranch?"

"Sure," Trace agreed as he put his hat on the stand and took a seat. He wasn't usually this early but still took his welcome for granted.

"Did you see Jeanette, by any chance?" Cassidy asked, going back to her work on the hem of a dress.

"No."

"Your mother had a bad day."

"I was just at the house."

"I'm glad. How was she?"

"Sleeping."

"Good."

Cassidy had asked all of this while looking at Trace, her hands working while they talked. It was not the first time Trace had seen her do this, and he finally asked about it.

"How can you sew and not watch what you're doing?"

"It depends on what I'm sewing. I've put in enough hems that I can feel with the needle how deep to go into the cloth."

She had made several more stitches in the moments it took her to say this, and Trace was quietly amazed. He would have commented again, but before he could say anything else Cassidy began to talk.

"I don't think you're going to need to be concerned about my going to Mr. Brickel's any longer. I doubt he'll be placing another order."

"Are you all right with that?"

"With not having to deal with him, yes, but the business would have been nice."

"What did he say?"

"He was not happy that I didn't stay for coffee."

"He expected that today, even when you'd made yourself clear last week?"

"Yes."

"And his response told you he was done with you?"

"Yes."

Trace didn't need to hear any more. Never having met him, the rancher still did not trust this man. There was no point in saying so, but he was glad Cassidy would have no further dealings with him.

Trace suddenly realized that Cassidy had put her sewing away and asked, "Are you ready to go?"

"I just have to get my bag."

Trace locked the shop door and waited for her at the bottom of the outside stairs. As soon as she came with her bag, he took it from her, helped her into the wagon, and headed out of town.

⁂

Cassidy settled into her bed at the ranch. She had accompanied Meg to her room when it was time to put Savanna down and was able to tell the other woman about the man who had come to town looking for her, sure that he was some sort of investigator.

It had felt good to talk about it. She had cried a little, as had Meg, but then Meg had prayed with her and told her they would trust God for whatever the future held.

Once Savanna was asleep, the two women had gone back downstairs and the four adults had played a game. It made for a later night than usual, but the time had been worth it. It had taken Cassidy's mind from her troubles and reminded her that God had provided these dear friends. He would go on providing everything else she needed.

⁂

"It's okay," Brad said quietly to his teary wife, holding her close on the dark porch at Jeb and Patience's. "It'll go by fast," he added, as much for himself as for her.

"You always say that," Meg said, "and it always does, but I still always cry."

Brad smiled and kissed her again. He had brought Meg and Savanna, with everything they needed, to town. He and Trace would leave in the morning from the ranch, along with a crew of five for the cattle drive. He hoped to be gone no longer than two weeks, but that wasn't up to him. The elements and the auction once they arrived in Burton would determine all of that.

Brad held her as long as he dared. The temptation was strong to stay with her in town, but he fought it. They kissed again, Brad squeezing the breath out of her with his pent-up emotions. He slipped back inside to give Savanna one more kiss; it was as hard to leave her as it was his wife.

Meg watched Brad ride away until the darkness covered him and she could no longer hear the horse's hooves. When Savanna was older, she would have to put up a brave front, but not this year. This year she would cry as always. She was suddenly glad it was almost bedtime. From the past she knew that sleep was the best thing for her.

Brad, his mind half in town and half on the trip he and Trace would start at daybreak, got himself home as fast as he could. He wouldn't cry, but he also knew that the best thing for him at the moment was sleep.

⁂

"Good morning," Patience greeted Jeanette, who was at the Dorns' door first thing Tuesday morning. "I thought we might see you."

"Too early?"

"Not at all. Come in and join us for breakfast."

Jeanette did not need to be invited twice. Meg and the baby were in town, and she had the entire day off. It was not an opportunity to be missed.

⁂

"Hello, Halston," Cassidy said with a certain level of surprise. The man appeared in her shop on Tuesday afternoon.

"Good day, Miss Norton. Is this a convenient time to place an order?"

"For Mr. Brickel?"

"Yes, ma'am."

Cassidy couldn't help herself. She had to ask, "So I'm forgiven?"

A smile lit Halston's eyes, even though he did not allow it to reach his mouth.

"So it would seem," he said a touch dryly as he proceeded to give Cassidy measurements for a pair of pants.

"May I ask you something?" Cassidy suddenly felt bold enough to enquire.

"Certainly."

"How does Mr. Brickel know about this store?"

"He's seen you walking and has asked about you."

"Asked whom?"

"He asked me."

Cassidy took a moment to digest this before asking, "What fabric does Mr. Brickel want?"

"Ah, yes," Halston remembered, producing a swatch of fabric from his pocket. "Might you have something like this?"

Cassidy took it and slipped into the rear to check her supply of cloth.

"I can match the fabric, but not the color," she said, coming from the back and bringing what she'd found. "Would you like to take some to Mr. Brickel to make sure?"

"I probably should, to be on the safe side," Halston agreed.

Cassidy cut a swatch and gave it to the man. She made sure he understood that she would not start to sew until Mr. Brickel was sure he wanted that color. Halston said he understood and then went on his way. Cassidy didn't have a lot going on, so she wasted the next ten minutes trying to figure out how she'd gotten back into the rich man's good graces.

※

"And Father," Rylan prayed as he finished the Bible study time with Chandler and Philip. "We ask You to be with Trace and Brad right now. Give them clear heads and help them to think well as they handle the elements, the cattle, and the unexpected. Please help them to be lights to the other men they're working with right now and to those at the auction.

"We ask in Your will to bring them home safely. We miss their presence and ask that You help Meg to do well while she parents on her own. Give her patience and grace as she works with Savanna, and bless her time with Jeb and Patience.

"Thank You, Lord, that they are all a part of our church family. Help us to be unified in You, Lord, so that our witness in Token Creek will be worth a second look. We trust You for all of these things and ask them in the name of Your Son, the Lord Jesus Christ. Amen."

The men visited a bit more before going their separate ways. They would not meet together again before Trace rejoined them, and that alone was a good reminder to keep that brother in their prayers.

※

"He what?" Cassidy asked Halston on Wednesday morning, aware that Jeanette was standing like a statue behind her.

"He wants the pants, and also for you to marry him."

"Halston—" Cassidy swiftly gathered her thoughts, working to keep calm, but for once that man cut her off.

"He wanted to ask you when you stayed for coffee, but that did not work out. He could think of no other way to ask you, so he sent word with me."

It was on the tip of Cassidy's tongue to argue that Mr. Brickel didn't even know her, but that was not the point.

"Please thank Mr. Brickel, but tell him the answer is no. Do you think he still wants the pants?"

"He does." Halston had anticipated this and asked that very question. "He would like you to deliver them when they are done."

"Very well, but I cannot linger. Make sure he knows that."

"Yes, Miss Norton."

This said, Halston nodded to both women and went on his way.

"You handled that with tremendous calm," Jeanette said, still shocked by the brief episode.

"It's easy to do when you don't take something seriously."

The two women stared at each other, and then Cassidy made a decision.

"I'm not going to speak of this, Jeanette, and I'd rather you didn't either. I respect Mr. Brickel's want for privacy. I don't wish to gossip about any of my customers."

"Of course, Cassidy, and just so you know, I'm proud of you."

"Thanks, Jeanette," Cassidy said sincerely, and both women got to work so Cassidy could get to her afternoon off.

"Do you have any idea how fun this was?" Cassidy asked Meg on Wednesday afternoon. The two women were alone in Patience's parlor. "I didn't have to rent a rig. I just walked down the street."

"A very strong advantage to Brad's going away," Meg said.

"Maybe the only one," Cassidy said compassionately.

"It's not that bad," Meg replied, already having a wonderful time with the aunt and uncle who were more like parents to her. "Jeanette was here yesterday, and then we took the baby to see Brad's mom. It was a good day."

"Did she respond?"

"There was no change in her at all, but Jeanette was emotional."

"She was a little quiet this morning," Cassidy realized. "I wonder if it was still on her mind."

"It might have been," Meg said.

The women visited for a few hours, and when Savanna went down for a nap, Patience stayed with her so they could walk to Jessie's to shop. It was the first time they'd ever done such a thing and made for an even more delightful afternoon.

Cassidy stayed for supper with the family but didn't linger long afterward. There was still plenty of light as she made her way home. She had actually turned the corner of her shop, intent on going up the stairs, before she spotted him.

Edson Sinclair, dressed in the dapper style he'd made his own, was sitting halfway up her stairs. For long moments Cassidy could only stare at him, hardly able to believe that her brother had come to Token Creek.

⇒ CHAPTER TWELVE ⇐

"HELLO, CASS!" EDSON'S VOICE was friendly, his smile real.

Cassidy stood very still while he came to his feet and joined her at the bottom of the stairs. He didn't insult her by hugging her, but his pleasure was hard to take.

"Nice town you have here," he continued when she was quiet. "Although why you would take Great Aunt Lara's maiden name and not keep the fine name of Sinclair is beyond me."

"What do you want, Edson?" Cassidy finally found her voice.

"Why you, dear sis," he said, his smile too charming to be real. "Or should I say your connections. They must be numerous in this town."

Cassidy shook her head. Nothing had changed. She was about to say that she would never help him, but he was talking again.

"It took me longer than I thought," he continued, his voice almost conversational. "I mean, you really hid. The investigator I hired had a tough time of it, and Mama was quiet."

"How is she?"

"Fine. I told her I'd found you. She wasn't pleased."

Cassidy felt sick. She had known it would not last, but to have gone this long...

"What's the matter?" Edson asked, actually managing to sound as though he cared.

"I won't help you, Edson. You must know that."

"You will if I say you will." The voice turned silky now, and Cassidy's chin came up. She was not afraid of this man or what he could do. She knew that in his heart he was a coward and would never lay a hand on her.

"Don't get uppity with me, girl," he surprised her by saying. "I wouldn't want to have to tell Neal that you need to be taught a lesson."

"What are you talking about?"

Edson looked across the street to a man sitting on a bench. Cassidy followed his gaze. Even from a distance she could see that he would not be kind. His body was thickset, making his head look small, and he looked out of place in the suit he wore.

"So you've found someone else to carry out your threats," Cassidy said to her brother. "How nice."

This time Edson smiled with real pleasure. "You know, Cass, I've missed you. I don't know any other woman who has your guts."

Cassidy ignored the compliment, took two steps up her stairway, and then turned back.

"I'm sure I'll see you around, Edson, but you're not welcome in my home or my business. Remember that."

Edson tipped his hat to her, but Cassidy did not respond. She turned and went up the stairs, slipped inside, and locked the door.

※

I don't know what's going on, Lord, Trace prayed from his bedroll in camp that night. The massive sky stretched above him, stars shining from every direction, but his heart was so heavy for Cassidy that he could not enjoy them. *Please take care of Cass. I know she needs You right now. Help her to be wise and trust in You, and to go to others for help. I admire her strength and independence, but help her to know when to reach to others. Help her to turn to Your Word and know that You are keeping her close. Help her to claim Your promises and believe what she knows to be true about You.*

And help me to trust. I want to be there. I want to know that she's all right. Help me to have the same trust in You that I want her to have, and know that You don't need my help. You have everything under control.

Trace had to remind himself of this several more times, but he finally embraced it and slipped off to sleep.

Cassidy knocked softly on Rylan's door early Thursday morning. It was barely light, but she knew he was an early riser. She pulled her sweater a little closer around her. The night had been cool, and the morning was still chilly.

"Good morning, Cassidy," Rylan said as he poked his head out to see who knocked. He came fully on to the porch, closing his door behind him.

"I'm sorry to bother you so early."

"Not at all," Rylan said sincerely, knowing she would not be standing on his porch at this hour of the day without good reason. "Are you all right?"

"My brother is here," Cassidy said without answering the question. "And he hasn't changed in the least."

"What does he want?"

"For me to connect him to the town. It will be like before: He'll want to know who has money and who doesn't so he can sell phony mine shares or persuade folks he has something else they should invest in."

"And does he actually think you're going to do this?"

"Yes. He's traveling with another man this time. He said his name is Neal. He looks like a thug in a business suit."

Rylan felt real fear for Cassidy's safety, but her face was disgusted, not afraid.

"Are you afraid?" Rylan asked, to make sure.

"Not for myself, but for others. And I know he could ruin my business."

"That's the least of my worries," Rylan surprised her by saying.

"What do you mean?"

"Just that. Your safety is all that matters."

"Rylan," Cassidy began. "That's very sweet of you but not at all practical. I have to make a living."

"Here, Cass," Rylan said, indicating one of the chairs on his porch with his hand. He'd suddenly realized he hadn't asked her to sit down. The sky was very light now, and as soon as Cassidy had sat, Rylan took a seat on the railing and began to talk. "So what's the worst that can happen? You go out of business and have to be taken in by a church family. I'm sure Jeanette would insist you live with her, and then you could look for work in town. It's not the ideal situation. I mean, of course you want to work for yourself, but you'd still be here, loved and protected by the rest of us, and life would go on."

Cassidy could hardly breathe. Was it really so simple? She had prayed for hours the night before, desperately wanting to trust but so afraid that her friends would be harmed because she had come to Token Creek.

"I never thought of it that way." Her voice was full of wonder.

"What had you planned to do?"

"Whatever I had to at the moment," Cassidy said, back to her practical self.

"What does that mean exactly?"

"Well, if Edson wants information about customers, I tell him no. If he gives someone a fake name, I'll make sure they know he lied."

"And what about Neal? How will you handle him?"

"He's a little tougher," Cassidy said thoughtfully, and Rylan noticed that she still showed no fear.

"I want to go to Sheriff Kaderly," Rylan began, but Cassidy was already shaking her head.

"It won't do any good right now. Edson has already served time for one of his crimes. Until there is a new offense, the sheriff can't do anything. And that's the whole problem: proving Edson did something and then having him stick around long enough to be arrested."

Rylan still had some ideas, however, and the two continued to talk for the next thirty minutes. By the time Cassidy left, her heart was a good deal lighter. She had thought about closing up shop and moving on but realized she could at least check with Rylan. She walked home to get ready for work, very thankful that she had.

⁂

"Good morning," Edson said to Cassidy and Jeanette just five minutes after they opened the door.

"I told you that you were not allowed in my store, Edson. I want you to leave."

"Without being introduced to this lovely woman you work with?" Edson said at his most urbane. He began to move in Jeanette's direction.

Cassidy moved between them, her chin going up, her eyes shooting sparks.

"I mean it, Edson. Move along."

Edson rolled his eyes like a child.

"Come now, Cass. I didn't think you really meant it."

"I assure you I did. Now do I have to send for the sheriff?"

The anger that lit Edson's eyes was fleeting, but Cassidy knew she had hit the mark. Tipping his hat in a mock salute, his eyes no longer friendly, he slammed out the door.

Cassidy turned to find Jeanette visibly shaken and went to her. She hugged the older woman and then began to explain.

"I'm sorry you had to go through that."

"Who was that, Cassidy?"

"My brother, and he's not a nice man."

"What is he doing here?"

"He moves around quite a bit, and he's come to see if any money can be made in Token Creek. I've told him I won't help him, but he's not taking no for an answer."

"But should you tell the sheriff anyway?"

"Not just yet," Cassidy said, speaking from experience.

"But maybe he's heard of him. Did you say his name was Edson?" Jeanette was frowning in thought. "Edson Norton. The sheriff might have a poster on him."

"It's Edson Sinclair," Cassidy said quietly. She watched the shock that covered Jeanette's face. "I'm sorry I didn't tell you before."

"Cassidy," Jeanette said quietly. "Is Edson Sinclair really your brother?"

"Yes."

Jeanette was stunned. This was a name bankers knew. Not that he would use his own name when conning some poor soul to hand money over to him for phony investments and the like. His real name was known all over Montana Territory by everyone in the banking world.

"Why is your last name not Sinclair?"

"It is. But when I left Billings, I took a family name so Edson could not find me."

"Oh, Cassidy," Jeanette said. She pulled Cassidy close for another hug, her heart turning over with compassion. It was a shock to learn of her connection to this man, but she was still her sweet Cassidy. Jeanette suddenly held the younger woman away from her.

"So much makes sense now," Jeanette said, her eyes wide.

"What do you mean?"

"Just who you are and how you do business."

Cassidy was confused by this statement, but Mrs. Potts had come in.

"Good morning," Cassidy greeted her. "How are you today?"

"I'm terrible," the lady said, tending to be dramatic. "I've torn two of my best shifts, and I can't find my best camisole."

"Come and look at fabric," Jeanette invited. "I know we have your sizes, Mrs. Potts. If you'll just pick out what you want, we can get right to it."

Cassidy watched Jeanette, surprised that she'd taken over, but as soon as Mrs. Potts had her back to the changing room, Jeanette nodded toward the window. Part of Edson could be seen past the lace curtains, standing outside looking in. Cassidy encouraged Mrs. Potts to take all the time she needed and then headed outside.

"What are you doing?" she asked him.

"I need a favor," he began. Cassidy began to open her mouth, but Edson put his hand up. "Just hear me out."

Before Cassidy could comment, he rushed on.

"I just need you to tell me who owns that big house at the end of the street. I'm sure you know them. Just tell me who lives there, introduce me as Ed Norton, your brother, and I'll take it from there."

"Edson," Cassidy began, a calm patience filling her; she almost felt pity for him. "That's not something I'm willing to do."

"Why not?"

"I'm not going to help you cheat someone," Cassidy said. She'd kept her voice low, but a man walked by and Edson glared at her.

"You're being unreasonable," Edson started, but this time Cassidy held her hand up.

"If by that you mean I'm done trying to reason with you, you're right. Do not stand around my shop," Cassidy said, and then noticed Neal across the street. "And take Neal with you."

Cassidy did not wait for a reply but headed back inside. She was tense for a time, but when Edson made no other appearances, she relaxed. Mrs. Potts took a good deal of time, but she left a large order.

Not until almost dinnertime did Cassidy realize she hadn't finished her conversation with Jeanette. Unfortunately that lady had gone home to dinner, and she was going to have to wait to find out what she meant.

◈

"Why don't you let me talk to her," Neal suggested when he and Edson were back in Edson's hotel room. "I'm sure I could make her see things your way."

"No." Edson's voice was sulky. "She's not afraid of you, and if you hit her, that ruins everything."

"Why?" Neal asked, disappointed over not being able to do his job.

Edson shook his head. "We have to be seen as a happy family. We can't do that if she's covered with bruises."

Neal looked affronted. "Bruises only show when I want them to," he said, but Edson had already made up his mind.

"Token Creek is small but too much of a plum to give up that easily. I'll stay clear of my sister for a time, and Cass will think I've lost interest. We've got all the information Bittner gathered while he was tracking Cassidy for us, and we'll just take our time with how we use it. Cheer up, Neal," Edson added when he noticed the other man's face. "I'm certain there's a profit to be made in this town and all the others."

◈

"You're just so good at business," Jeanette repeated.

"But I never worked with Edson," Cassidy pointed out, hoping Jeanette was very clear on that.

"Be that as it may, your family must have a natural bent for business, even though Edson has chosen to use his wrongly." Jeanette stopped for a moment and looked as fascinated as she felt. "It's an interesting combination, sewing as beautifully as you do, knowing how to run the business, *and* working so well with people."

"Thank you," Cassidy said, seeing it for the compliment it was but not getting overly excited as it was coming at such a difficult time.

"I've been wondering," Jeanette went on. "Will you warn people? I don't mean the sheriff, but should Chandler know that your brother is in town?"

Cassidy wasn't sure why she hesitated, but Jeanette couldn't help but notice.

"What's the matter?"

"I guess I'm just hoping he'll go away. I'm hoping Edson will figure out that there's nothing to be gained by staying and simply leave town."

Jeanette nodded, seeing how she would want that. It was hard not to jump in and tell Cassidy what she should do, but in truth she knew that Cassidy didn't need that. When Cassidy wanted and needed her advice, she always came to her. Jeanette thought that telling Chandler was the best idea, but it was not her news to tell. Another fine thing she'd learned from Cassidy over the months: keeping her mouth shut about customers and news that was not her own.

"What do you think?" Cassidy asked suddenly.

"I can see why you would hope he'd quietly go on his way, but I think I would still tell Chandler."

Cassidy nodded, needing to ponder this for a time. The very thought of confiding in Chandler made something inside her hold back, but she couldn't put her finger on what it was. It did not escape her thoughts that folks might feel betrayed. She had not lied about who she was, but neither had she been completely up front with everyone.

The women were working quietly along for a time—Cassidy's mind full of her brother and what his presence meant in her life—when Rylan came in.

"How are you?" he asked of Cassidy, taking for granted that Jeanette knew about Edson.

"I'm fine. Edson hasn't been around since this morning, and that's been a relief."

"But he did come here to the shop?"

"Twice."

Rylan's face gave nothing away, but as from the morning, he was concerned for her safety.

"What are you thinking, Rylan?" Jeanette asked.

"I'm not exactly sure what to think. I just want to make sure Cassidy is all right."

"Why don't you spend the night at my house, Cassie?" Jeanette suggested.

"That's a good idea," Rylan put in.

Cassidy looked as surprised as she felt and tried again to explain. "You don't understand. I'm not in any danger. Edson will find a mark, someone with money or who even looks like he has money, and cheat him out of it. At the very least, he'll cheat at a card game in one of the saloons at night. It might not be good for my business if folks connect Edson and me, but I'm not going to be physically harmed."

Rylan wished he believed that. He didn't know why, but it just didn't seem logical to him that it could be that simple.

"Well," Jeanette said before anyone could ask Rylan his thoughts, "if you change your mind—and not just tonight—you're very welcome."

"Thank you, Jeanette. I won't forget your offer."

Rylan did not stick around. He headed in the direction of home, forcing his mind to pray when he wanted to worry. He also asked God to help him to be more sensitive to things around him. Cassidy might not see danger coming, but that didn't mean he couldn't keep an eye out.

⚬❧⚬

"Do you see that woman?" Neal asked of Edson on Saturday morning. They were eating breakfast in the hotel and had taken a table by the window.

"What about her?"

"She's writing a book."

"And I care about that for what reason?" Edson asked, his voice a bit testy.

Neal shrugged as though he didn't care but still said, "It's on Token Creek. She knows about everyone in town."

The hired man suddenly had Edson's attention. The woman was not impressive. She talked to herself and looked half crazy, but Edson still watched her intently until she moved out of sight.

Cassidy did not know when she'd been so distracted. She'd kept on, looking normal to everyone, but thoughts of Edson and what his presence in town meant filled her mind.

I don't want to see my brother again, Lord, but You died for him, and if I could find a way to talk to him, maybe he would listen.

Cassidy lay in bed, her mind trying to think how that conversation would go. She didn't think it likely that he would be overly receptive, but did that mean she shouldn't try? She honestly didn't know.

Maybe he'll ask me, Lord. He knows the way Mama and I believe, but just maybe he'll ask me why I had to get away and why I won't help him.

Cassidy rolled out of bed, knowing the day awaited her. If she didn't get going, she would not have time for breakfast, and her Saturdays were too busy to go without that meal. Besides, she was done with Hiram Brickel's pants, and they had to be delivered today. She knew that that task would take some extra thought and time.

"It's Saturday already," Meg said to Patience at the breakfast table, Savanna at her breast. "The week has gone fast."

"Yes, it has. And whenever your uncle works for Jessie, the days drag a little, so I'm glad to have you."

"What time did he leave?"

"Just before you came down. He said to bring the baby over if you're up to it."

"I think I will. Jessie hasn't seen her either."

"I thought we would see more of Cassie while you were here," Patience commented.

"You mean in the evenings?"

"Yes."

"I wouldn't be surprised if she came tonight. I assume she's been busy."

"Well, I hope she does. I'll plan on her for dinner, and if she doesn't show up, we'll send Jeb to track her down."

Meg would have laughed at her aunt's tone and words, but Savanna had just fallen asleep.

⁕

What will you do if he wants to talk about his proposal? Jeanette's question lingered in Cassidy's mind all the way to the Brickel mansion, but in truth she didn't even expect to see the man. If he'd been angry about her refusal to stay for coffee, he must be livid about her not wanting to marry him.

Cassidy almost laughed at her own thoughts—the whole notion was ridiculous—but she was nearly to the Brickel mansion and tried to prepare her mind for whatever might happen. Mr. Brickel's answering the door, however, never occurred to her.

"Come in, Miss Norton," he invited, and Cassidy was so surprised, she obeyed.

"Is Halston ill?" Cassidy asked.

"Not at all, but I thought that I would see to things myself today."

"Oh, all right. Here are your pants," Cassidy said, handing them to the man.

"Thank you," Mr. Brickel replied, and Cassidy noticed that he didn't even glance at them.

"Are you going to try them?"

"Yes," Mr. Brickel agreed quickly, making himself look at the pants. "I'll be right back."

This said, he started away but came right back.

"Would you like to sit in the parlor, Miss Norton?"

"No, thank you," Cassidy answered, and then stood still as he walked away.

She discovered something just then. Far more disturbing than an angry, bellowing Mr. Brickel was one who was charming and kind. It simply didn't fit, and Cassidy didn't know what to do about it. She was still trying to work it out when Mr. Brickel returned.

"Are they satisfactory, Mr. Brickel?"

"Yes, thank you. Here is your money."

"Thank you, Mr. Brickel. I hope you enjoy your day."

"You really would be happy as my wife."

Cassidy had been turning for the door but stopped and looked at her customer. She did not want to do anything to encourage him in this line of thinking, but curiosity got the best of her.

"Why me, Mr. Brickel?"

"You would suit me perfectly, that's why. I also know you would be happy."

"How do you know that?" Cassidy found herself asking, not able to do anything else.

"Because you could do just as you please. If you wished to sew, you could. If you never wanted to sew again, you wouldn't have to. If you wanted to cook, the kitchen would be all yours. If not, we would hire someone."

Cassidy thought for a moment before asking, "What's in it for you, Mr. Brickel?"

"Sons."

Cassidy had not expected this, but she held the surprise from her face. She was not, however, able to disguise the spark of anger that lit her eyes. "Good day, Mr. Brickel," she said tightly.

"I won't give up," he said this time, not trying to detain her, but some of the force coming back into his voice. "I know we should be married."

Cassidy held her ground and spoke after taking a breath. "I would never want to do anything to deliberately hurt you, Mr. Brickel. My refusal is not meant to be cruel, but I hope you won't be long in this belief because it's simply not true."

Cassidy nodded again, telling herself to be calm, and this time slipped out the door. She thought if she couldn't see Meg and pour her heart out to her that moment, her head would burst. But she had a day of work ahead of her, and it wasn't fair to leave Jeanette alone on a Saturday. She only hoped that Meg would be free that evening and ready to hear an earful.

CHAPTER THIRTEEN

"Oh, Cass," Meg said compassionately when she'd heard about her friend's week. Cassidy had never planned to share Mr. Brickel's proposal, but after dinner, when they had some time on their own, everything came pouring out.

"He was so matter-of-fact about it, Meg, but I don't know how I kept from slapping his face. He just wants someone to give him sons. I felt horrible when he said that, like some sort of broodmare. I wished I'd never asked."

"How do you even know him?"

"I don't. He's seen me walking past his house. That led to my sewing a few things for him. That's all."

Meg didn't know why, but she wanted Brad home so badly that she ached. He loved Cassidy as she did, and she wanted to tell him all of this and hear from him what he thought they should do.

"Are you sure you're not afraid of your brother?" Meg couldn't help but ask next.

"Yes. He's greedy but not violent."

"But what about this Neal person?"

"I don't trust him at all, but there's no sense in harming me. I'm sure Edson knows that."

"I wish I shared your confidence."

Savanna was looking for her mother, and Jeb brought the howling baby into the kitchen where the women visited. Meg fed her, and then Cassidy had the pleasure of playing with her for the better part of an hour.

By the time Jeb walked her home, Cassidy's heart was much lighter. It had been a delicious meal and good to talk with a friend about life in the last few days. Nothing had been fixed. Cassidy was fairly certain that Edson was still in town, but having Meg know everything made all the difference in the world.

⁂

"I'm headed home," Cassidy said to the group she'd been talking to after church. Chandler, Heather, and Miranda all wished her goodbye, and Cassidy started off.

Cassidy did not sense that something was wrong until she was right in front of her door. It wasn't closed all the way, and she knew she'd locked it. Without having to think twice, she realized Edson was there. She opened the door, thinking she would tell him just what she thought, only to find both him and Neal inside.

"I can't believe you broke into my apartment."

"The door was open," Edson began, but Cassidy cut him off.

"Even if that were true—and we both know it's not—you have no business coming in uninvited."

"That's not very hospitable, Cass. I'm disappointed."

"And I'm weary of your little games. I want you to leave."

"Not until I get some information."

"I'm not negotiating with you, Edson."

"How well do you know Hiram Brickel?"

Cassidy only stared at him, her arms crossed.

"How about Jeanette Fulbright? I know you know her well. Is she as wealthy as she looks?"

"Have I ever told you what happened to me, Edson?" Cassidy

began, feeling tired and helpless and unable to find any other words. "It was life changing, I assure you."

"You're not going to start that, are you?" Edson suddenly wasn't so comfortable. "Mama tries that all the time, and I don't want to hear it."

"It's the only thing worth telling you," Cassidy said, realizing how true it was. "Nothing else has near the value."

Edson rose to his feet now, and Neal followed suit as he moved toward the door. Cassidy had not started this line of talk to chase them away, and in fact, she truly wanted to tell her brother about the way she'd come to Christ as a seventeen-year-old girl. Her mother had believed at the same time. Edson's retreating back made it obvious there was no opening here for that news.

"It's all pointless, Cass," Edson stopped at the door long enough to say. "If you won't help me, someone else will."

"I don't think so, Edson," she said quietly. "You need to leave Token Creek. You're not going to fool anyone here."

Edson left without another word, Neal in his wake. Cassidy felt shaken over the interchange. They had not threatened her in any way or messed up her apartment, but each time she spoke with her brother it seemed to take a little more out of her. Wondering how much more she could take, Cassidy started on dinner, not really caring whether she ate or not.

⁂

"She's not saying much, but she's been hit pretty hard," Sheriff Kaderly said to Rylan as the pastor came into Abi Pfister's small house on Monday morning. "She asked to see you the moment I got here."

"Hello, Abi," Rylan came close to say. Her face was turning black, especially around the eyes, and her mouth had a deep cut. "I'm sorry this happened."

"Why did it?" the woman rasped, able to see him with just one eye.

"Do you know who hit you?" Rylan asked, not understanding what she meant.

"Why did God?" Abi tried again, and Rylan pulled a chair up.

"Why did God allow this?" Rylan double-checked.

Abi nodded just a little, her one eye looking tear-filled.

"We live in a sinful world, Abi. Whoever did this to you was wrong, but if it's got you to thinking about God, that's a good thing."

"He could have stopped it," she said.

"That's true. I wonder how many other things He's stopped over the years that you know nothing about. For some reason, He let this go on."

"Please find out what happened," the sheriff whispered, suddenly near his ear. "I can't get anything out of her."

"Do you want to tell me what happened?" Rylan asked.

"I couldn't see him," she said.

"Why not?"

"Dark."

"And he just started hitting you?"

"No. He wanted to know things."

"What things?"

"About my book."

Rylan looked at the sheriff, both men frowning in confusion, but her answer did explain why the papers had been strewn about. Before Rylan could ask her anything else, the doctor showed up. Someone had been sent to find him, and that had taken some doing.

Rylan stayed out of the way, but by the time Doctor Ertz was finished, Abi was asleep. Rylan left word with Missy, the woman who had found her hurt, that he would be back later. Abi had started a line of questioning that Rylan was not about to drop. Until Abi said she didn't want to hear any more, he would keep answering her questions.

On Monday afternoon Edson walked away from the Brickel mansion nearly shaking with rage. That he'd not been able to get past the man who answered the door infuriated him. He knew his sister had gotten in, but not even at his most charming had he been able to persuade the man at the door that he had an investment Hiram Brickel would want to hear about.

His sister had said that no one would fall for his schemes in this town, but he knew that she'd not told the sheriff he was here. Planning to hit two other houses before the day was through, he went back to the hotel for a quick drink and tried to calm down.

"How are you?" Rylan asked when he was back at Abi Pfister's bedside.

Abi put a hand up in a small wave but didn't try to answer.

"Do you want me to talk to you any more about the question you asked earlier?" Rylan asked, not wanting to press her when she wasn't ready but certainly wanting her to know he was willing.

"I'll send Missy," Abi managed.

"When you're ready for me to come back?" Rylan checked.

Abi gave a small nod.

"All right. I'll plan on that. Do you mind if I pray with you before I leave?"

"No," Abi said, and Rylan bowed his head.

"Heavenly Father, thank You for Abi Pfister. Thank You that she's interested in others and wants to write this book about Token Creek. Please put Your healing hand on Abi, Lord. We don't know exactly how You're going to use this in her life, but help us to see Your hand working. Thank You, Lord, that Abi and I have had a chance to talk about You. Thank You for being the saving God that You are. Bless

Abi this night and help her to rest. I ask all these things in the name of Your Son. Amen."

The hand came up again when Rylan said goodbye. He left, still praying, hoping that Abi would do as she said and eventually send Missy to get him.

***

It was Wednesday morning before Edson went back to see Cassidy, and he was not happy. He asked to see her alone when he found Jeanette in the shop as well, and even though she didn't want to, Cassidy agreed. She walked into the rear of her shop, the part that was partitioned off, and Edson followed. He wasted no time.

"It's like this, Cass. You help me or I'll ruin you."

Cassidy wondered again how much more she could take, but her voice was calm when she said, "I don't know why you think threats will work on me, Edson. They never have before."

"You've built up a nice little business here, Cassidy. I can't think why you would want to see it ruined."

"I don't know what you're planning, but no matter what it is, I won't help you cheat people out of their money."

Edson's smile was not nice. "Don't say I didn't warn you."

Cassidy didn't say anything. She let Edson walk away, her heart heavy. Had Jeanette not come to check on her, she might have gone on standing in the back of her store all day.

"Come on," Jeanette said, having heard every word. "Start your day off now. Head to my house and tell Heather I said to pamper you."

It sounded wonderful, but Cassidy asked, "What if Edson comes back?"

"Unlike you, he scares me. I'll send for the sheriff."

Cassidy had to smile. She knew Jeanette would do it.

"Go," Jeanette sent her.

Cassidy took the offer. Heather was surprised to see her but recovered swiftly and knew just what to do. Cassidy soon found herself sitting in a comfortable chair, her feet propped up and a cup of hot tea in her hand. Letting the conversation with her brother fall away, Cassidy began to pray. She prayed for Edson for a long time and then for her future. It had always been in God's hands, but that was never more apparent to her than at that very moment.

⁂

There had always been quiet days in the business, but when both Thursday and Friday were almost without customers, Cassidy knew that Edson had been at work. She didn't know what he was saying or how he was going about it, but he'd been good at his word. He was ruining his sister's business. Cassidy wondered if he was even still in town or if he had done his dirty work and gone on his way.

One thing was clear, there was no point in Jeanette coming in and sitting around with Cassidy. She could do that on her own. It had been hard for both of them, but Cassidy had told Jeanette not to come in on Saturday. The older woman had argued, but Cassidy had pled her case, and Jeanette could see that she was right.

It was for this reason that Chandler found Cassidy alone on Saturday morning. The bank was open, but he'd left Mr. Falcone in charge, coming to Token Creek's dress shop looking for some answers.

"Hello, Cassidy," the banker spoke quietly.

"Hello, Chandler." Cassidy's voice was just as quiet. It was clear that he had something on his mind.

"I wondered if I might talk with you."

"Certainly."

Cassidy sat at her sewing machine, and Chandler took one of the chairs. He did not start right away, and Cassidy did not help him. His demeanor made her uncomfortable. Chandler had always been open and friendly with her, but everything about him today was guarded and suspicious.

"I understand your brother is in town," Chandler said at last.

"Yes."

Chandler had not expected her to admit this, and for a moment he was taken aback.

"So it's true," he said, forgetting all of his carefully planned questions. "Your brother is Edson Sinclair?"

"Yes."

"Why didn't you tell me?"

"For many reasons," Cassidy said quietly, feeling attacked and worse about this than about her lack of customers.

"Do you know how I found out?" Chandler asked, his heart telling him he'd been betrayed and still feeling the sting.

Cassidy didn't answer.

"He came in to see me!" Chandler sounded as outraged as he felt. "Edson Sinclair walked into my bank as though he owned the place and informed me that your name isn't Norton; it's Sinclair. He said that you'd helped him on many deals and that the very funds you used to start your business here in Token Creek was money you'd earned together!"

Cassidy said not a word.

"Nothing, Cassidy?" Chandler was not just hurt now; he was angry. "No explanation? No reason for why I had to find out from one of the biggest swindlers in the state that you're not who you say you are?"

Cassidy felt as though she'd been cut with a knife. That Chandler would treat her this way was beyond what she expected. From the customers it made sense, but not from the church family, and certainly not from her friend Chandler Di Fiore.

While Cassidy's mind was trying to make sense of the pain and confusion, Chandler suddenly stood.

"It's clear that I'm not going to hear any more from you now than I have in the past. So I'll just be on my way."

Even if Cassidy had been ready to speak, Chandler would not have given her time. He was out the door a moment later, not slamming it, but closing it with a finality that made his feelings all too clear.

Meg had gotten a bit of a cold and ended up running a fever that put her in bed. Jeb had heard the rumors about Cassidy and talked with Patience but not said anything to Meg until Friday night when she'd been feeling better. Meg wasted no time. Arriving just five minutes after Chandler left, she went to her friend and put her arms around her.

"I'm sorry I wasn't here sooner. I just heard. I'm sorry, Cass. I'm so sorry."

Cassidy didn't try to speak. She was too emotional for that. She could hold together with nearly everyone, but not with Meg. Meg's kindness and tenderness were too much, and Cassidy had held her tears for a long time.

"It's okay," Meg said, wanting her to cry it all out, her own tears coming. She held her friend, and prayed, and once again missed Brad so much it hurt.

"Here," Meg said at last. "Sit down."

Cassidy let herself be led to a chair, and Meg pulled the other one close.

"Do you want to talk about it?" Meg asked.

"I don't think I can," Cassidy said, tears closing her throat as she thought about Chandler's visit again.

Meg didn't press her but sat with her as long as she dared. She knew Savanna would be looking for milk long before she got back, but she couldn't bring herself to leave Cassidy alone.

Not until Cassidy assured her that she would be all right—with plans to close the shop early and go to her apartment—did Meg agree to leave.

When Meg got back to the house, she was given the good news from Jeb that Edson was gone. He'd been seen boarding the train with another man. She would tell Cassidy that. She would not, however, tell Cassidy she'd received a telegraph. Brad had been in touch. He and Trace would be home on Monday night. Her good news in the light of Cassidy's heartache seemed almost cruel.

❧

It did not escape the notice of several people that Cassidy was not in church on Sunday morning, but when all was said and done, only Rylan and Jeanette went to check on her. Jeanette was the first up the stairs, Rylan behind her.

Cassidy answered the door when she heard their knock, not overly surprised to see them. She invited them into the living room and asked if anyone wanted coffee.

"No," Jeanette said. "We just want to know how you are."

"I'm all right."

"Are you ill?" Rylan asked, taking in her pale features and thin cheeks.

"No, just tired."

"Is that why you didn't come this morning to church?" Jeanette pressed.

"No, that's not it." Cassidy forced herself to be honest. "I just felt it was best to stay away."

"Best for whom?" Rylan asked.

"For everyone," Cassidy explained. "I know that not everyone trusts me now. Some believe the rumors my brother started, and I thought I should stay away. At least today."

"I don't think that's true," Jeanette began, but stopped when she saw Cassidy's face.

"Did someone say something, Cassie?" Rylan asked.

Cassidy nodded, her face growing a little paler. Jeanette was stunned into silence, and Rylan's mind was working on how much he should know. He realized that Cassidy didn't want to speak of it, and he was not going to press her.

"Maybe at some point you'll want to tell me about it," Rylan said. He knew it was the right thing when Cassidy looked at him with relief.

"How about some dinner, Cassie?" Jeanette asked, her heart turning over Cassidy's pain. "Why don't you and Rylan both come to my house?"

It was clear that Cassidy was going to refuse, but Rylan spoke up.

"I think that sounds like a good idea, Cassie. You don't have to stay long, but we could give you a rundown of the sermon if you like."

"I would enjoy that," Cassidy agreed. It was tempting to stay behind closed doors, but she knew that one of Becky's meals would be worth the effort of getting out. She needed the fellowship too. It had been hard to stay home, but she still thought it had been for the best. The time at Jeanette's was probably just what she needed.

⚜

"So what will you do?" Jeanette was asking by the end of the meal. They had told her all about the sermon, even the comments shared by others, and which songs they'd sung. In that time Cassidy's demeanor had changed, and Jeanette knew this question would be welcome.

"It's funny, but it took coming here to realize what I should do," Cassidy admitted. "I've watched Becky working today, and Heather, and realized there's more to life than sewing. I mean, it's what I know how to do, but there are other jobs to be had."

"How soon will you look for other work?" Rylan asked.

"Not right away. Maybe folks will understand that I'm not like my brother, and business will pick back up. I've got about two months of savings I can live on, but after that, I'll have to look for something."

"Can you sell your building?" Jeanette asked, knowing Cassidy owned it.

"If it comes to that, I can certainly try," Cassidy said, but didn't elaborate. Her building was always meant to be her house fund. When that special man came along and wanted to marry her, she was going to be able to sell her building so they could buy a home together.

"It's good to have a plan," Rylan said, wondering even now if he should press her about the person or people from the church family who had believed her brother's lies.

"I think I'll head home," Cassidy said before Rylan could voice his question. "Thank you so much, Jeanette."

"You're welcome."

"How has it been for you?" Rylan suddenly asked Jeanette, realizing she was out of a job at the moment.

"Not going to work with Cassie?" Jeanette checked. "It's hard. I've been keeping busy around the house, but I miss her and seeing the townsfolk. It's an amazing opportunity to pray and do good works."

Cassidy realized this was part of the mourning she was feeling. She missed Jeanette, she missed Trace, and she missed the life that was hers such a short time ago.

Rylan walked Cassidy home, keeping the conversation between them light, but Cassidy was doing some heavy thinking. She realized she'd settled in in a way that had diminished God's presence in her life.

You're the only sure thing, Cassidy prayed when she got home. *I had forgotten that. I let the business, my friends, and this town make me feel settled and sure. Thank You, Lord, for sending Edson. I needed this reminder.*

To repent and remember what she'd been missing was good for Cassidy and gave her new purpose. She went to bed and rose at her normal time. She might not have any customers, but she still had a shop to open, and she was going to do just that.

⚜

"Jeb is going to take me home as soon as I'm ready," Meg told Cassidy on Monday morning. "But I didn't want to go without checking with you."

"Thanks, Meg," Cassidy said, giving her friend a hug. "I'm so glad the men will be home tonight."

"You'll come Wednesday?" Meg checked.

"I'll do better than that," Cassidy said with a smile. "If things are still this slow, I'll close for the day and be out after breakfast."

Her cheerful attitude, coupled with Meg's great need to see her husband, was too much for her. Meg cried and Cassidy joined her.

"I'm sorry, Cassie. I'm sorry you have to go through this."

"It's okay," Cassidy ended up comforting her friend. "I'm learning a lot. I'm sad and I'm hurting, but I'm learning a lot."

"Don't mind me," Meg said, taking a swipe at her eyes. "I just miss Brad, and I hurt for you. It's a double blow."

"How many times have I sobbed all over you?" Cassidy teased gently. "I think you're allowed a turn."

"But I'm not the one losing my business over a bunch of lies!" Meg said, knowing she could be outraged very easily.

Cassidy shrugged. "Edson said he would do it, and he did."

"Well, there are some people who are fighting for you," Meg said. "If Jessie hears things, she sets people straight, and so does Jeb when he's at the store and around town."

"Thanks for telling me," Cassidy offered sincerely, but she wasn't sure it would do any good. Even folks who had ordered things had not come back to pick them up. And since she was paid after the fact, she was stuck with some clothing she could probably do nothing with.

"I'd better go," Meg said.

"Thanks for stopping, and kiss that baby for me."

The women hugged again, and Cassidy saw Meg out the door. She smiled as she waved her off but knew that Wednesday was going to be slow in coming.

CHAPTER FOURTEEN

CASSIDY HAD GOTTEN OUT HER QUILTS, even the one she was working on upstairs. She chose the one she wanted to work on depending on the colors she was enjoying just then. She displayed them in the shop window and also inside, draped over an old steamer trunk she'd placed in a corner.

She had just settled in to work on the one she was putting together with rags, completely mismatched, when the door opened. Cassidy looked up to find Halston entering.

"Good morning," Cassidy said quietly.

"Good morning, Miss Norton. I'm here with a message."

"All right."

"Mr. Brickel would like to order another pair of pants, but he'd like to see a sample of your fabrics."

"That's no problem. I can cut those for you right now," Cassidy said, heading toward her fabric with a pair of scissors.

"He wants you to bring them."

The weight that landed on Cassidy's shoulders with these words made her stop and close her eyes. She needed this order. She needed any order, but she was not going to even discuss marriage with this man and knew that this was the only reason he wanted to see fabric.

Gathering herself, Cassidy turned to Halston and spoke. "I can't do that," she said. "Tell Mr. Brickel I'm sorry, but the answer is no."

Her face bothered Halston. He didn't speak but nodded in respect and slipped back out the door. He didn't hurry, but his mind was busy. Approaching the house and slipping in the kitchen in his usual fashion, Halston was not surprised to find his employer waiting.

"What did she say?"

"She said no, she will not come here."

Frustration covered the older man's features, but he was already coming up with a new scheme. "Go back and tell her—" he began, but for the first time Halston cut him off.

"No."

"What did you say?" The rich man had stopped to stare.

"I said no."

"No to what?" Hiram said, his face starting to look like a thundercloud.

"I won't go back and ask Miss Norton again. She's given you her answer, and she's very upset about other things right now."

"Did you tell her that I don't care who her brother is?" Hiram demanded. "Did you tell her I'll marry her no matter what?"

"I told her you wanted her to bring pants fabric, just as you requested. She's pale and thin, and I'm done tormenting the girl with your requests for marriage."

Hiram Brickel exploded in anger over this, but Halston ignored him. He turned his back on the man and began working on dinner. He listened for the word that he was fired, but it did not come. Halston did, however, eventually hear the front door open and slam. He turned from the bread he'd been slicing, stunned with the realization that his employer had actually left the house.

"I thought you needed business," Hiram said the minute he stepped inside Cassidy's shop.

"And I thought you were old enough to know what the word no meant," Cassidy said, a little bit ready for a fight. She had been discouraged after Halston left but soon got over that.

Hiram stared at her, his eyes narrowing a bit, and then began to walk around the shop. Cassidy watched him, not rising or moving the quilt from her lap, and not speaking either.

"This is nice," he said. "Feminine, but nice."

"Thank you."

"Do you think you'll have a business to sit in a month from now?"

"I would guess not, but I don't know."

Hiram wanted to repeat his offer, but Halston was right, she was thinner.

"Do you have enough to live on?" he surprised her by asking.

"Yes, thank you."

"I could look at that fabric while I'm here."

Cassidy stared at him, gauging what her answer should be and deciding she had nothing to lose. "Do you need pants, or are you looking for ways to keep asking a question I've already answered?"

"I do need the pants, but I can also see that you need a husband. It's perfectly clear that it should be me."

Hiram had a glimpse of what Halston had seen. Cassidy's eyes looked weary, almost desperate, as though she couldn't take any more. He didn't have the heart to press her.

"I'll look at that fabric now," Hiram said before Cassidy could frame a reply, "and leave you to get the pants to me when they're done."

Cassidy nodded and went to get the bolts of material. She had four that would be excellent for pants, and Hiram selected three of them.

"If things remain slow," Cassidy said in her honest way, "there's no reason I can't have these done for you by the end of the week."

"Do you mind delivering them?"

"I think I can do that," Cassidy said, "just as long as that's not misunderstood."

Hiram inclined his head in understanding, but his eyes were still watchful. He thanked Cassidy before going on his way, still certain he could persuade her to marry him. And because he was a man who liked a challenge, he was sure he was up for the job.

⁂

"Savanna…" Meg said her daughter's name in a sing-song voice, stepping into her kitchen. "We're home."

Savanna smiled at her mother, something the two-month-old did often, not caring where she was.

"Shall we open some windows?" Jeb offered, Patience coming behind him.

"Yes. It's stale in here."

A neighbor had checked on things every few days, but the house had not been opened.

With Savanna in her basket, the three adults worked until all of Meg's and the baby's trappings were inside. Patience was returning her niece with all clean clothing and a pot of stew that would last at least two days.

Meg's thanks to her family were heartfelt and, glad as she was to be home, just a little bit sad.

"Thank you for everything," Meg said while giving her uncle a long embrace. "We had a wonderful time."

"So did we, honey," he said before moving aside so Patience could hug her as well.

They both held the baby again, laughing in delight at the way she smiled up at them, and then took their leave. Meg waved them off from the porch and then went back inside. It felt as though she'd been gone much longer than two weeks, and even with dinner done and clothes clean, she could think of plenty she could do.

Meg ignored it all, sat with Savanna in the living room, and just enjoyed the feeling of being home.

⊱❦⊰

"Hello, Missy," Rylan greeted Abi's friend, even as he was surprised to see her come to the livery. She had lingered in the wide alley between the stalls until Rylan had noticed her

"Hello, Pastor," she said in return, and then just stood still.

"How are you?" Rylan asked next.

"Fine."

"How is Abi doing?" Rylan asked, sure that's why she'd come and not wanting to force her to say the words.

"She's sore but moving around some."

"Did she send you to find me?" Rylan asked.

"She just wants you to know she's not ready yet. Her head still hurts, and she can't think straight."

Rylan nodded with compassion. "Tell her that I haven't forgotten, and that I'm still praying for her."

Missy, who was a rather shy creature, smiled sweetly at him and went on her way without another word. Rylan wondered if Abi knew what a special neighbor she had. He might have gone on thinking about it for a while, but there was a man waiting for his horse to be shod, and Rylan had to get back to work.

⊱❦⊰

It was almost nine o'clock when Meg heard horse's hooves. Had they come earlier, she might not have gotten her hopes up, but at this hour she was sure it was Brad. She hit the front door at a run and kept right on running down the porch steps, across the twenty feet of yard that separated them, and into her husband's arms.

Brad had all he could do not to squeeze the life out of her. He could not believe how much he'd missed this woman. He kissed her, keeping it brief and allowing Meg to hug Trace too.

"How are you?" Trace asked.

"I'm fine," she said, her gaze taking in both men, "but it's been the longest two weeks of my life."

"We'll put the horses away and be right in," Brad said.

"I can do it," Trace offered, wanting to give Brad some time with his wife, but Meg surprised him.

"A lot has gone on, Trace, and you're going to want to hear everything."

Trace only nodded, forcing himself not to ask the questions that ran through his mind. Brad did go with him to the barn, and the two worked swiftly so they could get inside. Brad held a sleeping Savanna just to be close to her, and the four of them sat in the living room so Meg could explain. Not surprisingly, no one went to bed for a very long time.

The pants Hiram Brickel ordered were a blessing in more than one way. Cassidy was tired of quilting, and she'd cleaned everything she could lay her hands on. Having pants to work on gave her something to keep her mind and hands busy. So busy in fact that Trace was in the shop almost a minute before Cassidy realized someone was standing inside the door.

"Hello," Trace said quietly, not wanting to startle her.

"Oh, Trace." Cassidy couldn't stop her smile. She stood, wishing she could hug him but making herself stay by the sewing machine. "Welcome home," she said, her smile still in place. "Was it a good trip?"

"It was, thank you," Trace answered with a smile of his own.

"Everyone was safe?"

"Yes, nothing major."

"And the auction was a success?"

"Our best yet."

"I'm glad to hear it. You look good, but you've lost weight."

"So have you."

Cassidy's smile failed a little, but she worked to keep her voice light. "It's been an interesting two weeks. I suppose Meg filled you in."

"Yes, she did."

Silence fell for just a moment, and suddenly Cassidy felt afraid. Without thinking, she asked, "We're still friends, aren't we, Trace?"

Every vulnerable feeling inside her suddenly showed on her face, and Trace had all he could do not to react. He worked to keep his voice calm.

"Why would you even ask that?"

"I'm sorry, Trace." Cassidy could have bit her tongue out. She fiddled with the fabric in the machine and said, "Just ignore me."

"Ignoring you is the last thing I would do. Why did you say that?"

Stark pain crossed Cassidy's features before she admitted, "Chandler is pretty upset with me."

"Meg didn't tell me that."

"She doesn't know. I haven't told anyone."

"What did he say?"

"Oh, a lot of things." Cassidy looked around in frustration. "But it all boiled down to the fact that he believed my brother."

"That must have hurt."

"It did. I didn't know what to say."

"Does he have any idea that you're in love with him?" Trace asked, voicing his feelings to her for the first time.

"What now?" Cassidy asked, really looking at Trace this time, sure she'd heard him wrong.

"The way Chandler talked to you, it must have hurt more because you love him."

Cassidy finally heard what Trace said. She frowned at him in confusion before saying, "No, I'm not. Not at all."

Trace moved a little closer. "You're not in love with Chandler Di Fiore?"

"No."

Almost before Cassidy could see him move, Trace had stepped directly in front of her. His hat landed on the floor as he took her by the upper arms and said, "I should have done this a long time ago."

He bent his head and kissed her softly on the mouth. When he moved back, Cassidy was the first to speak.

"Why *didn't* you do that a long time ago?"

"Because I thought you had feelings for Chandler."

Cassidy's eyes closed in pain, and Trace simply put his arms around her. Cassidy held him right back, fighting the tears that threatened and losing the battle.

"It's okay," Trace said quietly when a sob escaped her.

Cassidy found that his tenderness was more emotionally draining than Meg's. Not able to say a word, she cried for a time. Trace's undemanding hold and quiet words were simply too much for her heart.

"Better?" he asked after a time, and Cassidy nodded. Trace had given her his handkerchief, and after Cassidy used it she looked up at him.

"I have so much to tell you," she said.

"We have time," Trace said. "It doesn't all have to be said in one day."

Cassidy had always known Trace was special, but to have it directed at her in this way, almost started her tears again.

"I'm headed to see Chandler," Trace said, surprising all thoughts of crying right out of her.

"Right now?"

"Yep." Trace sounded very sure.

"Why, Trace?"

"I want him to hear from me that I've thrown my hat in the ring where Cassidy Norton is concerned. I also want to hear from him why he talked to you the way he did."

Cassidy looked into his face, her heart a mix of comfort and concern. She didn't think that she would have the guts to do this, but this was who Trace Holden was. He liked things on the table and not simmering under the surface.

"I'll check in with you later," he said, stepping away just a bit.

"All right."

"Are you okay?" he asked before he moved very far away.

"I think so," she said, still trying to take it all in.

Trace reached with one finger and stroked down her cheek. Cassidy's gaze softened instantly, all worry leaving her eyes, and Trace smiled at her. Repeating that he would check in with her later, he went back out the door.

Trace was not angry or in a hurry, but Chandler had seen him coming. The banker had been nothing short of miserable for days now, and he didn't know if he was glad to see his friend or not.

"Welcome back, Trace," Chandler greeted, but with none of his normal cheer.

"Thank you. Are you free for dinner today?"

"I am," Chandler said, surprised but not put off. "What's up?"

"We need to talk about some things."

Chandler knew he'd seen Cassidy, and he was relieved. He found he wanted to talk to someone about it, and it never once occurred to him to go back to Cassidy herself.

"I'll come back about noon," Trace said.

"I'll plan on it," Chandler agreed as he watched the cowboy walk away. Once Trace left, Chandler tried to get some work done, but there was too much on his mind. He opened the other teller's window and hoped that working with customers would get his mind back onto banking.

"Were you a good girl?" Brad asked his daughter, who was still trying to place this "stranger" who held her. Eventually she smiled at Brad, something that delighted the returning father. "I can see that you must have been," he murmured, continuing to speak quietly to her.

Meg didn't interrupt. She was snuggled under Brad's free arm, just quietly watching him get reacquainted with his daughter.

"How about you take a nap pretty soon?" Brad asked Savanna next. "Then I can have your mother all to myself."

"Don't say those things in front of her," Meg chided him quietly.

"You would object?" he asked, turning to her with brows raised.

"No," Meg said, not able to stop smiling, "but I don't want Savanna knowing about such things already."

Brad smiled at her, but he was serious. He continued to enjoy his daughter, but the moment Savanna showed signs of fatigue, he suggested they tuck her into bed and have some time to themselves. Meg wasted not a moment settling the baby down in her bed and getting her arms around her husband.

Trace stopped only long enough to tell Cassidy he had a dinner appointment with Chandler and then took himself to Jeanette's. He found that lady working at her desk and gladly returned her warm hug.

"I missed you," she told him, her hands still touching him, her eyes studying his face.

"I missed you too. How are you?"

Jeanette sighed. "It's been a time, Trace," she said as the two got comfortable. "I'm sure Meg told you."

"Yes, and Cassie."

"You've seen her? How's she doing?"

"She's going to be all right," Trace said with a confidence Jeanette loved.

"You're going to see to that yourself?"

"Yes, ma'am."

Jeanette smiled. "It's about time."

Trace smiled a slow, satisfied smile but didn't share any more.

"How is my mother?"

"The same. Some days I'm glad about that, and some days it makes me mourn."

Trace had taken the small sofa in Jeanette's office, and she had taken a nearby chair. It was quiet for a moment, but then Trace asked a question of Jeanette that he sometimes asked of himself.

"Do you ever wish she would just die and be done?" Trace asked.

"Not so much now. I did at first, when it seemed she was in so much pain. I don't know why she's still here. I don't think it's for her. I think God wants to teach me some things."

Trace nodded. He'd had some of the same thoughts but never quite knew what to do with them.

"Do you think she's in pain when she cries and frets?"

"I don't know. I guess she must be remembering something. It's at those times I think she might return to us, but it's never happened."

"Sometimes I think that would be great, and sometimes the idea scares me."

"Why does it scare you?"

"If she could speak, I would want—and probably expect—her to be the mother she was." Trace shrugged a little. "That's highly unlikely. I would never want her to think I'm disappointed in her. My father already did too much of that."

"How much do you remember about their marriage, Trace? I mean, I don't think of teenage boys as being observant."

"We weren't, but things come trickling back. He was a restless man, and I remember the looks on her face. She felt like a failure, and my father did that to her."

"I don't know why they married," Jeanette admitted. "It was not something I ever wanted to ask. I just wanted to support her, and I was glad when she moved close enough so I could."

The room was quiet for a time, but Jeanette was not done.

"Brad has chosen better. He's chosen to follow God first and then find a wife. He and Meg will never be where your parents were."

"You're right about that," Trace agreed, knowing it to be very true.

"And you, Trace. You'll be the same way. If you and Cassidy marry, your marriage will be wonderful."

"It sounds like you're doubting." Trace had to mention the obvious.

"I didn't mean to say 'if.' I'm sure it will happen."

"But you have something else on your mind," Trace said, having watched her carefully.

"Only what a hard time this has been. Cassidy is strong—she'll put it behind her—but it might take a little time."

Trace nodded but didn't speak. He didn't doubt that Cassidy was the woman for him. He knew their life together would be wonderful, but he had not been around to meet her brother or see the full effect his visit to Token Creek had had on her life.

Trace eventually went in to visit with his mother, but his mind was still on Cassidy, and how slowly he might have to be willing to go.

CHAPTER FIFTEEN

"I DIDN'T KNOW HOW MUCH could go on in two weeks' time," Trace said when he and Chandler had made themselves comfortable in the hotel dining room.

"I don't know about two weeks ago, but life changed for me when Edson Sinclair walked into my bank last week."

"Why was that, Chandler?" Trace asked, wanting to give him the benefit of the doubt.

"Up to that point, I thought Cassidy was who she said she was."

"And why does Cassidy's having another last name change who she is?"

"It's not that simple, Trace," Chandler said. He truly hated to disillusion the man about Cassidy, but it had to be said. "You don't know the things her brother told me. The very money she used to start her business is money she earned while helping him."

"And you have this on Edson Sinclair's authority?" Trace asked, glad that Meg had spilled all she knew.

"Yes," Chandler said, not sure he liked Trace's tone and doubting himself for the first time.

"So you take the word of a known swindler over Cassidy's."

"I went to Cassidy. I asked her, and she would not explain."

"Asked or attacked?"

"Asked," the banker said, but he knew it wasn't the full truth. His had been questions, but he'd been emotional and his mind had been made up.

"When has Cassidy ever refused to answer your questions?" Trace asked pointedly. "That alone should have told you something was wrong."

"Her brother is Edson Sinclair," Chandler stated slowly, as if this explained everything. "If she's so innocent, why did she hide that from all of us?"

"She didn't. Meg has known Cassie's full story all along. I believe Rylan has known too," Trace added, willing to bet that when the two of them talked alone on that Sunday many weeks past, Cassidy had told their pastor her story.

While Chandler was digesting this, Trace laid it on the line.

"Cassidy did not tell me everything you said—only she did ask me if I was still her friend. When I wanted to know why she would even think such a thing, she made it clear that you were the reason. We're not talking about some business associate here or a bank customer. You went to a sister in Christ in such a way that she now doubts your friendship. You've got some repair work to do."

Their meal arrived just then, the kitchen running way behind, but Chandler didn't touch his. He had honestly felt betrayed. Everything Edson said had made complete sense. But that wasn't the worst part. He'd not given Cassidy a chance to explain. He'd gone to her in agitation and attacked when the town had already deserted her.

"I have to talk to her," Chandler said at last.

"I'm glad you plan to do that, but there's one other thing you need to know: I made my feelings clear to Cassie this morning, and I was not rejected."

Chandler nodded, not sure how he felt about this. He cared for Cassidy and had wondered if there could be more between them, but he'd never acted on it or even talked to her about it—he'd just assumed she would always be there. Now it was too late.

"I didn't know you felt that way," Chandler said at last.

"For a long time," Trace admitted.

Chandler realized he was disappointed in himself, but he also saw something else: Trace was a good friend. Not many men were willing to put things on the table the way he'd done today. And Chandler, having realized what he needed to do, found his heart unburdened for the first time in days. He went ahead and ate his lunch, using the excuse to pray. He was confessing to God how wrong he'd been and asking Him to give him the words to make things right with Cassidy Norton that very day.

"Welcome back," Rylan said to Trace when he tracked him down in the livery.

"Thank you. How are you?"

Rylan smiled. "It's been an interesting time," the big man admitted. "I'm doing well, but it's not been easy."

"I've heard some of it from Meg and Cassie. A lot certainly went on."

"How is Cass today?"

"Doing well. I'll see her again before I leave town."

"Trace." Rylan's voice grew serious. "Someone from the church family was pretty hard on her. I don't know who. Did she talk to you about that?"

"Yes. It's been taken care of."

"Good." The word was said with heartfelt sincerity. "I was very concerned and seriously considered bringing it up on Sunday morning. We can't have that and still grow in unity and holiness."

"You might end up hearing about it," Trace said, realizing such an action on Chandler's part would not surprise him. "But I think it's being taken care of right now."

"Good," Rylan said again, his heart remarkably blessed that folks were making such choices. He didn't need to know the facts, only that whoever had hurt Cassidy was making sure that not another day passed without reparations.

⚜

"Hi, Cassidy," Chandler said when he got to the shop. He'd planned to come right away, but Mr. Falcone had had to take his dinner. Nevertheless, Cassidy was alone.

"Hello, Chandler," the seamstress said. She stood up from the sewing machine but was still keeping her distance.

"I've come to apologize to you," Chandler wasted no time in saying. "I was harsh on Saturday and didn't even let you talk. I'm very sorry."

"Thank you, Chandler. I appreciate that."

Chandler looked into her thin, pale face, and really saw for the first time how this had taken its toll. Not asking, but wanting them to be back on their old footing, Chandler took a chair. Cassidy sat back down at the machine and waited.

"How did two people like Cassidy Norton and Edson Sinclair come from the same family?"

Cassidy had to smile a little. "Edson was out of control from the time he was little. My father, who's dead now, was never around. He gambled a lot, and my mother had to work so we could eat. Edson and I were on our own quite a bit. I would wait for the times when my mother could be home, but Edson was always off getting into trouble."

"Did he not feel any responsibility as your older brother?" Chandler asked, thinking of his own younger sisters.

"I'm older," Cassidy surprised him by saying.

Chandler looked as stunned as he felt. "But you're only twenty-three."

"Yes, and Edson is twenty-one. He's always looked older, and he started conning people and making a name for himself at a very young age."

Chandler was out of words. He thought about the man who had come to his bank and realized he would never have guessed. A woman walked by the window just then, and Chandler was pulled back to the present.

"How is business? Pretty slow?"

"Yes. I've only had one person place an order this week. Someone did come to pick up something she'd ordered last week, but it's been very quiet."

"How long can you last?"

"No more than two months."

It was on Chandler's tongue to say that maybe she'd be married by then, but he didn't think he could do that and not give himself away. He deeply regretted not pursuing Cassidy long before now.

"It looks like you're working right now," he said instead.

"Yes. Thankfully the order I received was fairly large."

"I'm glad," Chandler said as he stood. "If there's anything I can do, Cass, please tell me."

"Thank you, Chandler. You've already been a huge help."

Chandler said goodbye, and Cassidy saw him to the door. The days were cooling fast, but she still stood outside, looking up and down the street. Token Creek looked the same to her, busy as ever. It was within her shop that things had changed.

Going back inside, Cassidy started again on Hiram Brickel's pants, but she'd made up her mind. She would do as she said and not even open the shop in the morning so she could spend the entire day at the ranch.

⁂

"How are you?" Trace asked when he found Cassidy alone in the afternoon, putting a hem in a pair of men's pants. He'd spent all day in town and needed to get home soon, but not without seeing this woman.

"I'm doing fine. How was your day?"

"My day was great," Trace said, smiling into her eyes.

Cassidy smiled back, sensing a new feeling of freedom inside her to do so.

"Did Chandler come?" Trace asked.

"Yes. Thank you for taking care of that."

"Did your conversation get at all personal?"

"No, nothing like that. Did you think it would?"

"Well, I'm not sure he was overly pleased with all of what I said." Trace looked at her. "You're sure you don't have special feelings for him?"

"Very sure," Cassidy said.

"I'm glad to hear that," Trace said, a smile starting.

Cassidy watched him, her heart doing funny things in her chest.

Trace saw the warmth in her eyes and knew he had to leave.

"I'd better get going."

"All right. I'll be out tomorrow."

"I'm counting on that."

Cassidy smiled at his tone but also admitted, "I'm so glad you're home."

"That makes two of us." Wanting to stay, Trace made himself say, "Have a good night, Cassie."

"You too."

Trace wanted to hug and kiss her in the worst way, but he forced himself not to. With just a gentle touch to her cheek again, using just one finger, he moved toward the door.

Cassidy didn't move at all. Her heart was still acting up inside her chest, and at the moment she couldn't feel her feet on the floor.

❦

"I kissed Cassidy," Trace announced at the supper table that night as though he were discussing the weather.

"What brought that about?" Brad asked.

"I found out she doesn't have feelings for Chandler."

"So you talked?" Meg asked.

"Not much," Trace admitted.

"You kissed but you didn't talk?" Meg clarified.

Trace nodded, and Meg looked at him. She then looked at her husband but still didn't speak. Her face thoughtful and a little confused, she went back to her food.

"Well," Brad said slowly, "you've done just what a man would do, Trace."

"We didn't keep kissing." He knew he had to explain a little. "But the door is open, even if I didn't do it in the right way."

He sounded so uncertain that Meg bit her lip. Nevertheless, she had to ask about her friend.

"And Cassie's okay?"

"She was by the end of the day. She cried a lot when I saw her this morning, and she says she has a lot to tell me. I told her we have time. I didn't know any other way to stake my claim. At least I don't have to hold back in the same way. At least I know she'd welcome my suit."

"Meg?" Brad had seen the tears flood his wife's eyes. "Are these tears okay, or are you upset with Trace?"

"I'm not upset," she managed before she broke down. Savanna began to fuss from her cradle in the living room, and Meg was glad for an excuse to escape.

Trace watched her go and then looked at his brother. "You're sure she's all right with me?"

"Ah, Trace," Brad said, wondering how he could explain. "We've wanted this for so long. We knew Cass was the one, but Meg never wanted to ask her and risk putting some kind of strain between the two of you.

"And all of this doesn't change the fact that Cass has just been through a huge ordeal. Meg's not questioning your motives, just your timing."

Trace nodded, glad he'd asked. Without Brad and Meg's blessing he would not proceed. And he needed Meg's take on things. She knew Cassidy well and had been around for the ordeal, as Brad put it.

"I'm sorry." Meg came back, the baby in her arms. "I don't know what came over me."

"I'll take her," Trace offered, no longer hungry. He settled Savanna on one arm, kissing her brow and seeing that she was already headed back to sleep. When he looked up, Meg was staring at him.

"I love you, Trace," she whispered.

"I love you too, Meg."

Meg's tears had started again, but she forced herself to go back to her supper. Brad finished his as well, but he didn't taste a thing. His eyes were on his wife, and his mind was asking God to help them in every way. The next few weeks were sure to be as eventful as the last.

※

"Oh, hi, Pastor," Cassidy said when she answered the knock on her door that evening.

"Hey, Cassie, is this a bad time to join me for a walk?"

"Not at all. Let me grab a sweater."

"I didn't get a chance to come by the shop today," Rylan explained when she came out and they walked down the stairs. "But I wanted to know how you are."

"I'm doing well, thank you, Pastor Rylan."

"I'm glad. Trace stopped by and said you were, but I thought I would check."

"I appreciate it. He took care of something specific today that had been weighing on me. That was very helpful."

"That's good news. Do you think you've seen the last of your brother?"

"Yes. He moves around a lot, and I doubt he'll see a reason to come back."

"And your mother? Will you feel free to see her now?"

"If my business falls apart, there's nothing keeping me from visiting her. I've already sent her a letter. I'm sure to hear back from her any day."

"I'm glad for you, Cassie. What a relief."

"Yes, it is," Cassidy agreed and laughed a little. "When Abi Pfister gets wind of all of this, my life will be a whole chapter in her book."

"Did you not hear what happened?" Rylan asked. He then went on to explain the way Abi had been hurt. Cassidy was sorry to hear it but glad that Rylan was going to have further contact with her.

"Why would someone beat her up?" Cassidy asked.

"She said they wanted information on her book. It made no sense to Sheriff Kaderly or me."

"I'll pray for her," Cassidy said, thinking how frightening the attack must have been.

The two had walked full circle. They'd gone down by the mill before turning back and returning to Cassidy's shop. It was also growing dark.

"I'll let you get in out of the cold."

"Thanks for stopping," Cassidy said sincerely. "Your support in all of this has been wonderful, Pastor. Thank you."

"Your business might not survive this, Cassie, but you're safe and still a part of our church family. I thank God for that."

Before heading up the stairs, Cassidy smiled and told him she was thankful for the same things. Rylan waited until she was safely inside before heading for home.

⌘

"Well now," Trace said softly, meeting Cassidy's buggy as he always did and helping her down, hours earlier on this day. "This is a nice surprise."

"I left a note on my door," Cassidy said, "saying I would be open again on Thursday."

"Well done," Trace praised her.

Meg was close behind, hugging her friend and trying not to cry. "Have you had breakfast?" she asked.

"Not much."

"Well, come in because I'm going to feed you all day."

Cassidy laughed and went along to the house. Trace watched them go and then took care of the horse and buggy. From there he wasted no time getting into the house, not having to pretend anymore that he had other places to be.

"The trees out here are amazing," Cassidy said, taking in the colors that were turning fast and telling everyone that October was approaching. The two were on a ride before dinner. Meg had to feed the baby, and both men had already planned to take it easy all week.

"My mother saw to that," Trace said, his eyes on the trees as well. "She brought plantings of several varieties of maples when we moved here from Pennsylvania."

"How old were you?"

"Almost six."

Cassidy smiled, trying to picture him.

"What an adventure this must have been for you and Brad."

"It was. We got into more trouble that first month than all the other years combined."

"Why was that?"

"Oh, just so much going on and we thought we could do it all. Our father took the switch to us over and over, but we were pretty willful."

They rode for a little while in silence, but Trace's curiosity got the best of him. "What were you like as a child?"

"I don't know," Cassidy admitted. "Just a normal little girl, I guess."

"I don't think so," Trace argued.

"Why not?" Cassidy asked on a laugh, sounding as incredulous as she felt.

"No one with your guts and independence comes from a normal childhood."

"I don't know if that was an insult or not," Cassidy said.

"It wasn't," Trace assured her.

Cassidy took some time to think on what he said and finally admitted, "I was alone much of the time. I guess that would account for the independence. But I don't find myself very gutsy, even though my brother said the same thing."

"He said that when he was just here?"

"Yes. I stood up to him, and he complimented me."

"Why are you able to?"

"I always have. Edson doesn't scare me for myself, just for others."

"How do you mean?"

"I'm afraid he's going to cheat people I know, and they'll lose all they have. He's done it so many times."

"Do you think he'll come back here?"

"I doubt it. None of his schemes worked, or he would have flaunted that in my face. There's no reason for him to return."

"You're sure?"

"Yes. Edson doesn't go where there isn't a profit."

This made sense to Trace, and he hoped it would be true. Cassidy didn't need her brother coming in and out of her life and making her miserable. The damage he'd done already would be felt for a long time.

"What are you thinking about?" Cassidy asked when he was silent.

"Your brother. I'm almost glad I didn't meet him."

"He's very charming. Neal, on the other hand, was not."

"Who is Neal?"

Cassidy wasn't sure how Neal had been left out of the story, but then maybe she hadn't told Meg about him. She filled Trace in, and he did not look happy. He pulled his mount to a stop, and Cassidy naturally stopped with him.

"I want you to take a gun back to town with you."

"Trace," Cassidy said patiently. "They're not going to come back here. I'm sure of it."

Trace did not look convinced, but Cassidy thought nothing of it. She learned otherwise after dinner when he took her out to work on her shooting lessons again.

***

"How are you?" Meg asked Cassidy when the men went to feed the stock. Supper was almost ready, but they had some time alone.

"Oh, Meg," Cassidy said with a smile. "I feel like this is all a dream and I'm going to wake up any moment."

Meg smiled before saying, "Should I pinch you?"

Cassidy laughed but then had to ask, "Why did you never ask me if I had feelings for Trace?"

"What if you hadn't?" Meg asked, having anticipated this question. "It would have made you feel awkward. I would have hated doing that to you."

"Did you not suspect?" Cassidy asked, thinking she'd been transparent so many times.

"I hoped, but you would laugh and have a good time with Chandler and Rylan too, and even with Philip. You were very relaxed around everyone in the church family, and that's not usually what it looks like."

Cassidy had to agree. Since knowing that Trace had feelings for her, she blushed easily, something that was not normal for her.

"What are you thinking about?"

"Just the newness of it all. I've been holding myself in check for so long. It might take some time to realize my special feelings for Trace are welcome."

"They're welcome," Meg said, sounding a bit dramatic. "Brad has been asking God to send you our way for a very long time."

"What do you mean by that?"

Meg explained the way Brad prayed almost every night that God would bring a godly wife for Trace. Meg ended up telling the story and then laughing until she was red in the face because she had managed to shock Cassidy into complete silence.

And that woman was still thinking about what Meg had said when it was time to help her put on supper. She knew Meg was serious, but such a thing had never occurred to her. Not until Brad prayed for the meal more than an hour after the conversation did she really take it in, and only because he ended his prayer with "And, Father, we have asked You for many years to bring Cass into Trace's life, and now it's Your will and timing. We thank You from hearts that are awed by Your love. Amen."

⟞ CHAPTER SIXTEEN ⟝

"WHAT'S THIS?" TRACE ASKED when Cassidy handed him a wrapped bundle a little while after supper. They had just finished the dishes and were at the kitchen table.

"Open it," Cassidy said quietly and waited, her eyes watchful.

Trace tore back the paper and began to smile.

"You made me a shirt?" Trace asked the obvious, looking as pleased as he felt.

Cassidy nodded, feeling suddenly shy.

"You could not have made this last night."

"No. It was a while ago."

Trace nodded, his eyes holding hers until Cassidy forced hers to her lap.

"How did you know my size?" Trace asked to break the tension between them.

"I'd helped Meg with Brad's."

"I keep telling you," he started to tease. "We're nothing alike."

Cassidy only shook her head and laughed at his innocent expression.

"Thank you," he said finally.

"You're welcome."

Trace suddenly leaned back in his chair and studied her. "I never considered this part."

"What part of what?" Cassidy asked, smiling at his look of pleasure.

"The part about having Cassidy Norton as my girl."

"What are you talking about?" Cassidy asked on a laugh, partly because he was so funny and partly because she was so delighted to hear him call her his girl.

"I can have all the new shirts I want."

"You think so, do you?"

"Of course."

"Fabric costs money, Trace Holden. Don't forget that."

The change in him was visible. His face lost all its teasing, and he even reached for her hand where it sat on the table.

"I meant to check with you about that. How are you doing?"

"I'll be good for a few months," she told him sincerely but with his same serious tone. "Then I'll have to look for work."

Or marry me, Trace thought, but he didn't say it, fairly certain it was too soon for such talk.

"You'll keep me informed?" Trace asked instead, wanting to say so much more.

"Yes."

Trace kept her hand for a little longer. Cassidy could have sat and talked to him all night, but an hour later she said it was time to get home. Trace took her back to town as he always did, but tonight was different. Tonight when she said goodbye, there was no need to keep her eyes from showing the things she'd been feeling for a very long time.

*

"Hello, Mrs. Potts," Cassidy said to that lady on Thursday. "How are you?"

"That's just what I've been wondering about you. Are you still in business?"

"Yes, I am. Did you need something?"

"I needed something yesterday," that lady stated.

"Well," Cassidy replied, deciding to be honest, "business has been very slow, so I took the entire day off."

"I need a skirt," the other woman said next, as though Cassidy should have known this.

"I have several fabrics you might like. Dark or light?"

"Dark, I think. Blue or black. I don't care for brown."

Cassidy moved without haste to retrieve the fabric she had in mind, but her heart had started to pound a little fast. She hadn't expected this. Mrs. Potts was a valuable customer, and to keep her business was a wonderful surprise.

They worked together for the next thirty minutes. Mrs. Potts was well pleased with her choice and even more pleased to learn she could have the skirt on Saturday.

"Just so you know, Cassidy," Mrs. Potts said when they had finished and before heading toward the door, "I never believed any of those things I'd heard. And no one had better spread such rumors in my hearing."

Before Cassidy could even thank her, she went out the door. Cassidy thanked God instead, wondering if maybe it was His plan that she keep her business after all.

⁂

"How did it go yesterday with Cass?" Brad wanted to know. They were in the barn together, still enjoying the week off but getting out of Meg's hair for a while.

"It was good."

"Did you talk about the future?"

"We talked a little bit about her business, and that was it."

"Will she try to keep the business after you're married?"

"I doubt it, but we haven't gotten that far."

Brad studied his younger brother. "You've gone about this backward, but I think it can still work."

"I don't know how either one of us did it," Trace admitted, "but the feelings are all there."

"How you kept them from each other, your true feelings?" Brad clarified.

"Yeah. It didn't happen overnight, but I sure couldn't tell what she was thinking before I kissed her."

"And she would say the same about you."

Trace nodded in agreement, but he wasn't sorry for any time they might have lost. If the truth be told, he wouldn't change a thing. Cassidy was his friend. He believed she would someday be his wife as well, and in his thinking that was the finest way to go about it.

⚜

Cassidy didn't have to think about sewing when she sewed. Hiram's pants were a little bit tricky in places, but for the most part, her mind could drift to other things. It was for this reason that she put the pieces together on Thursday afternoon. She didn't know why she hadn't caught it before, but it was astonishingly clear. Neal had beat up Abi Pfister. He hadn't wanted information about her book but about the townsfolk. It was just the sort of information her brother would have been looking for, and clearly Neal was working with him for that very reason.

Feeling upset but trying to hold her emotions in check, Cassidy closed the shop thirty minutes early and went to Abi's house. She wasn't sure she'd be welcome, but she was going to try. No one answered the door. Cassidy tried for a good five minutes before giving up and going to see Rylan. He answered right away.

"I need to tell you something," Cassidy said, wasting no time when he joined her on the porch. "Neal—the man who works with my brother—I'm sure he's the man who attacked Abi Pfister."

"Why do you think that?"

Cassidy explained her theory. It sounded logical to Rylan save for one aspect.

"How would your brother and Neal know Abi would have information on the residents of Token Creek?"

"I didn't hear from my brother for about a week after our last meeting. I knew he was in town, but he wasn't coming to see me because I was not helping him. I'm sure he used that time to gather what information he could. With the way Abi goes about her research, she would be a hard person to miss. I'm sure they thought she could tell them who the wealthy folks in town were, and Edson could make his mark."

Rylan could not help but agree and asked, "Have you told Abi this?"

"I was just there and no one answered. I wanted you to know so you can tell her how sorry I am."

"It's not your fault."

"I don't know about that. If I had warned everyone, my brother and Neal wouldn't have stuck around. If everyone had been onto their game, it would have chased them out of town."

"Don't take this on yourself, Cassie," Rylan warned in all sincerity. "It's clear to you now, but you don't know how it would have all turned out. Neal's violence could have been turned on you. They would have seen your interference as a good reason for retaliation."

Cassidy had not thought of that. Her heart had been heavy, and she'd been full of guilt, but Rylan had suggested an aspect she hadn't thought of. And she needed to hear it. She had been certain that Edson would not send Neal after her, but in truth, with a man like that there was always a risk.

"Are you all right?" Rylan asked.

"Yes. And thank you for what you said. I've been a little naive about what Edson is capable of. I think I needed to be more cautious than I was."

"I'm going to let Sheriff Kaderly know your theory. I'm sure he'll agree with you."

"And Abi? Will you please tell her, and tell her how sorry I am?"

"I will, Cassie, but I don't think you need to apologize. I'm sure she'll see it the same way."

Cassidy thanked him, said she was getting cold, and walked home. She wished Trace were in town. It was the kind of thing she wanted to talk to him about, and not being able to left her feeling a little empty inside. Of course she was learning swiftly that not seeing him and talking to him every day left her feeling that way no matter if she had news to share or not.

⁂

Hiram's pants were pressed and ready to go. Cassidy had decided to take care of the delivery first thing rather than leave a note on the door, but it also meant opening a little late.

She walked swiftly toward the Brickel mansion, determined to keep things brief. She was hoping that Halston would come to the door where they could make a swift exchange and the seamstress could be on her way.

"Good morning," Hiram said, answering the door, looking so pleased that Cassidy knew he'd been waiting for her.

"Good morning, Mr. Brickel."

"You're wearing your hair down," he said. "I like it."

"Here are your pants," Cassidy said pointedly, holding out the stack.

"Thank you. They look fine, and you can call me Hiram."

"I'm glad you're pleased," Cassidy said, ignoring the personal remark. "I have to get right back and open the shop."

"Isn't Mrs. Fulbright watching things for you?"

"She doesn't work for me anymore," Cassidy explained.

Hiram had been so busy trying to think of ways to persuade her to marry him that this fact had escaped him. He didn't let on about this but realized it did complicate matters.

"I'll come when you close this evening. You'll have time to talk then."

"No, I won't. Trace Holden will be coming for me, and I won't have time."

"Trace is someone special?" Hiram asked, keeping his voice even.

"Yes," Cassidy said as she turned toward the door. She wanted to be paid but could see it was going to take some doing.

"Is he the reason you won't marry me?"

"One of many, yes," Cassidy said, not beating about the bush. "Please send my payment, Mr. Brickel. Good day."

Cassidy was back out the door before he could object. It would not have surprised her to see him later that day, but at the moment she did not have time to worry about it. It was always possible that someone would want to give her business, and for that reason alone she was determined to be open.

❧

"How are you?" Rylan asked of Abi, sitting across from her in the hotel.

"I'm fine," she said in a voice that did not inspire confidence.

She had finally sent for him. The weather had turned cold, so they could not go for a walk or sit outside. Abi had looked at him strangely when he said he would not come into her house alone, but she had still agreed to meet in public.

"Did you speak with Sheriff Kaderly?" Rylan asked when Abi stayed quiet.

"Yes. Why did Cassidy Norton tell on her own brother?"

"What he did was wrong. Cassidy knows that. She's very sorry about what happened to you."

"She came to the house," Abi said. "I couldn't get to the door, but Missy saw her."

"She tried to talk to you before she came to me."

"And then you went to the sheriff?"

"Yes."

The table fell quiet for a moment, but Rylan didn't let it last. "Your bruises look like they're healing."

"Some say I deserved it," Abi said quietly. "Said my book was nothing but a nuisance."

"Did that make you mad?"

"Yes! I work hard. Folks don't know."

"Is your book more important, or are people more important?"

"What are you talking about? The book is about people."

"Some of whom are not even alive or do not live in Token Creek anymore. I think your book is an interesting idea, but you don't care whom you insult or how you treat folks. That's not going to endear people to you."

"So that's why I got hurt? God is punishing me?"

"You got hurt because a sinful man wanted something he thought you had. I do not think you deserved what happened to you, and I don't think God feels that way either, but He allowed it to happen for a reason, a reason we may never know. At any rate, I hope you won't ignore that or be so angry about it that you can't hear anything I'm saying."

"And you think you have all the answers?" Abi asked, her face flushing in agitation.

"Not at all," Rylan said gently, "but if you recall you asked for me, and when I came you had some serious questions about God. I hope you'll want to talk about that again."

"I'm afraid of what He'll do to me next," Abi admitted.

"Why are you afraid of Him?"

"He's God. He can do anything."

"Who taught you about God?"

"My grandfather was a pastor, but then he left my grandmother. I don't know why. I haven't cared for pastors for a long time."

"I can see how you would feel that way," Rylan said, thinking how hard it must have been. "How will you know you can trust anything I have to say?"

"Kaderly says you're all right. He says you've helped lots of folks."

Rylan nodded and then asked, "Do you want to know why I am the way I am?"

Abi nodded, for once her book the furthest thing from her mind.

"I've read in my Bible that God sent His Son to die for all men," Rylan continued. "I've also read that the only way to have a relationship with God is through His Son. I need that relationship. I need it more than I need my next breath. So I did what the Bible said. I believed on the Lord Jesus Christ to save me from my sins.

"I didn't go around beating on other people, but I still was and am a sinner. I wanted salvation for my sins. God offered me that and a life as His child. I accepted and believed. I don't always do the right thing. I still sin, but the shed blood of Jesus was poured out for my sins, and I'm forgiven.

"There is nothing sweeter in all of the world than being forgiven. And the best news is, there's room for all. For all who see things God's way and believe on His Son, there is forgiveness and life as His child."

Abi thought she might have forgotten to breathe while he was talking. Her grandfather had tried to scare folks into doing things God's way. Pastor Jarvik spoke of forgiveness, and Abi would have been a liar if she'd said she wasn't interested.

"Do you talk about this on Sundays?" Abi eventually asked.

"This and much more."

"What time do you preach?"

"The service starts at ten o'clock."

Abi nodded, relief coursing through her. She could hear more. She could think on what he'd said and hear more about it in the morning.

"I think I'll come."

"I hope you will," Rylan invited.

Abi didn't say anything for a moment. Rylan was about to ask her if she'd changed her mind and wanted some coffee or something to eat, but she suddenly grew intense.

"I want to go see Cassidy Norton. Will you go along?"

"Certainly," Rylan agreed, surprised but still willing.

There was no further discussion. Abi got to her feet, and Rylan paid for his coffee. With their coats back on, they started down the street.

*

"You're welcome, Mrs. Potts. I hope you'll enjoy it."

"Has anyone else been in?" that lady said, something of a bee in her bonnet concerning Cassidy's situation.

"As a matter of fact, Mrs. Ferguson from next door asked me to mend some clothing. She found holes in some of her winter wear."

"Good!" Mrs. Potts said, taking her leave a moment later, leaving Cassidy smiling in her wake. She was getting ready to start on the mending when Rylan walked in, Abi with him.

"Hello," Rylan greeted, entering first. Abi had started to hang back and entered rather slowly behind him.

"Hello," Cassidy said in return.

"Is this a good time?" Rylan asked.

"Certainly," Cassidy said and turned directly to the other woman. "How are you, Abi?"

"I heard what you did," Abi said with her typical lack of social skills.

"I'm just sorry you got hurt."

"Did you get hurt?"

"Not like you did," Cassidy said, not quite sure how to answer. She fought the urge to look at Rylan, wishing she knew exactly what to say.

"Why didn't you tell people who your brother was before I got hurt?" Abi wanted to know.

"I didn't want him to find me," Cassidy said quietly.

Neither Rylan nor Cassidy could tell what Abi was thinking. She glanced around as though she was going to say more, but didn't.

"I have to go" was what abruptly came out.

The pastor and seamstress both said goodbye as Abi moved toward the door, but Abi didn't answer. Rylan made sure that Cassidy was all right before he went on his way, but it was any man's guess as to whether the local author would be in church in the morning.

* * *

"How was your day?" Trace asked once they had cleared town on their way to the ranch. He had brought blankets and had Cassidy well wrapped for the ride.

"It was interesting," Cassidy said, wondering where to start. She didn't think he knew about the marriage proposal. She had not talked with him concerning Neal hurting Abi. Rylan and Abi's visit was on her mind, and Sheriff Kaderly had come the day before to question her about her thoughts on Neal. She knew she just had to start somewhere and did.

"Has Meg talked to you anymore about Hiram Brickel?"

"No. Is he still ordering things and expecting delivery?"

"Yes, and all with the express purpose of getting me to marry him."

Trace slowly turned his head to look at Cassidy, waiting for her to laugh at her own joke. Her face told him it was no laughing matter.

"When did this start?" Trace asked quietly, working to control his emotions.

"The day after you left," Cassidy said, remembering it very clearly. She gave a brief overview of what had gone on and then fell quiet. Trace was quiet too, and Cassidy worried a little.

"Are you upset with me?" she asked when he stopped the wagon in the yard, making no move to get out.

"No," Trace said simply, but in a tone that left her no doubt. "I think we need to talk about what you should say in the future to Mr. Brickel and how you should handle this, but *you're* not the one in trouble."

Trace had climbed out and was waiting to help her down, but Cassidy did not move. She sat looking at him. "What are you going to do?" she asked.

"If you can't make it very clear that you're off limits, I will."

Cassidy nodded, still thinking on it. Trace helped her down, and she found herself drawn into his arms.

"You look like you're worrying," he said quietly, hugging her close.

"I had so much to tell you, and I only got to one topic."

Trace was going to say they had the rest of the evening but took one look at her tired eyes and changed his mind.

"Come for the day tomorrow."

"I was going to ask all of you to join me for dinner."

"Can you have us next week? I think you and I need to talk, and that's probably going to be easier here."

Seeing his point, Cassidy nodded. Trace let her go so she could head into the house and warm up.

"How did you sleep?" Meg asked of Cassidy when the women met in the kitchen on Sunday morning.

"Very well. It's so wonderfully quiet out here."

"Yes, it is. I'm glad you didn't hear Savanna."

"Were you up much?"

"No, just for about twenty minutes at three o'clock."

"Do you fall right back to sleep?"

"I didn't at first, but I do now."

Both women heard Brad calling from upstairs. Meg heard the baby crying at the same time and left the kitchen. Cassidy sat down to her coffee and toast. She was trying to decide if she wanted anything more when Trace joined her.

"You're wearing your shirt," Cassidy noted with pleasure the moment she spotted him.

"How does it look?" he asked, looking pleased himself.

"Very nice," Cassidy said, feeling a bit of pride in her workmanship as well as in how good the medium blue shirt looked on the handsome Trace Holden.

"You know," she teased him a little, "if I could just have you model that this morning for the church family, I might get a few more orders."

"Maybe I could stand up front when Rylan is done and make an announcement," Trace teased right back, turning as though he were on display.

"Nice shirt," Meg commented when she came back, Savanna in her arms.

"Do you want me to take her?" Cassidy offered.

"Have you eaten?" Meg and Trace said at the same time and laughed.

"Yes," Cassidy said.

"What did you eat?" Trace pressed the point.

"Toast and coffee."

"I'm about to make eggs. I'll put some in the pan for you."

"Was that a not-so-subtle hint about how I'm taking care of myself?" Cassidy asked, but she didn't turn down the eggs.

"No," Trace denied, working to look innocent.

Meg handed off the baby and helped with breakfast. Cassidy made herself stay seated. It was nice to come here and be cared for, and with the things that had come into her life lately, she realized this was just what she needed.

CHAPTER SEVENTEEN

THE HOLDENS AND CASSIDY arrived in plenty of time for the service. They sat together, a normal occurrence, but Trace and Cassidy sat closer than usual. They were talking about Cassidy's conversations with Rylan, Sheriff Kaderly, and Abi until Cassidy noticed something.

"What do you keep staring at?" Cassidy asked, having watched Trace's eyes and the way they strayed.

"Your hair," he admitted. "I like it down your back."

"Thank you," she said.

For a moment their eyes met, but both soon looked away. Their new awareness was both sweet and powerful, but the sermon would be starting soon. For this time their minds did not need to be on each other.

⁂

Abi Pfister was not on time for the service but did slip in before Rylan began his sermon. She sat in the back, not removing her coat but appearing to listen closely to every word he said. Rylan spoke on the fear of God but also on hungering after God.

"How greedy and hungry are you for God's blessing?" Rylan asked.

"Our sin keeps God from blessing us as He wishes. He's waiting to pour out His blessing upon us, but too often our sin keeps that from happening in full measure.

"Look in Psalm 119 with me. Listen as I read, starting in verse fifty-seven: 'Thou art my portion, O Lord: I have said that I would keep thy words.' Did you hear the promise of the Psalmist here? He's taking God's words seriously.

"Now the next verse. 'I entreated thy favor with my whole heart: be merciful unto me according to thy word. I thought on my ways.'"

Rylan stopped in the middle of verse fifty-nine and looked up. "I've read that part over and over. 'I thought on my ways.' How often do I stop and think about what I'm going to do or what I'm planning to do? Listen to the rest of that verse and the next. 'And turned my feet unto thy testimonies. I made haste, and delayed not to keep thy commandments.'

"Did you catch it? The writer stopped and thought about what he was doing and made haste to keep God's commandments. This is someone who understands that he must hunger after God's blessing. In order to receive that blessing, God's commandments must be obeyed."

Abi was not missing a word, even the ones she didn't completely understand. She had some questions, but as Rylan concluded and had the congregation bow their heads for a closing prayer, she slipped from her pew and back out the door. She didn't mind talking to Rylan about what she'd heard today, but she didn't know if she trusted anyone else.

Folks visited after the service in the usual way. While Heather and Cassidy talked, Chas snagged Trace before he could move ten steps.

"Did my eyes deceive me," the older man asked, "or are things a little warmer with you and our Cassie?"

Trace did nothing to hide his smile, and Chas' shoulders shook in silent laughter.

"I just have one thing to say," Chas dropped his voice a little.

"What's that?"

"It's about time."

Trace laughed out loud this time.

"I had begun to think all of you were blind," Chas admitted.

Trace was still laughing when Chas thumped him on the chest and went on his way.

⁂

"Jeanette wants us to come to dinner," Brad told Trace after Chas walked away.

"Okay," Trace said with little enthusiasm, causing Brad to look at him.

"What's up?"

"I told Cass to plan on coming back with us so she and I can talk."

"I'm sure that won't be an issue at Jeanette's. There are more rooms to work with there, and you know she'll understand."

Trace nodded, and Brad said he would make sure Jeanette knew. Trace went to find Cassidy and tell her about the change in plans. Ten minutes later all of the Holdens, together with Jeanette, Heather, and Cassidy, climbed into the Holden's wagon for the ride to the house.

⁂

"How are you, Chandler?" Rylan asked that man when the building was almost empty.

"I've been better," Chandler answered truthfully. "How are you?"

"I'm fine, thanks for asking, but can we talk about what's bothering you?"

Chandler nodded, even as he admitted to himself that it would feel better to talk about what he was thinking.

"If you don't mind leftovers," Rylan offered, "you're welcome to join me for dinner."

"I don't mind," Chandler agreed, and when the last folks left the church building, the two men walked to Rylan's house. It was warm in the kitchen where Rylan began to heat up leftover chicken and dumplings and slice a loaf of bread.

"Did you bake this yourself?" Chandler asked, already impressed.

"No. My bread is all right, but Heather brought this from Jeanette's. Becky's bread is exceptional."

As Rylan worked on the meal, he began a gentle conversation, starting with Chandler's work.

"It's been a little busier than usual," Chandler said. "A number of houses are being built or worked on—folks trying to get things done before it's too frigid to move. Building always assures a need for money."

"Nice for the banking business," Rylan said.

"Yes, it is," Chandler agreed, but he didn't sound overly pleased. Rylan decided to plunge in.

"What's troubling you?"

"I figured out a little too late that I have feelings for Cassidy," Chandler answered, saying exactly what he was thinking.

Rylan nodded and kept listening. Like Chas, he had not missed the change in Cassidy and Trace's relationship.

"Trace has spoken up, and clearly Cassidy feels the same way. I was thinking that she might have feelings for me, but I guess I was wrong."

"You never spoke to her about it?" Rylan asked.

"No. I was waiting to see if I would just somehow know. Why is it that the moment Trace tells me I can't have Cassidy, I'm sure she's the one?"

"Maybe you've been competing with Trace and not realized it. As long as he kept his distance, you were free not to have to choose or make up your mind where Cassie was concerned."

"Is that your way of saying that as soon as I get over not winning, I'll realize it wasn't about loving Cassidy at all?"

"So you feel that you love her?"

"Yes, I do," Chandler admitted, his heart heavy in his chest. "I also treated her as no one should have. I've repented to her and to God, but I still feel awful about it."

In the next two hours the men talked about everything that had gone on in Chandler's life in the past ten days. He had had much to repent of—anger, fear, and jealousy—and it helped to tell Rylan about it. Rylan could not give him any comfort about having Cassidy for his wife. It looked to the pastor as though Trace and she had an understanding. But Chandler still felt better for having unburdened himself.

By the time he left Rylan's house, his outlook was greatly improved. He couldn't think about Cassidy without pain, but he had begun to take Rylan's words to heart. Chandler prayed for Cassidy and her future, asking God's blessing on her life, even if he was never going to be in the picture.

❧

Trace and Cassidy had taken up residence in the small parlor when dinner was over. The door was open, the fire blazing high, and they sat in the chairs close to the flames so they could talk and be warm on this chilly day.

"I'm concerned about Mr. Brickel's intentions toward you," Trace admitted. "I don't want you put in that position, and I don't want him getting it into his head that he has to take more drastic measures to persuade you."

"Why would you think that might happen?"

"I don't think it will, but it's not out of the scope of my imagination. I would rather you did not go back to his house, even if it means passing up an order."

Cassidy nodded and said, "His orders have been large, but they're not going to make or break things for me at this point."

"And you need to say whatever works," Trace said next. "You

haven't made your dress, and we haven't talked to Rylan about a date, but that doesn't mean this wedding isn't going to happen."

Cassidy nodded, suddenly warmer than the fire merited. It got worse when Trace spoke again.

"You tell Mr. Brickel that a certain rancher is very much in love with you and does not appreciate his interference."

Again Cassidy could only nod, wondering if her face looked as warm as it felt.

"I'll tell him," Cassidy managed, but her voice was very soft.

"I think it's a good thing we didn't share the sofa," Trace said. The softness in Cassidy's eyes was getting to him.

They had more to talk about and covered a lot of ground. But Trace wisely kept his place on one side of the fire, and Cassidy stayed on the other.

⁂

Cassidy tried not to worry as she worked to fall asleep. She had been so certain that her mother would have written her by now, but it hadn't happened.

Trust is hard at times like this, Lord, she prayed from her bed on Sunday night. *Does everything in my world look right if there's a letter for me tomorrow, or is everything in my world right at this moment because You are in charge?*

Cassidy knew the answer to this was the measure of faith. Hers felt small right now as she wanted to worry about her mother and felt a very deep ache to have contact with her. She fell asleep asking God to remind her that He was watching over Rhonda Sinclair wherever she was and that Cassidy could trust Him for His plan no matter what.

⁂

Rylan found a note on his door on Monday morning. He didn't

know if it had come early that morning or late the night before, but he hadn't heard a thing. He was headed out to check with Pete Stillwell at the livery and see how much he was needed that week but instead went back inside long enough to read it. The note was from Cassidy.

Dear Pastor Rylan,

If you think it appropriate, I would like to tell my story to the congregation. They have been warm and kind, but I would feel better explaining to everyone why I came to Token Creek as Cassidy Norton and not Cassidy Sinclair. If you have time this week to discuss this with me, I would appreciate hearing from you.

Sincerely,
Cassidy

Rylan put the letter in his pocket and went out the door. He would go ahead to the livery and maybe even check on Abi, but he would also make time to pay a visit to Cassidy, today if he could manage it.

⁂

"How are you?" Jeanette asked Cassidy on Monday morning, not having had a chance to visit with her the day before.

"Doing well. Business is still slower than I'd like, but I haven't had to touch my savings."

"That's what I wanted to talk to you about," Jeanette said, taking one chair and waiting until Cassidy was comfortable in the other chair. "I assume you and Trace are going to set a date one of these days?"

Cassidy smiled and said, "I'm assuming the same thing."

"I'll bet you are," Jeanette had to laugh, but soon went back to business. "Tell me something. If Trace wasn't in the picture, and you had to make a decision about the business based on only that as your future, how would you handle it?"

"Like I always have. As long as I can pay my bills, I'm in business. If I don't have money to buy fabric and supplies—and now I have to add wood to the list—as well as for food to eat, I have to make a change."

"When do you think you'll know?"

Cassidy looked at nothing in particular and thought out loud. "This is the fourth of October. I've had a little bit of business, but I don't want to take myself down to nothing trying to make this work. I'm thinking that things will have to go back to the way they were very soon, or by the end of the month I'll be closing."

"What if you were only open a few days a week?"

"That wouldn't help me unless I find other work. I don't pay rent on the building, so I don't have to take that into account, but as I said, I have to eat and replenish my supplies."

Jeanette looked thoughtful, and Cassidy watched her. However, it wasn't long before her curiosity got the best of her.

"What's going on, Jeanette?"

"Well, it might only be a dream that can't come true, but if you still have enough business and don't have to close completely, I want to buy you out."

Cassidy looked stunned, but Jeanette was not done.

"I talked with Brad about it yesterday, and he could think of no reason for me not to try it. I don't want to be open every day like you are—maybe four days a week—but I would still like to do this if Token Creek will support it."

"Jeanette," Cassidy began, but she could not find the words.

"Do you think I can do it?"

"Yes! You sew beautifully," Cassidy said, and she meant it. "And I think being open less is perfect."

"If work piled up, I could hire someone to help me or even send things with you if you're interested."

"I'm very interested. You do realize I own the building?"

"Yes. I would buy that from you and probably rent out the apartment. And if for some reason it didn't work, I could rent out the shop to some other business owner."

Cassidy was not surprised that she'd thought this through. Jeanette had a good head for such things.

"Well," Cassidy said, a smile on her face, "if I still have a business, you've got yourself a deal."

Jeanette put her hand out. They shook and then laughed like girls before they hugged.

"So tell me," Jeanette began, wanting to know about some of the details she wasn't sure on. There was nothing outstanding to report. Jeanette knew enough about Cassidy's ways to know how she did things and that the business had been a profitable venture before Edson Sinclair came to town.

Jeanette was getting ready to leave when Cassidy remembered one more thing she should share.

"Hiram Brickel didn't pay for his last order."

"Really?" Jeanette asked, surprised. "That won't do at all. I'll just go along and collect it for you."

"You don't need to do that," Cassidy said calmly. "Trace said he would speak to Mr. Brickel if I couldn't make myself clear, but I've decided instead to let it go. I only mentioned it so you would understand the gap in the account book."

Jeanette looked thoughtful before saying, "I have to see Chandler at the bank. The Brickel mansion is only two more blocks over. I believe I'll just stop in and see if Token Creek's richest man is willing to make good on his own debts."

Cassidy had to laugh at the mischevious look in Jeanette's eyes before the older woman started on her way. Cassidy went so far as to walk her outside, smiling at her coated figure as she moved away from the shop. She prayed for Jeanette's day and also that Hiram would willingly part with the money he owed the dress shop.

⁂

"Hello," Halston greeted the handsome woman at his door, recognizing her from the dress shop.

"Hello," Jeanette greeted in return. "I'm here on behalf of Cassidy Norton. She tells me that Mr. Brickel owes her money from his last order."

"Please come in," Halston invited. "I will check with Mr. Brickel on the matter."

Jeanette looked around from her place by the door, seeing what Cassidy had seen on her first visit. Everything was lovely. The ceilings were very high, and in every direction was evidence that no expense had been spared.

"Where is Cassidy?" Hiram suddenly appeared and questioned as he walked closer to Jeanette.

"She's at her shop," Jeanette answered calmly. "I was coming this way and told her I'd stop for her money."

"You're Trace Holden's aunt," Hiram stated, staring hard at her. "I am."

"Is she really going to marry him?"

"Yes, she is," Jeanette said, glad that this had been confirmed in several ways over the weekend.

"When?"

"They haven't told me the date."

Several moments of quiet followed this statement. Jeanette wasn't sure what to do, so she simply held her tongue. When Hiram did speak, his voice was quiet and even, but there was anger in his eyes.

"Halston will pay you. Tell Cassidy I will not trouble her again."

Jeanette was given no time to reply. Hiram went back the way he'd come and shut the door behind him. Halston came swiftly to give her Cassidy's money and with quiet efficiency, not lacking in charm, saw her to the door.

Jeanette took herself back toward the bank, finding it in her heart to pity Hiram Brickel. That Cassidy should marry Trace was all too clear. Jeanette wondered if the man would ever believe that and stop making himself miserable.

⚜

Tuesday brought warmer temperatures. The cold spell had started turning the leaves on the trees vivid reds, yellows, and oranges. The hills surrounding the town were awash in a kaleidoscope of color. Token Creek had settled into a gentle Indian summer. Folks were moving around town a bit more, and Cassidy noticed the activity the moment she unlocked her shop door. A customer wasn't long in arriving.

Mrs. Aliota came in just after Cassidy opened. She had visited only one other time in the history of the business, but Cassidy still had the measurements she'd taken.

"It's not for me," Mrs. Aliota said after just a few minutes. "My husband needs shirts. He says he doesn't, but he does."

"Do you know his size?" Cassidy asked.

"No, we'll have to guess."

Cassidy was not thrilled with this idea, but Mrs. Aliota could order what she liked. She at least knew who Trace and Brad were and was able to tell Cassidy that her husband was not as tall or broad. When she took her leave, Cassidy had an order she hadn't expected but no real confidence it would work out.

She was working numbers in her head, trying to figure out a scaled-down version of Brad's shirt—Mrs. Aliota had picked the same fabric—when the door opened and Rylan came in.

"Hi, Cassie," the big man said. "I got your note."

"What do you think?" Cassidy asked.

"I like the idea. I want our church family to be open about such things. I'm even planning to cut my sermon short so folks can ask questions. That is, if you don't mind."

Cassidy didn't know why, but she could have wept. It was such a relief to speak of it, and to have Rylan support her.

"What does Trace think of your doing this?" Rylan asked.

"I just thought of it this morning and wrote you that quick note. I'll tell Trace all about it on Wednesday."

"Good. If for some reason he wants you to hold off, just let me know."

"I'll do that," Cassidy agreed, looking forward to hearing Trace's views.

"So when's the big day?" Rylan asked without warning, his eyes sparkling a little too much.

Cassidy stopped and stared at him, knowing from long experience when she was being teased. "I can't imagine what you're talking about," she said innocently.

"You must think I can't see a thing from that pulpit."

"What did you see?" Cassidy had to ask.

"Two people who were suddenly more than friends."

"Do you object?" Cassidy had to ask.

"Object?" Rylan asked, knowing them both well enough to be bold. "I wonder how it could have taken so long."

Cassidy laughed with more than just pleasure. Having Rylan's blessing, not that she'd doubted, was a relief too. They were still talking about the changes that had occurred between her and Trace, sharing like the friends they were, when another customer arrived.

With just a swift word about checking with her later in the week, Rylan went on his way to work, and Cassidy soon found herself with another order.

⇻ CHAPTER EIGHTEEN ⇺

"How are you?" Rylan asked Abi. She'd come by the livery just as he was finishing on Tuesday afternoon, and the two walked as they talked.

"I didn't know the Bible said those things," Abi said, feeling anxious about what she'd heard but also hopeful.

"What exactly?" Rylan checked.

"That sin keeps us from God's blessing."

"And what do you think about that?"

"I don't like it."

"I don't like it either. That's why I choose to obey God. I want His blessing."

Abi snorted a little. "You probably don't know how to do anything else."

"You know that's not true," Rylan corrected her. "I told you I sin every day. I need saving as much as you do."

"I'm afraid," Abi admitted, almost too softly for Rylan to hear.

"Of what?"

Abi didn't answer him. Rylan walked with her a bit more, but she didn't speak.

"Do you want to tell me?" he asked after they'd walked another block. Abi stopped and looked at him.

"I want what you have, but I'm afraid."

"Do you know what scares you?"

"Just God. Not pleasing Him and not having His blessing."

Rylan nodded. "When I feel that way I take comfort in His Word. It's full of promises for His children."

"What if I'm not His child?"

"Then that's the first thing you need to take care of, Abi."

She had no argument. With sudden clarity that this man was right, Abi asked Rylan to pray with her then and there. Believing that Christ died for her sins, Abi trusted in the work of the cross and gave her life to Jesus Christ.

⁂

"Thanks, Chandler," Cassidy said to the banker.

"You're welcome," he said in return. "It's nice to have you bringing something in."

Cassidy shook her head a little. "I thought it might be over, but I don't think I have to close my doors just yet."

"I'm glad for you, Cassie," Chandler said, and he meant it. His heart was still agonizing over this woman, but that would never mean that he didn't wish her the best.

Cassidy went on her way, headed toward home. She had already checked with Jessie. There was no letter from her mother. As she walked the distance back to her apartment, Cassidy made up her mind. She would write to her mother again. There were no guarantees that the first letter had gotten to her, so she would simply try again.

I'm going to trust that you are able to read this even if you're not able to write back. Cassidy started the second letter before she even worked on supper. The first one had been brief. She had been too emotional to say much past telling her mother that she was all right and that they could communicate again. This time Cassidy told her mother about herself, Trace, the church family, and her business.

Jeanette has been working for me for many months, she explained near the end of her letter.

She's older and does not need the money but loves to sew. I can't think of how hard it would have been without her. And she wants to buy the shop. We talked this afternoon and put together a plan. She won't try to be open as many days each week but plans to keep the business going. Trace and I will use the money to build a house.

I can't tell you how pleased I am to be able to write that. You're going to love Trace. He's an amazing person. When things are settled, there is no reason I can't come to see you. Maybe Trace can come too.

I've missed you so much. I wish I could give you a better report on Edson, but as long as this finds you well, I won't worry about that. Please write as soon as you can, Mama. I want to know if you're all right. I ache to have some word from you—anything at all. I'll write again in a few days and in the meantime believe that all is well.

> I send this with my love,
> Cassidy

Cassidy cried as she wrote her name—not tears of fear, but tears that spoke of the ache to touch her mother and be hugged by her. Cassidy eventually ate some dinner, but she wasn't very hungry. She spent the evening asking God to help her be strong until she could be with her mother again.

※

Trace and Brad had already headed out on the range when Cassidy arrived at the ranch. She had not told Trace that she'd be free on Wednesdays from now on and had no one to blame but herself for having to unhitch the horse and put her into a stall. Meg was close by, watching her efforts while she got the job done.

"I'm glad Trace wasn't around to watch that," Cassidy said, thinking she would have to tell Rylan that he was not in danger of losing his job. She had managed fine, but it was obvious she didn't do it every day.

"It's all right," Meg comforted. "Trace is no good with a needle."

Cassidy liked this. She chuckled her way into the house, washed her hands, and then took Savanna from her mother. "Good morning," Cassidy said softly to the baby, kissing her cheek and holding her close. "How is my Savanna today?"

"Grouchy," Meg said dryly. "All these smiles you're getting right now are an act."

"Is that right?" Cassidy asked the baby. "Were you cranky?"

Both women laughed when Savanna smiled with pure contentment.

"Meg," Cassidy teased. "I don't think you should tell me these tales. This child is clearly an angel."

"Not ten minutes before your buggy came in the yard, that *angel* was howling as though I were pinching her."

"What did you do to make her stop?"

"I put her down and walked away. I let her cry for a little while.

When she stopped, I checked on her. She'd found a spot to look at on the crib and was fascinated by it."

As if to prove her mother's point about her mood, Savanna began to fuss again. Cassidy tried to talk her out of it, but she was having none of it. Meg took her and nursed her to sleep, the women talking all the while.

"How did things go for you on Sunday?" Meg asked. "Did you and Trace talk about getting married?"

"We didn't talk about a date—just that it will happen."

Meg nodded, not wanting to give her friend negative ideas but wondering if she was missing something.

"Does Trace tell you he loves you?"

"He did in a roundabout way on Sunday, and I liked hearing it, but I still want to talk to him about that."

"What exactly?"

"We spend so much time talking about my problems that we never get to discuss us. There are things I want to know about his feelings."

"I think he'll be able to tell you," Meg said, not afraid of giving anything away. "Brad was talking to him about noticing you a long time ago."

"What did Trace say?"

"He said he held back because of Chandler. I don't think it ever had anything to do with his lack of feelings."

Cassidy smiled, and Meg smiled with her.

"We're going to be neighbors," Cassidy said to her friend with a smile.

"Neighbors?" Meg said on a soft laugh. "Without money to build a house, you'll be living here."

Cassidy smile was huge when she said, "Jeanette's buying the business. We'll have money to build a house."

"That's right!" Meg said, unable to believe she had missed that.

The two fell to discussing house plans, how long it would take to build, and how much Cassidy wanted a large porch. They talked all the way through Savanna's nap and Meg's feeding her again. They didn't start to sew for almost two hours.

⁂

Trace spotted the extra horse in the barn the moment he returned. He didn't know Cassidy was coming early and swiftly headed to the house. He came through the kitchen, washed his hands, and then went to the living room. He found Meg alone but was not fooled.

"Where is she?" he asked his sister-in-law.

"Where is who?" Meg asked, almost looking convincing.

"Tell me something, Meg," Trace said, enjoying himself. "Did she actually think I wouldn't notice the extra horse and the buggy parked right outside the barn?"

Meg only smiled, and Trace began to look around. He skipped the upstairs and wandered into the office, back into the living room, and then into the kitchen. There was a rather deep pantry in the corner of that room, and Cassidy was just coming out. She shot around the back way, but Trace knew this house much too well. Darting through the door that led from the dining room, he caught her in the back hall before she could reach the stairs.

"How are you?" Trace asked when he cornered her, just keeping his distance and his hands to himself.

"I'm fine."

"I didn't know you would be here already."

Cassidy looked pleased. "My sign now says 'Closed Wednesdays and Sundays.'"

Trace smiled into her eyes before his went to her hair.

"Your hair is back up."

"It got warm again."

"Oh," Trace said, not having figured that out.

"I have a lot to tell you," Cassidy said, thinking about Jeanette's offer, "but I want to talk about us today too."

"Okay. Where do you want to start?"

"You're not free now, are you?"

"I can be in about an hour. Will that work?"

Cassidy nodded and sighed a little, just pleased to be in the same room with him. She hadn't seen him since Sunday. Waiting one more hour would be no effort at all.

"Did you know Jeanette wanted to buy the business?" Cassidy asked, all of her plans to talk about just the two of them flying out of her head.

"Not until we got home on Sunday night and Brad told me."

"I'm so excited, Trace. I think Token Creek can keep it going. I think it will work for Jeanette."

"Did you have orders today?"

"Between yesterday and today, I have five. And Jeanette went to see Hiram Brickel and got my money for me."

"How did that work out?"

Cassidy told him the story, and Trace knew no end of relief. He'd not been holding Cassidy's hand as they walked, but he took it now. The enormousness of his feelings told him he'd been more worried about that than he realized.

"Good," he said quietly, and Cassidy looked at him.

"Were you worried?"

"Yes," Trace admitted, looking back at her.

They didn't talk for a little while, both thinking about the past days and events they'd been through.

"I did something a little bit big yesterday," Cassidy said after a few minutes, and then explained about her note to Rylan.

"This Sunday?" Trace asked.

"Yes. What do you think?"

"I think it's a good idea. It might be hard on you, but I like the idea of folks being able to ask questions. Everyone will know all at one time what happened."

"That's what I thought. I'm glad you don't object."

"Did you think I would?"

"No, but Rylan asked me what you thought, and I realized I hadn't had a chance to check with you. Rylan said I could cancel if I needed."

"As long as you're up to it, I think you should plan on it."

"I might not hear much of the sermon," Cassidy admitted.

"I'll fill you in later," Trace said, and Cassidy loved the way he understood her.

Trace had some things he had to get done before supper, so they walked back to the house. Cassidy realized then that they hadn't talked about their own future. She tried to be patient and was happy to help Meg with supper, but she had plans. As soon as supper was over, she wanted more time alone with Trace Holden.

"You look tired," Brad said to Meg, finding her alone in the dining room. Trace, Cassidy, and Savanna were in the kitchen.

"Really?" She looked surprised. "I feel fine."

"I don't think so," Brad said, working hard not to smile even a little. "I think you need to turn in as soon as Trace leaves to take Cassidy back to town."

Meg caught it then. It had taken longer than usual but still had the usual effect. Her husband's warm gaze filled her with pleasure. She moved to his side of the table, pressing close to him in the guise of adjusting one of the plates.

"I think you're right," Meg agreed softly, enjoying the little flames that lit his gaze.

Brad kissed her before she could move away, telling himself to

be patient. Trace and Cassidy would be on their way in just a few
hours.

⚜

"When did you first realize you had special feelings for me?"
Cassidy asked. Meg and Brad were doing dishes. Savanna was sleeping
on Trace's shoulder, and Cassidy was sitting beside him on the living
room sofa.

"That would have been in April, maybe May."

"What happened then?" Cassidy asked with a frown.

"You came with me to visit my mother for the first time."

"I remember that happening but nothing special about it."

"Well, you would have needed to know that I had been thinking
about getting to know Lilly Karlen."

Cassidy nodded. She knew Lilly but not well. She was a shy woman
whom Philip Leffers was just starting to court.

"It's been a long time ago now, but one Sunday Jeanette had us over
with the Karlen family. I don't hold this against Lilly, but she could
not deal with even visiting my mother on the porch. Her parents
and brothers went out and met her, but Lilly just about panicked.
That changed the way I viewed her.

"When you came along and talked to my mother like you do
everyone else, I started to see you differently. I didn't fall head-over-
heels in love right then, but I began to notice things about you. The
more I watched, the more convinced I became that you were perfect
for me."

"But you didn't want to say anything?"

"I couldn't tell what you felt about me. You were kind to everyone,
including Chandler. I even wondered for a while if you might have
feelings for Rylan. It wasn't that you did anything special, but you
were warm and caring with everyone."

Cassidy looked at him. She had had no idea. Not a clue.

"Your turn," Trace said, but before Cassidy could get started,

Meg and Brad came from the kitchen. Brad wanted to talk about Cassidy's business.

"How will you and Jeanette work this? Have you had a chance to discuss it?"

"As a matter of fact, she came to see me yesterday afternoon, and we talked about it. I've had enough orders the last few days to make me think the business will survive. Jeanette plans to take over from me all during this month. If that works, I'll just work for her until she no longer needs me."

"Have the two of you set a date?" Brad asked.

"Not yet," Trace said, taking that one.

"Are you anxious about that, Cass?" Brad wished to know.

"Not at all," she said. It was enough to know that her future was with Trace. There was no need to rush. Not until she and Trace were on the road back to town did she learn that he wasn't feeling quite so patient.

"The weather is changing fast. Without a lot of warning, we could be in deep snow. If the snow is on the ground, I can get to town in the sleigh without a problem. But if we're in a blizzard or a white out and I can't be with you on a day I normally would, that would be hard. A few weeks of that I could stand, but not a whole winter."

"So what are you thinking?"

"How does next month look to you?"

"You mean you want to get married in November?" Cassidy checked with him.

"Yes."

Cassidy was not expecting this. She wasn't doubtful about wanting to marry Trace, but next month was not what she'd had in mind. Cassidy was still working it through when the buggy came to a halt. She turned to find Trace watching her.

"Problems?"

"No," Cassidy said without thinking.

Trace's brows rose in unbelief. "You're sure?"

This time Cassidy stayed quiet.

"You can tell me."

"Do you realize that I haven't even told you I love you?" she asked. "*And,*" she added with a bit of strength, "you haven't even officially asked to marry me?"

"I do realize that," Trace admitted.

"Those things might seem silly to you, Trace, but they're not to me."

"They're not silly to me either. I know you love me, and I'm looking forward to the time you're ready to tell me. I will ask for your hand, down on my knee, but I keep waiting for a special time when we won't be interrupted, and so far that's not happened."

There it was again—the softening of Cassidy's eyes that always got to Trace's heart.

"What are you thinking?" he asked.

"That you're wonderful. I didn't know you were planning that."

"Yes, ma'am," he said softly. "We need to keep our heads so we don't miss anything but not so much that this feels like a business arrangement."

Cassidy sighed a little and asked, "So what happens now?"

Trace looked out over the horse's head. "Why don't we stop in and see if Rylan is available to talk. We'll tell him what we're thinking and get his advice."

"What about Brad and Meg? Are they ready to have us living there as husband and wife?"

Trace smiled as he put the buggy back into motion. "Brad asked me right before I left what I was waiting for. I mentioned that very thing to him—that we'd be sharing the house for a while—and he dismissed it with three words."

"What were the words?"

"'What's the problem?'"

Cassidy could not hold her laugh. Trace took that for a yes and headed for Rylan's.

"Jeanette?" Trace called to his aunt when he slipped in through her front door much later that night.

"Who is it?" she asked, coming from her parlor, a book in her hand and a small pair of spectacles perched on the end of her nose. "Trace?"

"Yes. Can I talk to you?"

"Of course. What can I do for you?"

"I need your help with a surprise," Trace started.

"For Cassie?" Jeanette guessed.

"She's the one," Trace answered with a smile.

Jeanette all but rubbed her hands together before saying, "Just tell me what I need to do."

"I've got a job," Abi said to Rylan, catching him on his way to the livery on Friday morning.

"Where are you working?" Rylan asked.

"I'm writing for the newspaper."

"How did that come up?"

"I took some of my stories to the publisher and he bought two."

Rylan smiled and asked, "Will you still be able to use them in your book?"

"I'm not working on it just now."

"Why is that?"

Abi shook her head but didn't look agitated. "I don't know," she finally said. "I just don't want to right now."

"All right," Rylan said. He wasn't sure if the book was earning her any money as she wrote or how that all worked. He'd never asked, and she'd never shared. Instead he asked, "How are you doing with the verses I gave you?"

"I memorized them."

"That's great. Are they making sense to you?"

Abi smiled a little and said quietly, "I have hope in the Lord now."

"Do you want to say those verses for me?" Rylan asked, knowing he had just about that much time.

Abi quoted two she had learned from the Psalms. "'Let Israel hope in the Lord: for with the LORD there is mercy, and with him is plenteous redemption. Let Israel hope in the Lord from henceforth and for ever.'"

"I think you just made my day."

Abi looked pleased without smiling. Rylan, however, didn't even attempt to hold his smile. He looked at the woman whose hunger for God was new but still very real and believed again in his heart that God could save the people of Token Creek.

Cassidy was on the verge of closing on Friday evening when Timothy, the man who worked for Jeanette, came into the shop.

"Good evening," he spoke formally and looked serious.

"Hello," Cassidy greeted him, not having met him more than a few times.

"I was asked to give you this," Timothy stated, handing a piece of paper to Cassidy.

"Thank you," she said automatically, not realizing until too late that Timothy was not staying around for anything else. "Goodbye," Cassidy called after him and then opened the letter.

Your presence is requested for supper at my house tonight. Please come at half past five.

It was signed by Jeanette, and Cassidy had to laugh. That woman had just been there—they'd worked together all day—and not mentioned a thing about it. Cassidy wondered what she was up to but didn't give it great thought. Closing the shop, she went up to her apartment, taking some time to freshen up and change into one of her Sunday dresses before heading toward Jeanette's.

CHAPTER NINETEEN

CASSIDY WAS ALMOST TO JEANETTE'S FRONT DOOR when it opened. Timothy was there yet again, bowing formally and bidding her to enter.

"If you'll come this way," he invited once Cassidy had laid aside her coat, making the seamstress think that Jeanette had lost her mind. She followed Timothy, however, watching him step aside as he neared the doorway of the small parlor. He told her to go right in, and when Cassidy did, Trace was waiting inside.

"Trace," Cassidy said in soft surprise. "What are you doing here?"

"I'm waiting to dine with Cassidy Norton."

Not until that moment did Cassidy see that a small table, set for two, had been placed in the middle of the room, not far from the fire. Candles flickered from the table's center, fine plates and crystal gleaming in the light. Cassidy was looking around, still trying to find her bearings, when Trace came toward her.

"First things first," he said, taking her hand and leading her to stand with him in front of the mantel, the fire crackling beside them. Still holding her hand, Trace went down on one knee.

"Oh, Trace," Cassidy said, her voice catching in her throat as she watched him.

"Cassie," he said, his voice deeper than usual, "will you marry me?"

"Yes," Cassidy whispered, not able to manage more.

Trace kissed the back of her hand before standing up again. He took her into his arms.

"I love you, Trace." Cassidy said the words she'd been longing to say, her own arms around his neck.

At the moment Trace couldn't say anything at all. He lowered his head and kissed her softly on the mouth.

"Forgive me?" he asked when he could breathe.

"Why do you need forgiving?"

"For setting a date before I'd proposed."

"I'm not sure there's anything to forgive, but if you need that, I'll say yes."

Trace could have gone right on holding her, but that would have to wait. With special care, he took Cassidy to the table and held a chair for her. The moment she was seated, he excused himself and left the room.

Cassidy didn't hear anything, but Trace came back just a minute later, taking the seat across from her. Before Cassidy could ask what he was up to, food began to arrive. Becky had clearly outdone herself, and she and Heather began to wait on them, delighted with the whole idea.

Large bowls of black bean soup were set before Trace and Cassidy, along with biscuits that Becky had coaxed to an impossible height. Cassidy was still so surprised by the whole evening that she could only stare. Not until they were left alone could she find her voice, but then she heard piano music playing in the distance. Cassidy looked across at Trace, hardly able to believe he had done all of this.

"That's Jeanette, isn't it?"

"Yes."

"You planned it all."

"With Jeanette's help."

"I won't ever forget this," Cassidy said, realizing it was true.

"Shall we do it every year?" Trace asked.

"Yes, please."

"Try your soup," Trace invited, so pleased over her obvious enjoyment that he was having a hard time sitting still.

The soup was as delicious as it looked and smelled. And it was only the beginning. Pot roast followed, crowded all around by fat potatoes and carrots, with more of Becky's biscuits and a tub of fresh butter always at hand. Their coffee cups were not allowed to become empty, and when their plates were, chocolate cake, frosted between all three layers, came to the table.

Cassidy's skills in the kitchen were fine, and if she had a recipe she could make anything, but she never had time for special desserts, so this ended up being her favorite part of the meal. "That was amazing," she said as it ended, thinking that to do this every year would be such a treat.

"I could eat another piece of cake," Trace admitted.

Cassidy groaned. "I don't know if I can even move."

Trace laughed before asking, "Shall we head to the ranch?"

"I have work tomorrow," Cassidy hated to remind him.

"No, you don't," Trace said. "Jeanette's taking over for the day."

Cassidy could not stop her smile. This might have been the sweetest surprise of all.

"What do you think?" Trace asked.

"I think I love you," the future Mrs. Holden said.

Trace smiled and said, "Let's go home."

❦

Cassidy had been right. She didn't hear more than a half-dozen words on Sunday morning, and long before she was ready, Rylan was wrapping up his sermon and preparing for her to come.

"As all of you must know," the pastor started, "Cassidy has had some difficulties in the last weeks, all resulting from a visit made to Token Creek by her brother. She asked me if she could share her story with you, the very reason she came to Token Creek, and I thought it a fine opportunity for you to hear from her what really happened. Cassidy," Rylan invited before taking a seat in the front pew.

Trace gave Cassidy's hand a squeeze before she moved to the front. She was not able to hide her nervousness. Many people smiled at her, and she knew she would simply have to start.

"My younger brother is Edson Sinclair. If you've not heard the name before, Edson is known all over the territory—especially by banks—for conning folks and rarely getting caught in the act. He has served jail time, but it was brief and for only one charge. He came here looking like himself, but he often uses disguises, and there are few accurate pictures of him.

"My family is from Billings. My late father was never around much. He gambled for a living but rarely brought any money home. My mother worked cleaning homes until she hurt her back and was forced to take in mending so we could live. Eventually she started her own dress shop, working out of a small bedroom in our home. That's where I learned to sew," Cassidy added, not sure if that was important or not.

"Even though Edson began playing card games and getting into trouble at a young age, he didn't involve my mother or me for many years. And when he did start to target the customers that came to the house, selling phony mine shares and such, we were not at first aware. When my mother became aware, she reported Edson."

Cassidy took a breath. History had so painfully repeated itself here in Token Creek that it was hard to talk about.

"My mother's business was nearly destroyed by Edson's actions. Folks who had trusted her now became suspicious. We had made a good business. We were working hard and supporting ourselves, but our church family was small, and they could not keep us going with just their patronage.

"My mother begged me to move away and try again. But then

history repeated itself," Cassidy said, managing a smile that was very crooked before continuing.

"But that's not really what I wanted to explain to you today. My mother gave me money that her mother had left her, money that she'd kept tucked away for years. She sent that money with me, told me to take my great aunt's maiden name, and sent me off. We did not have contact until after Edson found me. Not since I came to Token Creek have I sent letters or tried to contact her for fear that Edson would find me.

"Changing my name was not done with the intent to deceive my church family or the folks of Token Creek. I didn't tell people the name I was born with so that Edson could not track me. Obviously it didn't work. I'm sorry if you have been hurt by Edson's presence and anything he might have said or done. I wonder if I should have handled things differently, but to speculate on that is fruitless."

Cassidy stopped and took another breath, feeling as though she could cry but fighting the urge.

"I don't know if I covered everything or not. I would be happy to take questions if you have them."

Chas Vick's hand went instantly into the air. Cassidy smiled at his kind expression, and he asked his question.

"How is business right now, Cassie? Are you going to make it?"

"Yes, I think the business will survive. Jeanette has offered to buy both the building and the business. Orders picked up this week, and folks seem to have forgotten or forgiven the things Edson said about me."

"Have you been in touch with your mother?" Patience Dorn wanted to know.

"I've written to her but not heard back. I'm working on a plan to visit her, but I don't know when."

The room fell quiet for a moment. Cassidy forced herself not to look at Trace. She thought his eyes might make her even more emotional.

"What will you be doing when Jeanette buys your business?" Brad asked, and Cassidy had all she could do not to laugh. She looked at him a bit sternly, an effect that was spoiled by her smile.

"Last night Trace Holden asked me to marry him, and I said yes."

As might be expected, there was much laughter and applause. Cassidy felt her face going very red, and this time it did help to look at Trace, who winked at her.

For a while, there were no questions. Cassidy thought it might be time for her to sit down, but finally Philip Leffers raised his hand.

"What is something you wondered if you might have done differently?"

"I wonder if I should have contacted Sheriff Kaderly the moment I knew Edson was in town. And whether I should have told Chandler at the bank. I don't know if alerting folks would have worked. As it was," Cassidy's voice dropped a little, "someone was physically harmed because of Edson's presence in town. Had I raised the alarm, the physical violence might have come on me instead. To tell you the truth, I wish it had. I'll always wonder if I could have done a better job."

Listening to her, Chandler felt a jolt go through him. Such a thing had not occurred to him. He did wish that Cassidy had come to him, but her being harmed had not played into his thoughts. The idea made him slightly queasy.

"I don't want to cut things off," Rylan said, suddenly standing and going up front, "but I'm going to. It's past the time we usually let out, and I want to be sensitive to folks' plans and the needs of little ones.

"That doesn't change the fact that Cassidy would still answer your questions. Maybe hearing her story brought even more questions to your mind. You can see her or talk to me, and I'll make sure Cassidy hears your questions. Thank you, Cassie," Rylan said, turning to her, "for being willing to share your story and answer all questions. You've encouraged our hearts."

Cassidy nodded at him, her face still warm, and went back to her pew. Rylan closed in prayer, but Cassidy didn't hear it. She hadn't thought it was going to be so hard, but it was. Trace had taken her hand, not bothering to ask if she was all right but just staying close while the congregation converged.

⚜

"Let me get this straight," Rylan demanded, catching Trace while the others crowded around to speak with Cassidy. "You came to my house on Wednesday night, looking to set a date, but you didn't ask Cassie to marry you until last night?"

"Is that what she said?" Trace was too quick. "You know, she was a little upset. I asked her *last* Saturday. I'm sure that was the day."

Rylan's head went back as he laughed. He clapped Trace on the shoulder and told him he'd see him that week.

⚜

"Oh, Cassie," Patience cried as she hugged Cassidy and told her she would pray for her.

"Thank you," Cassidy said, her heart turned with gratitude.

And Patience was just one of many. Nearly everyone in the church family checked in with her, asking other questions or stopping to give her a hug. Not until the room was nearly cleared did Cassidy see Abi waiting.

"Did you mean that?" the older woman asked.

Cassidy knew exactly what she meant and wasted no time in saying yes.

"But if I'd not gotten hurt, I wouldn't have sent for Pastor Jarvik," Abi said, making it sound like more of a question than a statement.

"Clearly God had a plan. I'm glad it included your being here."

Abi looked uncomfortable for a moment, but she eventually thanked Cassidy and moved on her way. Trace took Cassidy's hand and led her to where Meg and Brad were waiting. None of them had ever seen Cassidy looking so drained, and Meg's eyes searched her face.

"Can you take me in for the afternoon, Meg?" Cassidy asked.

Meg didn't answer but put her arms around her friend.

"It's over now, Cass," she whispered in her friend's ear. "You can get on with your life."

Cassidy nodded, trying not to think about her mother, wanting only to go to the ranch and spend time with her future family.

❧

Trace sat alone in the living room oiling his rifle on Sunday afternoon, parts of Rylan's sermon going through his mind. The pastor had said that believers in Christ must be perfectly content at all times but never stop walking, never stop working to strengthen their obedience.

Trace thought this one of the most profound concepts Rylan had ever spoken about. It was easy to be content right now and want to stay right where he was. Cassidy loved him, and he loved her more deeply than words could express. They would be married in six weeks' time and, as soon as weather permitted, building a home.

But amid these thoughts, Trace knew that any real contentment must come from his relationship with his unchanging Savior and God. Lately Cassidy had so filled his head that his time in the Word and prayer had been halfhearted. In those circumstances, any claim to contentment with God was false.

Trace began to pray, his heart as well as his attention undivided. He confessed to the Lord that he had let Cassidy get between them and that he no longer wanted that.

I confess to You, Lord, that I have pushed You out of the center of my heart. Help me to see that for the sin it is and not to repeat this act against You. You are holy and worthy of my whole heart. Please help me not to forget this. Help me to guard my unfaithful heart.

Very soon I need Your help to be the husband Cassidy needs. I won't know how to do that if I'm not first obedient as Your child. Give me a renewed hunger for You, Lord. Help me to see how much I need You and to stop depending on myself.

Trace reached for the Bible that Meg kept on the living room table. He turned to the verse Rylan had emphasized in the fifth chapter of Matthew and spent some time committing it to memory. His hunger for God needed to increase, and he needed this verse in his heart to remind him.

⚜

Cassidy came quietly down the stairs four hours after arriving at the ranch. She had blinked her way owlishly through dinner and finally Brad, of all people, had told her to give up and head upstairs.

Because she had a room of her own, she simply hung her dress on one of the closet hooks, climbed into bed, and was asleep a minute later. She slept deeply for more than two hours and woke feeling human again. She even thought of her mother and prayed for her without needing to cry. That, in and of itself, told Cassidy she had been short on sleep.

"Well, hello," Trace said before Cassidy even spotted him. He'd heard her on the stairs before he'd seen her skirt.

"Hello," Cassidy said with smile, sitting close beside him.

Trace took her hand and asked if she'd slept.

"Like a hibernating bear. It was wonderful."

"You took your hair down," Trace commented, brushing his hand down the soft, straight, dark blonde mass.

"It was a mess from my nap, and I didn't try to do anything with it."

"I'm not complaining," Trace said, enjoying the view.

"Well," Cassidy replied, growing practical, "enjoy it now, because next summer I'll have to get it off my neck."

"I like it up too," Trace said kindly, "just not as well."

"That was a gallant thing to say," Cassidy teased him, knowing how much he preferred it down her back.

"Do you know the first time I noticed your hair down?"

"When was it?"

"The night Savanna was born. When I came back from getting Doc Ertz, I found you in the kitchen with your hair down." Trace shook his head a little. "It took quite a bit of effort not to tell you what I was thinking right then."

"I had no idea."

"You also had no idea after we moved in here and you fell asleep, I put a blanket over you. I watched you sleep for a long time."

Cassidy's mouth opened in surprise, and Trace leaned to kiss that mouth before smiling at her.

"Tell me, Trace," Cassidy asked at last, "why did it take so long to find each other?"

"I think we found each other a long time ago. We just couldn't take the chance of talking about it. And speaking of which, did you ever tell me when you knew you loved me?"

"I cared for a long time," Cassidy said by way of an answer, "but I didn't know that I wanted you in my life forever until you got worried about me in town on Saturday nights. I wanted to kiss you right on the spot."

"I would have liked that," Trace said softly, and Cassidy just looked at him. Trace looked right back until both realized they were on dangerous ground.

"How about a game of horseshoes?" Trace asked.

"I think that's a good idea," Cassidy agreed. She rose to get her sweater. The two were outside a few minutes later, their hands holding horseshoes and working to keep their distance.

"Savanna," Brad spoke with quiet firmness into the face of his crying daughter, bending over her cradle but not picking her up. "We have trained you to think that you need to be held all the time. I'm sorry we did this. You're dry and your stomach is full. You do not need to be held right now." Brad watched her cry, working to harden his heart, and eventually walked away.

Meg was waiting for him, her eyes watching him, knowing how hard it was going to be. It was true that they had done this. There were always arms waiting to hold Savanna, and the two-and-a-half-month-old was starting to cry for no reason.

"She'll be all right," Meg said, as much for Brad as for herself.

"But will I be?" Brad asked, hearing the kitchen door just then. "Don't pick her up," he said when Trace came in. He'd just returned Cassidy to town.

"Why not?"

"She's getting held too much and starting to expect it."

Trace took a seat in the living room with his brother and sister-in-law, but he was clearly not relaxed.

"Okay," he said at last, "is this making either of you as miserable as it's making me?"

The words were no more out of Trace's mouth when the crying shut off. Little noises from the cradle told them she was not asleep. Meg whispered that she might have found her fist.

"Now can I pick her up?" Trace asked, just stopping himself from heading that way.

"No," Brad said, wanting the same thing.

"How are your plans coming?" Meg asked, hoping to distract herself.

"Good," Trace answered. "We walked out to where the house will be, and Cass got pretty excited."

"Did she tell you about the porch she wants?" Meg asked.

Trace was answering when Savanna started up again.

"Please, Brad," the younger man asked.

Brad nodded and Trace wasted not a second. Brad spoke when Trace was settled back in a chair, the baby cuddled close against him.

"We have to start working on this, all of us. It's not fair that she thinks she's the center of the universe."

Nothing else Brad could have said would have gotten to Trace's heart faster. His own realization that very afternoon that he'd pushed God out of the center was still fresh in his mind. And he loved this baby enough to want nothing less for her than that God would be at the center of her life.

⁂

"When will you change the hours?" Cassidy asked Jeanette on Monday morning. They had worked on the details already, getting ready to finalize the sale.

"I think I'll put an ad in the paper." Jeanette was thinking out loud, not answering the question yet.

"That's a good idea. Why did I never think of that?"

Jeanette laughed at the younger woman before adding, "I'll probably make the changes on the days and hours right at the beginning of November. You'll still be around to help me, but if you get busy and can't, I'll be able to manage."

"That sounds good," Cassidy was saying when they were interrupted. Halston came in the door, and Cassidy's heart sank. She did not want to work with Hiram Brickel again.

"Good morning," Halston greeted. "I'm here to place an order."

"Certainly, Halston." Cassidy would never take her feelings out on this kind man. "For Mr. Brickel?"

"As a matter of fact, no."

"Oh," Cassidy said, and watching her, Jeanette wanted to laugh.

"I need two shirts," Halston informed her, just holding his smile.

"Well," Cassidy said, still working to recover. "If you'll just allow me to take some measurements…"

Halston had to smile then. He could see that she was surprised, and like Jeanette, he'd found this very amusing. Cassidy never did catch that she was being laughed at, but it didn't matter. It was another order, and it confirmed what she'd hoped all along: Token Creek would support the business again.

CHAPTER TWENTY

"HELLO, CASSIE," JEB GREETED on Tuesday afternoon, having come to the shop, a place he'd never before visited.

"Well, hello, Jeb. How are you?"

"Fine. I have a letter for you. Jessie mentioned that you'd received one, and I thought you might want to see it right away."

Cassidy froze a little right then, but Jeb just smiled at her.

"Here you go," he offered, coming close enough to hand it to her.

"Thank you," Cassidy said, looking down at it. "It's from my mother."

"I hoped it was." Jeb took in her suddenly anxious face. "Are you going to be all right?"

"I don't know."

"I'll tell you what," Jeb offered, his feelings as fatherly toward her as they were toward Meg. "I'll just sit myself down right here in a chair, and you can go in the back and read. If someone comes in, I'll explain that you're busy and take a message or something."

"Okay," Cassidy agreed, feeling breathless but also excited. She didn't go in the back but stood right where she was and opened the letter. Jeb moved to a chair to give her privacy, but Cassidy never noticed.

> *My darling Cassie,*
>
> *I can't tell you what your letter meant to my heart. I got both your letters, but I've broken two fingers on my right hand, and writing has been almost impossible.*
>
> *I'm sorry about Edson. He was here and tried to tell me he'd not seen you, but then I showed him your letters and that stopped his lies. I ache for what you've been through, but I take comfort that if someone is willing to buy the shop, you must still have a business. Maybe it helped that Edson wasn't around long enough to do as much damage.*
>
> *I want to meet your Trace. My back is bothering me again. I don't think I could stand the train ride, or I would try to come for the wedding. Do not delay the day for me, but please visit when you can, and please bring Trace. I must meet this special man who has won my girl's heart.*

Cassidy had to stop. She felt as though she had run a long way, her breathing coming hard. A noise behind her reminded her of Jeb's presence.

"She's all right," Cassidy turned to say. "My mother is fine."

"I'm glad, Cassie." Jeb came to his feet. Cassidy's color was high, but he could see she was going to be all right. "Can you see her soon?"

"I think so. I'll have to work that out with Jeanette and Trace."

"Maybe after the wedding?"

"Maybe."

Jeb smiled at her smile. "I'll get out of your way now."

Cassidy stepped forward to hug him and was hugged warmly in return.

"Thank you, Jeb."

"You're welcome, Cassie."

Cassidy waved him off from the door and went right back to her letter.

When I sent you away, I did not reckon with how hard it would be to have you gone from home. I was thankful every day that you could be safe and doing well in Token Creek, but my life has felt almost empty without you.

Please write again and tell me about the church family and all your friends. Meg sounds like the sister you always wanted. And Jeanette! I wish I could meet this special woman.

My hand is beginning to ache, (I wasn't paying attention and fell down the front steps), but I'll write again. You do the same. The only thing that has kept me going is knowing that God is watching over my girl and keeping her close to Him until we meet again.

All my love,
Mama

Cassidy hugged the letter to herself, read it all over again, and began to pray. *Thank You, Father. Thank You for taking care of my mother. Thank You she is well. Please keep her close to You, Father, just as she prays for me. You know I want to see her again, and I ask, in Your time and in Your hand, that Trace and I will find a way. Until then, please help me to keep my trust in You alone. I may want to go home but not be able to, Lord. Help me to be content in You, no matter what else might happen.*

Cassidy suddenly remembered she had work to do. She headed to the sewing machine to start her jobs for the day, but her heart still prayed. Trace had shared with her some of his thoughts from Sunday. Cassidy did not want to find contentment in getting a letter from her mother but in knowing she was right with her God.

⁂

"Well, ladies," Chandler said on Wednesday morning from his desk chair in the bank. "It's official. Jeanette Fulbright is now the new owner of Token Creek Apparel."

"Thank you, Chandler," Jeanette said, but Cassidy was looking at the older woman.

"We didn't talk about rent."

"For what?" Jeanette asked, confused.

"The apartment. I'm going to be there for more than a month."

Jeanette had all she could do not to laugh. It was the last thing she was concerned about, and Cassidy had already refused to take a dime of payment for the weeks before the wedding that she would work for Jeanette.

"If you won't let me pay you for working for me, I won't be taking any money for rent."

Cassidy opened her mouth and then shut it again. She smiled at being caught out.

"Deal?" Jeanette asked.

"Deal," Cassidy agreed.

Chandler smiled at this exchange, knowing that it was unconventional but also that it was going to work. If these two women had a reputation in town for anything, it was integrity.

"Well, Chandler," Cassidy said, finally turning to him. "We're going to breakfast at the hotel to celebrate. Can you join us?"

"I might be able to do that," Chandler replied, not sure his heart could take it but hating to say no in the midst of their pleasure. "Let me check with Mr. Falcone about minding the store."

The three left the bank just five minutes later, their spirits high. They laughed and talked like the old friends they were, and even though Chandler had to work at guarding his heart more than one time, they had a wonderful celebration.

"You're late," Trace teased his fiancée, meeting her in the yard and not able to hold his smile.

"I'll have you know, Trace Holden," Cassidy said, much too pleased with herself, "that I just sold my business."

"This morning?"

"Yes. Because we're closed, it seemed the most logical day. Jeanette and I went to the bank and sealed the deal. And then," she rushed on before Trace could say anything else, "to celebrate, we went to the hotel for breakfast. Chandler even joined us."

"I'm sorry I missed it," Trace said, helping her down and hugging her close.

Cassidy's heart was so full she threw her arms around his neck and squeezed him. "And that's not the best part," she said, her blue eyes sparkling into his. "I've had a letter from my mother."

"Is she all right?" Trace asked, growing serious.

Cassidy brought the letter from her coat pocket and handed it to him. "Go ahead. Read it."

Not able to resist, Trace kissed her before he opened the letter. Cassidy watched him read, smiling almost all the way through.

"This is great. When should we go to see her?"

It did amazing things to Cassidy's heart to hear Trace say *we*.

"I don't know. I could probably go anytime because Jeanette has just about taken over, but maybe it would make more sense to wait until after the wedding."

"We'll figure it out," Trace said, taking her arm and directing her toward the house. It was cold again, though not as cold as it was going to be, but Cassidy's cheeks were already red from the buggy ride out to the ranch.

Meg was waiting with coffee, and Cassidy was able to share her news all over again. Trace could not stay around all day but said he would be back in for dinner. The women started on some baking and then moved to sewing, all the time working on when Cassidy should see her mother. By the time the men came in to eat, Meg and Cassidy were ready with a plan.

❧

The Vicks asked Trace and Cassidy to join them for dinner on Sunday. Miranda kept the meal light and easy. Cassidy claimed two-month-old Nellie, saying she was happy to eat with only one arm. And Miranda, being sensitive to her son's heart, put Trace next to Franklin at the table.

"How is Quincy?" Franklin wasted no time checking on Trace's horse.

"He's doing well. I think the next time I have him in town I can stop by so you can have a ride."

The eight-year-old looked at his parents, his eyes telling them Trace had made his day.

"What do you say?" his father prompted.

"Thank you," Franklin said softly, hero-worship all over his face.

Watching from across the table, Cassidy's heart melted at the sight and knew that their own children would feel the same way.

"Was there something else you wanted to hear about, Frank?" his father asked to remind him.

"Oh, yeah! Can you tell me about your cattle drive?"

"Sure," Trace agreed. "It started a month ago and went for about two weeks. Brad and I, four other hands, and a cook left from our ranch early one morning. We had eight hundred head of cattle to drive to Burton."

"Why Burton?" Chas asked.

"The Burton railroad is equipped to take cattle to Chicago. It would cost a lot of money to try to send them from Token Creek."

"So you went on the train?" Franklin checked.

"No, just the cattle did that, but not until they'd walked for about five hundred miles."

"Did you sleep on the ground?"

"We certainly did. We had a chuck wagon for our food, and Tinker Hayworth, an old cowboy you might have seen around town, cooked for us. Then the four other hands helped us drive the cattle."

"Did you wear your chaps?"

"I did," Trace said, and then answered the question he knew would be next. "I had my gun belt on and my pistol with me. My rifle was on my saddle."

"Did you have to shoot?"

"A few times, but not at anyone."

"Did anyone get hurt?"

"There were a few injuries but nothing too serious."

"What did you eat?"

"Lots of beans," Trace said with a smile, "and beef stew and biscuits. Pancakes for breakfast."

Franklin was opening his mouth again, but his father broke in.

"Why don't you eat a little, Frank. Trace can do the same. I'm sure he'll have time to answer all your questions."

"Yes, indeed," Miranda said softly, "before Chas starts with his."

"What is this about?" Trace asked.

"Nothing," Chas tried to say, but he couldn't stop his smile.

"Someone wants to know about the two of you." Miranda told on her husband. "He wants to know how the wedding plans all came about."

Both Cassidy and Trace smiled at Chas, who worked to look innocent.

"I'm just asking out of concern," the other man said, his voice telling them he was not the least bit sincere. "I know Rylan has spoken with you, but as a fellow elder, if he's missed something, we can talk about it."

The adults all laughed at this, but that topic was going to have to wait. Franklin, who had all but swallowed his food whole, had more questions for the cattle rancher.

"From our viewpoint," Chas said when the adults were alone in the living room an hour later, "one week you were friends, and a few weeks later you were more."

"In a way that's how it happened," Cassidy said.

"Not with our feelings," Trace elaborated, "but with telling each other our feelings."

"How did that come about?" Miranda asked, telling the couple that she was as curious as her husband.

"While I was gone," Trace started, "Edson visited, and you both know what happened with that. I didn't see Cassidy until I came back from the cattle drive." Trace tried to weigh how much he should share, and seeing no reason to speak about the part Chandler had played, continued. "That had been a hard time for Cassie, and when we talked about it, it came out that her heart was available."

"Not really available," Cassidy said with a smile. "Or rather, available just to you."

Trace smiled down at her where she sat beside him in the living room, and Chas, the old romantic that he was, grinned at the two of them.

"What happened next?" their host asked.

When both Trace and Cassidy smiled, Miranda put the pieces together.

"I think someone got kissed."

When the smiles grew, the married couple laughed.

"Then what?" Chas knew there was more.

"We had some things to talk about, but we'd been watching each other for a long time. I knew Cassidy was the woman I wanted for my wife. I had seen her in nearly every situation, and there was nothing I objected to."

"And for you, Cassie, was it the same?"

"Oh, yes. Trace was taking care of me long before he made his feelings known. Between him and Brad, I knew I would never go without. I just didn't know Trace felt the same way I did."

"How did you pull that off?" Chas had to ask. "I watched both of you, and every once in a while, I thought I might see something, but then nothing would happen."

"We've wondered that ourselves," Trace said. "It seemed like it would have been so easy to talk about a future together, but if one of us didn't share the intensity of feelings, we would have ruined an amazing friendship. Neither one of us was willing to take the risk."

"So you just kissed her," Miranda guessed.

"That about sums it up. We didn't keep kissing—we had a lot of talking to do—but that broke down the gate, and I at least knew that my interest was shared."

Chas' sigh could be heard all over the room. "I'm telling you," he said, while the others laughed at him, "this heart business is fun stuff, but it wears a body out."

"Do you know," Trace said, "I believe Jeb Dorn said that very thing when Brad and Meg finally found each other."

Chas realized he'd never heard their story, and that's what he wanted to talk about next. From there, they moved to the morning sermon, which had been on hungering after God, and then played a game with the children. It ended up being a perfect afternoon of fellowship.

⁂

"What is it that bothers you so much?" Rylan asked of Abi. The two were using Jeanette's parlor to talk, and that lady was in attendance as well. Abi had been visibly upset in church and afterward when Rylan had tried to speak with her about it.

"I tried to talk to Missy," Abi admitted. "I tried to tell her that God died for me, and she said I thought I was better than her. I don't think that!" she said in obvious agitation. "I'm not like that."

"Did she ask you about this, or did you volunteer?"

"She asked. I've been careful, just like you said, but she asked."

"Then you can't worry about it. If you had gone next door intending to shove your beliefs on her, then you would need to apologize, but you need to just give this time. She'll see that you don't feel that way. Your life will prove it to her."

Abi shifted in her seat, clearly not at peace.

"Do you feel like you've lost your friend?" Jeanette asked.

"Yes," Abi said, looking relieved at being understood. "She's been a good neighbor and a friend. She's never criticized me or been upset with me before. I don't like it this way."

"It's hard when that happens," Rylan commiserated. "I wonder if Missy might be feeling the same way."

"What do you mean?" Abi asking, frowning in confusion.

"Like she's lost a friend."

It was on the tip of Abi's tongue to say that she hadn't gone anywhere, but that wasn't true. She was changing. She was home more, and not stalking the streets of Token Creek looking for a story. And she was no longer outraged by what had happened to her. At one time she wanted the law to find the man named Neal and hang him from the nearest tree, but no longer. She had forgiven Neal, and even though she thought he should be behind bars, she trusted God to take care of her.

"Are you all right?" Jeanette finally asked.

"I just never thought of it that way." Abi came to her feet. "I think you must be right. I have to go."

Rylan hoped to eventually find a way to talk to her about her abrupt way of exiting a conversation, but not today. He and Jeanette said goodbye from their seats, not given time to see her to the door.

"I think you helped her," Jeanette said.

"Maybe. I don't know."

"She's a fascinating person, isn't she?"

"Yes. I think she's seen and experienced more in her fifty-eight years than any of us can imagine."

"Is she really fifty-eight?" Jeanette was surprised. Abi Pfister was not a young woman, but neither did she look nearly sixty.

Rylan had to laugh before saying, "She said being nosy has kept her young."

Jeanette laughed with him before asking, "Do you suppose she would want to have a Bible study with me? Do you think she trusts me enough for that?"

"I was thinking about that very same thing. I don't know if she trusts you or not, but if you're willing, I'll ask her."

The two talked about the possibilities for a while longer. Rylan was much encouraged by Jeanette's willingness and offer.

"How about some of Becky's chocolate cake?" the hostess offered a while later.

"That sounds good," Rylan agreed. "Can we eat it while I visit with your sister?"

Jeanette smiled. "Theta and I would both enjoy that."

***

"Can you make me a new suit?" Trace asked as he and Cassidy began to walk toward Cassidy's from the Vick house.

"Certainly," Cassidy said.

"In time for the wedding?" Trace asked.

"I think so. Do you have an old suit?" She could not remember. "I don't think I've seen you in it."

"I got one for Brad and Meg's wedding. I don't wear it anymore because the jacket is too tight in the shoulders. I've worn the pants on Sunday for a long time, and they're starting to show their age."

"Let's go into the shop and see what I have for fabric."

Trace was all for that. They picked out exactly what he wanted; Cassidy got the measurements she needed; and then they headed to Jeanette's. Trace wanted to visit his mother, and naturally Cassidy wanted to go with him.

***

October was swiftly drawing to a close. The days were busy for Trace and Cassidy with wedding plans as well as plans to visit Billings and Cassidy's mother for their honeymoon.

Jeanette was busy as well. Her ad was written up and ready for the newspaper, and her sign, with the new store hours, was ready to go into the window at the close of the day.

The first day of changes would be Tuesday, the second of November. Things hadn't been altered all that much, but on the last Saturday of the month, both women felt a little excited about the changes and the store's future. Cassidy would have more time to work on her and Trace's wedding clothes, as well as her packing. Moving to the ranch was quite a venture. Meg and Brad didn't really have room for her furniture, but if she and Trace were going to have something to sit on in their new home someday, they needed to hold on to it.

And business had stayed active. Things had been quiet at the beginning of the week, but on Thursday and then again today, she and Jeanette had run their legs off. Cassidy would be headed to the bank for Jeanette, who wanted to head straight home because she was having company. There was an impressive amount of cash to deposit. Indeed Cassidy was just about to head out when the door opened.

"Hello, Cassie!" Edson Sinclair greeted cordially, not having changed at all.

Cassidy didn't speak but watched Neal come in behind Edson. He shut the door and locked it.

"What are you doing here, Edson?" Cassidy asked, knowing that Jeanette had come from the rear of the store.

"Ah, you're both together," Edson said by way of an answer. "Perfect. I'll tell you, Cass, you've been one busy little lady."

"What do you mean?"

"Mama shared your letters with me. She was thrilled to see me and tell me you'd sold your shop and gotten engaged."

"Mama shared my letters with you because you tried to lie about having been here," Cassidy spoke plainly.

"Oh." Edson's voice was almost comical. "She wrote about that, did she?"

"Yes. Now I want you to leave."

"That's not going to happen." Edson's voice became silky, and Cassidy's heart began to pound a little faster. She watched Neal move toward Jeanette and tried to step in, but Edson caught her arm in a surprising grip.

"Now you listen, Cassidy *Norton*," Edson snarled, his voice low with fury. "You're going to do just what I say, or Neal is going to use that knife on Mrs. Fulbright's throat. Do you understand?"

"Yes," Cassidy said, her eyes watching Jeanette's face drain of color as Neal took hold of her. The knife was already in his hand, and Cassidy began to shake.

"Please don't hurt her," she begged softly, remembering what had happened to Abi.

"We won't have to if you'll head to the bank."

"The bank?" Cassidy was confused for a moment.

Edson gave her arm an angry shake. "Yes, the bank! You're going to withdraw the money Mrs. Fulbright paid you for the business and bring it back to me. You have fifteen minutes to do this, or Neal uses his knife."

Cassidy looked at him, her eyes huge. "Edson," she tried. "It will never work. I never take that much out. Please let Jeanette go."

"Shut up!" he barked. "You're a great little pretender, coming to this town and setting up a business in a false name. You can fool anyone with those big, blue eyes. Now you do as I say, or the old woman dies."

Cassidy could see he was completely serious. She nodded, but Edson gave her arm one more squeeze.

"Fifteen minutes, Cassie. Don't be late, and don't try anything funny."

Cassidy looked into Jeanette's face, seeing her fear but also that she was trying to be brave. Her look gave Cassidy the courage to shoot out the door. She had fifteen minutes to help her friend, praying all the while that nothing would go wrong.

CHAPTER TWENTY-ONE

CASSIDY MANAGED THE WALK TO THE BANK, albeit rather swiftly. She entered the door calmly enough and made a beeline for Chandler. Unfortunately, his first remark completely rattled her.

"Cassie, where is your coat?"

"What?" she asked, not realizing she looked as upset as she felt.

"Your coat? It's freezing out."

"Oh, I'm all right," she said and tried to smile. "Chandler, I need to make a withdrawal."

"Okay. How much?"

"Five hundred."

"Dollars?" Chandler questioned her, alarms going off in his mind.

"Yes, and I'm in a bit of a hurry."

"Cassidy, something is wrong," Chandler said.

"That's right," Cassidy said, not sure that Edson had not followed her and might be watching from across the street.

"Where is Jeanette?" Chandler asked.

"At the shop," Cassidy didn't hear the high timber of her voice. "Please, Chandler. Please get the money."

Chandler went behind the counter, knowing something was very wrong but gathering the bills. He didn't want to send the money with her, but any amount was worth far less than her life or Jeanette's.

"Are you sure, Cassidy?" Chandler asked when he had the money ready.

Cassidy took it and looked at him, her eyes begging. "Please just go back to work, Chandler. Nothing can go wrong."

Chandler took a seat as soon as Cassidy turned from his desk, but his eyes were on the windows. As soon as Cassidy moved out of sight, he would find Sheriff Kaderly.

⚜

Trace pulled the wagon to a stop outside Cassidy's shop the way he always did. The weather was getting cold these days, and he turned to make sure he'd remembered the blankets. Not until that moment did he see the sign in the shop window that said it was closed. Trace didn't think he was running late but then remembered that Jeanette had plans to change the days and times.

All thoughts of this went out of his head, however, when he looked up to see Cassidy walking swiftly toward him. In the back of his mind he too wondered where her coat was, but at the moment he was just glad to see her.

"Hey, Cass."

"What are you doing here?" Cassidy blurted, not having seen him until he spoke.

"What am I doing here?" Trace asked, wondering what he'd done wrong. It took a moment for him to really see Cassidy's face.

"What is it, Cassidy?"

"Edson and Neal," she said in a rush. "They have Jeanette."

"Inside?"

"Yes."

Trace's eyes flicked to the window and saw nothing. Without moving his body or his head, he said, "Stand right there, Cass. My rifle is in the wagon."

"Neal has a knife," she whispered, shaking almost violently. "He'll use it."

"When I give the sign, do as they told you. I'll be coming in right behind you."

Trace moved to the wagon, fear gripping him that he was being watched, but knowing he didn't have a choice. Cassidy had stopped outside the door, but when Trace nodded to her, she tried the handle. It was locked, and it took a moment for Edson to open it. When he did, he found the barrel of a rifle coming over his sister's shoulder directly into his face.

"Easy now," Edson said, backing his way into the room.

"That's what you need to tell your friend," Trace countered. He'd already entered, pushed Cassidy behind him, and watched Neal's knife come to Jeanette's throat.

"We just want our money," Edson tried.

"Who's money?" Trace asked to stall.

"The money Cassidy said I could have," Edson lied.

"Or you'll what?" Trace had his eyes only on Neal now. "Kill my aunt? I can't let you do that. Or maybe—" Trace suddenly swung the rifle until it was nearly touching Edson's nose, not bothering to finish the sentence. "Now how about you tell Neal to drop the knife."

"You heard him," Edson said, not bothering to hide his fear. "Let her go."

"We can do this," Neal urged, saying his first words.

"No, Neal," Edson said, studying the eyes of the man with the rifle. If Jeanette Fulbright was his aunt, this was Cassidy's intended, and Edson could see that he was not afraid to use his weapon.

Trace's eyes had gone back to watching Neal, but he hadn't moved the gun. For that reason, Neal thought he could make it. He pushed Jeanette away from him, shoving the knife into her back at the same time, but also giving Trace a clear shot. Trace fired the gun. Neal and Jeanette went down at the same time. Cassidy dodged around Trace and ran for Jeanette. At the same moment Trace put a fist into Edson's jaw, knocking him out cold.

"Jeanette!" Cassidy called her name, touching her as she knelt beside her and staring at her bloodless face. Jeanette didn't answer. Folks began to arrive, Sheriff Kaderly and Chandler among them. Someone ran for the doctor, and for a moment there was general mayhem.

"Here, Cass." Trace was beside her, trying to find a pulse in Jeanette's neck. "She's alive," he said before removing the knife and pressing his handkerchief onto the wound.

The minutes that followed were a blur. Cassidy felt hands move her so Doc Ertz could come through. She was not even aware that Chandler had taken this on himself, not wanting her to notice Neal's body, which lay unmoving past Jeanette's.

When Jeanette was finally moved, the blood that had spread on the back of her dress was almost more than Cassidy could take, but she wanted to stay close to her. Chandler held her out of the fray, and when he saw that she was going to follow the wagon to Jeanette's house without her coat, he again stepped in.

While Chandler was helping her with her coat and gloves, she caught herself and said something that astounded the banker. He didn't think it a good idea but couldn't bring himself to argue. He helped Cassidy down the street.

⚜

Trace's mind was completely centered on his aunt and the fact that his hand was working to stop the flow of blood. He asked someone to go for Brad, and when he looked up and found Rylan nearby, he had all he could do not to weep.

"How bad is it?" Rylan asked right after the doctor had taken Trace's place and Jeanette was transferred into the house.

"I don't know yet."

"Has someone gone for Brad and Meg?"

"I think so."

"Where is Cassie?"

"I don't know," Trace said again, and Rylan just stayed close, no more questions coming from him.

Jeanette was settled in her own bed with as little fuss as those carrying her could make. Stopping the bleeding became the next order of business. Trace hated not being needed, but he stayed out of the way as much as possible and prayed, glad to catch sight of Rylan from time to time.

Almost an hour passed before he began to look for Cassidy. Trace assumed she was in the house, but she was not upstairs. Brad and Meg had already arrived, and when he checked, Heather and Becky had not seen her. Not until Trace had gone downstairs and was almost to the front door did he see Chandler. That man stopped him.

"I thought you would want to know that Cassie went to the sheriff's office."

"Did she say why?"

"No. Her brother was taken there, and she was going to go no matter what, so I made sure she made it. I also returned her money to the bank. She dropped it in the shop."

"Thanks, Chandler," Trace said, trying to gather his thoughts. "Rylan is somewhere here in the house. Will you let him know that I've gone to get Cassie?"

"Certainly."

"Thanks," Trace said, and started out the door. Chandler stopped him long enough to hand him a coat. Trace went out the door without another word.

Even with the blanket around her and her coat on, Cassidy shivered violently. Sheriff Kaderly watched her, wishing someone would come, not knowing what to say or do. She had been sitting outside her brother's cell for nearly an hour. Edson Sinclair had not gained consciousness, but that hadn't driven Cassidy away. When the door opened and Trace walked in, the lawman had all he could do not to sigh with relief.

"Cassie?" Trace said quietly, and that woman stood and walked into his arms.

"How is Jeanette?"

"They think they have the bleeding stopped."

"You should be there," Cassidy said.

"Yes, but I was worried about you."

"I'm all right," she said with more strength than she felt. "I have some things to say to Edson."

"He's not going anywhere," Trace said, concerned about how violently she shivered. "We'll ask Sheriff Kaderly, but I'm sure he's going to hold him."

"That's right," the sheriff said from behind them.

"I want you to come to the house with me."

Cassidy began to shake her head, but Trace was having none of it.

"I want you to," he said, not sure she was thinking clearly. "Your brother can wait."

Cassidy was going to plead her case again, but Trace gave her no chance. He took the blanket from her shoulders and put it on the bench. Thanking the sheriff, he ushered her to the door.

"You'll hold him, won't you?" Cassidy got in before Trace could get her away.

"Yes, Miss Norton. He'll be here."

"I want to talk to him," Cassidy said.

Trace didn't trust the sound of her voice. He thought she would be sobbing any moment, which he knew might be for the best, but it didn't happen. Her hand safely tucked into his, she allowed herself to be led down the street. Trace prayed for her and for himself. At the moment, it didn't seem that life would ever be the same again.

*

"She's asking for you" was the first thing Trace and Cassidy heard when they reached Jeanette's. Trace helped Cassidy with her coat, even though she was still trembling, before leaving his own nearby and following Cassidy up the stairs. They entered Jeanette's room, going slowly to the bed and saying her name.

"Jeanette?" Cassidy tried when Jeanette didn't hear Trace. She finally opened her eyes a bit.

"Cassie?"

"Right here."

"Trace?"

"I'm here," the man said.

Jeanette sighed.

"Just rest," Cassidy said.

Jeanette closed her eyes, and Cassidy turned away from the bed. Meg spoke to her in the hall, but she didn't answer. Meg would have gone after her, but Trace was there. He followed her down the stairs and into the small parlor, where he'd asked for her hand in marriage. He then watched the way she crowded as close to the fire as she could get.

"Why did I go to the jail?" she suddenly asked, her face telling how stricken she felt.

"I don't know," Trace had to admit. "It must have made sense to you at the time."

"Jeanette could have died, and I wouldn't have been here. I'm sorry, Trace. I'm so sorry."

Trace came close, and Cassidy clung to him, holding on for all she was worth. Trace didn't know when he'd felt so tired and cold, but it was a relief to touch this precious woman. Still managing to keep Cassidy close, he pulled the sofa closer to the fire and got blankets for both of them. Wrapped up but still shivering, they sat close to each other and the fire and tried to make sense of what had happened.

"Rylan?" Jeanette asked the person by the bed. She thought it might be Brad.

"He's here in the house somewhere. Do you want him?" Brad answered.

"Did he pray?" Jeanette asked.

"Yes. Just a little while ago. We weren't sure you were awake."

"Savanna?" Jeanette asked next.

"Meg is feeding her, and you need to stop taking care of everyone else."

Jeanette managed a smile, and Brad felt tears rush to his eyes. There was so much he would say if his throat would just work.

"I'll make it, honey," she said to him, her hand rising to take his.

Brad did nothing to stem the tears that slipped down his cheeks. This was the only mother he'd known for nearly ten years. Not having her in his life was not something he'd ever considered. Brad asked God to give them more time for the simple reason that he knew his heart needed her.

"How are you?" Cassidy asked after a long stretch of quiet in the small parlor, finally warm, some of the shock receding.

"Awful," Trace said. "My heart feels like lead in my chest."

"I'm sorry," Cassidy said. "I'm sorry I wasn't here with you."

"It's all right," Trace said, his hand gently touching her face before taking her hand again. "You were upset too."

Cassidy nodded, thankful for his understanding but wishing she'd been there.

"What do you want to say to Edson?"

Cassidy shook her head in wonder. " 'How much longer, Edson? How many more people need to be hurt or die so you can have money you didn't work for?' I want to hear from his lips why he thinks he has the right."

"I don't know if that's the best thing to do," Trace said. "But I don't think I have the energy to discuss it right now."

Cassidy nodded. She did want to discuss it, but it didn't matter when. Earlier, when she was so hurt and angry about what had happened, it made complete sense. But now she realized that she didn't have to have her say. She would ask Edson those questions if she had the chance, but if not, Edson still had to answer for his actions. He was grown up enough to ask those questions of himself and make changes if he so desired.

Cassidy was about to tell Trace what she'd decided when Rylan joined them.

"How are you?" he asked, taking a nearby chair.

"Just fair," Trace said honestly. "A lot is still a blur."

Rylan did not want to ask a lot of probing questions, even though many were on his mind. God had a plan for this day—Rylan was confident of that—but it didn't change the fact that part of the plan was trauma and heartache for some of his flock.

The three were talking quietly, not dwelling on any one topic overly long, when Becky arrived with a tray of food.

"Now, Becky," Rylan began. "You do not need to be waiting on us."

"Yes," she said quietly. "I think I do."

The three thanked her, not missing her red eyes or the slow, weary way she moved as she left them. No one would have said they were hungry, but the aromas coming from the assortment of dishes she had assembled smelled good. Rylan had a small plate of food and then went to find Brad and Meg. Rylan sat with Jeanette while the couple ate. Arrangements were made to have someone head to the ranch and see to the stock. The family had plans to stay very close to Jeanette.

***

"How long do I have to stay here?" Edson asked from his cell on Sunday morning. He well remembered the last time he'd been jailed and did not like it.

"That's hard to say," Sheriff Kaderly answered from the desk, not bothering to look at the other man.

"What happens next?" Edson asked, his memory failing over this part.

"I'm sure that depends on the condition of Jeanette Fulbright."

"Has anyone been in? Cassie?" Edson asked, sounding pathetic to the sheriff's ears and astounding the man when he didn't even ask about Jeanette's condition.

"She was here."

"When?"

"Yesterday."

"Is she going to get me out?"

"It doesn't work like that, Mr. Sinclair."

Edson had more questions, but Kaderly was done. He left while the prisoner was still speaking, wondering if the man had a lick of sense to his name.

⁂

"You didn't have a choice," Brad told Trace in plain terms. The men were alone for the first time.

"I hope you're right."

"I don't want you to trouble over that." Brad sounded firm.

Trace did not look convinced, but Brad was not done.

"I was on a walk early this morning and saw Sheriff Kaderly. He found two more knives on Neal. If you hadn't shot him, he could have used those on someone else—you or Cassie or someone right outside the shop who got in his way."

Trace's eyes closed at the thought, even though he hated thinking about what he'd done.

"I wish it had been me," Brad went on to say. "I wish I could take it for you."

Tears had come to the older brother's eyes, and seeing them, Trace felt his own fill his throat. Not many men were blessed with brothers like Brad Holden. It was not something he took for granted, and he was never gladder than now.

Trace could not speak—his throat would not work—but his nod told Brad he understood. Not five minutes later, Rylan was at the door, both men very glad to see him.

"Many of you have asked me what you can do," Rylan said from the pulpit after he'd explained what had happened the evening before. "Thank you for that. I was at the house this morning. Jeanette is resting comfortably. The bleeding has stopped, but it was significant. It will take some time for Jeanette to regain her strength, but at this time Doc Ertz believes she'll do well.

"Immediate needs include the ranch, since Brad and Trace are at the house for the rest of the day. Stock was seen to last night and this morning, but if someone could go tonight and tomorrow morning, that would be a help.

"I would not worry about meals right now. Becky likes to have something to do, and townsfolk were making deliveries when I left last night. Cassidy is not going to try to keep the shop open, but I have the key if someone would be willing to do some unpleasant cleanup."

It would have been impossible for Rylan to miss the tears in some folks' eyes, and he continued gently. "I was comforted by some verses from Psalm 119 this morning. And I would like to read them to you. 'This is my comfort in my affliction; for thy word hath quickened me. I remembered thy judgments of old, O LORD; and have comforted myself. Let, I pray thee, thy merciful kindness be for my comfort, according to thy word unto thy servant.'

"We can turn to God because we know He never changes. The comfort He has given His children for generations is still ours today. God does not protect us from every hurt that can befall man. Death and injury are with us always, but God's comfort is also there. As you pray for Jeanette and her family, ask God to help them remember His plan and His comfort. And that He is a God who saves again and again."

Rylan took time to pray and then had the other three elders come and pray as well. The service was dismissed early so folks could volunteer and get organized to help. Rylan planned to head to Jeanette's when everyone had cleared out. He was sure the family would benefit from knowing he had more offers for help than he could use.

"How are you?" Cassidy asked, sitting close to Jeanette's bed. For the time being, it was just the two of them.

"Tired," Jeanette answered, but there was a smile in her voice.

"It's nice that you have nothing to do," Cassidy teased gently.

"It's nice that you're not hurt. That's what scared me the most."

"Then we have something in common. I was terrified for you."

They looked at each other for a long time. It had been awful and would be awful in their minds for a long time, but it was over.

"I'm so glad you're going to be my girl," Jeanette said, her hand squeezing Cassidy's just a little. "You have been for a long time, but marrying Trace will make it official."

Cassidy smiled, not telling Jeanette that she had been thinking they might have to postpone the wedding. They couldn't get married without Jeanette. That wouldn't do at all.

Trace joined them just then, smiling when he saw Jeanette's eyes open. He leaned down and kissed her brow and stood close.

"I'm sorry you had to do that," Jeanette said. "I'm sorry, Trace."

Trace didn't try to answer. He was sorry too and would wonder for a long time if there was some other way he could have handled it. Jeanette was alive, though, and right now that's all the more his mind could take in.

In light of all that had happened, it was a ridiculous thing for

Trace to have on his mind, but he could not stop thinking about what he'd seen.

Jeanette was fairing well. Brad, Meg, Savanna, and Trace were back at the ranch, one of them coming in to check on her every day. Cassidy had been to see her brother, but when he showed no remorse, wanting only for her to find a lawyer who could get him out, she kept her words and time brief and left Edson Sinclair to his own thoughts.

And in the midst of all of this, Trace had to talk to Rylan. He actually had many questions for that man, but one in particular was weighing heavily.

"Trace," Rylan welcomed him almost a week after the incident. "Come on in."

"Thank you. Do you have a minute?"

"Yes. Have a seat."

The men sat in Rylan's parlor, and Trace wrestled with how to ask his question.

"What's up?" Rylan asked, seeing the other man hesitate for the first time.

"A lot of images keep running through my mind from last Saturday, some more disturbing than others."

"I can imagine."

"Has Chandler ever talked to you about any feelings he might have for Cassie?"

"What did you see?" Rylan asked, buying a bit of time. This was the last thing he'd expected.

"I can't quite describe it, but I think he might love her. I'm not questioning anything he did that day. He took care of her when I couldn't, but something in his face lingers in my mind—a yearning or longing when he told me she'd gone to the sheriff's office."

Rylan nodded. "Chandler has talked to me. He does feel like he loves Cassidy, but he knows he can't love another man's wife. He's working hard to keep his feelings in check."

"When did this all start?"

"He's cared for Cassidy in a special way for a long time, but for several reasons he's not acted on it. Then you made it clear how you felt, and he realized he waited too long. He's examined his heart, hoping it was more like competition than real feelings of love, but that's not what he's found."

Trace didn't know what to say. He was glad he knew but not sure what should happen next.

"How can he stay here?" Trace asked, thinking how hard it would be for him if the situation were reversed.

"I'm not sure he can. He's actually considered moving on."

Trace didn't want to lose his friendship with Chandler, but neither did he wish this on any man. He'd gone too many months loving Cassidy and not knowing where he stood. Chandler couldn't have Cassidy. At least Trace had been able to live with hope.

"Listen, Trace," the pastor said. "I can see you're bothered by this, but you shouldn't be. You didn't do anything wrong. If Cassidy had feelings for Chandler, she would not be marrying you. It's difficult for Chandler, but he's working hard in the midst of it."

"I don't want him to have to leave. He's a friend to both Cassidy and me, but if he's going to be miserable—" Trace cut off because Rylan was nodding in agreement.

The two talked for a bit longer, and Rylan was able to assure Trace that the situation was being handled. Then he asked his last question. "Will you tell Cassie?"

"No." Trace was sure about this. "She's too tenderhearted. It would bother her a great deal and make her uncomfortable around him. I don't think others know. I think for Chandler especially, that's best."

Rylan agreed. Trace thanked him and then made his way to Jeanette's. Once again, he told himself he was glad he knew, but it didn't make it a whole lot easier.

CHAPTER TWENTY-TWO

CASSIDY WOKE ON SATURDAY MORNING, glad that there was a sign on the shop door stating it was closed until further notice. She didn't want the business to die—she had finished and delivered everything that had been previously ordered—but she didn't have the energy to keep things going on a daily basis right now.

Her visit to Edson had been such a horrible disappointment. He was still thinking of no one but himself. A man was dead, but all her brother would talk about was wanting her to find him a good lawyer.

And then the questions had set in. The plaguing doubts about how she'd handled everything last Saturday. Should she have fought Edson or Neal? Might Neal still be alive if she had begun to fight her brother, or would Jeanette be dead right now because of it?

And the wedding. Should it be postponed? Trace had not said anything about that, but then they'd seen very little of each other all week. And when they were together, they hadn't spent the time talking about their lives. The events from last Saturday were still too fresh. Jeanette was not quite out of the woods, and Trace still had a ranch to run.

Cassidy slowly climbed from bed, working not to worry but failing as more and more thoughts crowded into her mind. She heated water for a bath, just wanting to talk with Trace and wondering when that was going to happen.

❦

"No sign of Cassidy?" Trace asked of Becky, whom he'd tracked down in the kitchen.

"Not yet. Shall I send her up when she arrives?"

"Actually, until my aunt and Heather are done, I'll be in the front parlor, but thank you, Becky," Trace said to the cook, wanting to talk with Cassidy while Jeanette was occupied.

Heather was helping Jeanette, who was moving very carefully, take a bath. Trace had not rushed into town, but he had hoped to talk to both Jeanette and Cassidy and felt let down when neither was available. He made himself comfortable in the front parlor, knowing he would hear the door.

He didn't have long to wait. Cassidy arrived about ten minutes later. Trace met her the moment she stepped inside, ready with a hug.

"Good morning." Cassidy greeted him warmly, returning the hug and sighing a little. "How are you?"

Trace stepped back without answering. "I'm fine," he said a bit slowly. "How are you?"

Cassidy noticed vaguely that his eyes searched her face, but she was more concerned with him than herself.

"Are you really fine?" Cassidy asked, not having registered Trace's question to her. "You must be getting worn out with this schedule."

"A little," Trace admitted, knowing that things were going to have to change. He sincerely hoped that Jeanette's bath meant she was well on her way to normal health because Cassidy Norton needed him. Meg Holden took care of him when she took care of her husband. No one looked after Cassidy but Cassidy. Jeanette and Meg certainly tried, but both of them were unavailable right now, and so was he. There were dark smudges under Cassidy's eyes, and she was thin, the thinnest Trace had ever seen her. Trace, however, opted, at least for the moment, to keep these thoughts to himself.

"How is Jeanette?" Cassidy asked next.

"She's having a bath, so I hope that's a good sign."

"So you haven't talked to her yet?"

"No. Heather will come for me as soon as she's done. Come here," Trace commanded, taking her hand. "Sit down and tell me about you."

"I think you know everything," Cassidy said, smiling at him at little.

"We just haven't had much time to talk," Trace offered, "and I'm wondering how you are."

"I keep worrying," Cassidy admitted but didn't elaborate.

"About what?"

"Everything." Cassidy said this and no more.

Trace worked to keep his own worry at bay. This answer concerned him. It wasn't like Cassidy. The woman who was usually so open with him was not talking.

"Do you want to tell me about it?" Trace tried.

"Oh, Trace," Cassidy began, her heart working to protect him. "It's just a lot of silly things. We don't have to get into anything right now."

"I'll tell you what," Trace decided quickly. "I'm going to run up and see how Jeanette and Heather are doing. I'll come back, and maybe then we'll have time to talk more."

Cassidy stayed where she was when he left, but not for long. A noise coming from the direction of the kitchen reminded her that Becky might be glad of some help.

"How are you?" Trace asked Jeanette. Heather had just tucked the covers back around her and gone to check on Theta. Jeanette's sister had done well during the ordeal, surprising everyone.

"Weary. Never has getting clean been such an effort."

"You didn't start bleeding again, did you?"

"No. The wound is in good shape. Doctor Ertz was here last night and gave me a good report."

"That's good news."

"I have to sleep now, Trace."

"Okay, but I need to tell you something. I'm getting Cassidy out to the ranch today and keeping her there for a while. Brad or I will try to come in tomorrow, but I've got to see to Cassie right now, and Meg thinks Savanna has a cold."

"Oh, my," Jeanette said, wanting to help in the worst way.

"We'll be all right. Will you be?"

"Yes, Trace," Jeanette murmured, her voice fading. "Go ahead. You know Rylan will come, and I've got Timothy and the girls."

Trace kissed her cheek before she completely drifted off, and then he slipped back out of the room. He didn't find Cassidy right away but eventually ran her to earth in the kitchen, her sleeves rolled up, working over some dough.

"How is she doing?" Cassidy asked, wiping her hands and getting ready to visit upstairs.

"She's doing well. The doctor was here last night and gave her a good report. The bath wore her out."

Cassidy headed out of the kitchen, but Trace caught her at the bottom of the stairs.

"You can certainly go and see her, Cass, but she's not going to wake up. She could barely stay awake to speak to me."

"Okay. I'll just run up and take a peek at her."

Trace trailed along, not impatient but ready to talk to Cassidy as soon as she had seen Jeanette. It didn't take long, but Cassidy was still full of surprises.

"Maybe I should sit with her today," Cassidy suggested once she and Trace were back in the hall.

"She's just going to sleep," Trace said. He had Cassidy's arm and was taking her toward the stairs. "And besides, we're running away to the ranch."

"We are?"

"Yes. I talked with Jeanette, and she knows that Brad or I will be back tomorrow."

"Where will I be?"

"At the ranch."

"What about Meg?"

"Savanna is sick. They'll be at the ranch too."

He had actually gotten her to the front door, her coat on, before she dug her heels in.

"What's going on?"

Trace put his hands on the sides of her face, framing it, his thumbs stroking softly across her cheek bones.

"You're tired and thin and taking care of everyone but yourself. I didn't see it until today. I can't do anything about the past, but today I can start to fix this. You're worried, and I suspect working too hard, and something is very wrong. I'm taking you away to the ranch so you can rest and we can talk. That's what's going on."

"Oh," Cassidy said, her voice so surprised and adorable that Trace had to chuckle. He also had to kiss her. It took a little longer than he planned to leave for the ranch.

⚜

"Out with it," Trace had said when the wagon was in motion.

He had gotten an earful. Cassidy had cried and said things almost before he could take them in. It had been painful to write to her mother. Did he want to postpone the wedding? All the customers' clothes were sewn and delivered, but that had meant seeing Hiram Brickel again when she delivered Halston's shirts, and she could tell that he wanted to ask her yet again to marry him. She was low on food but didn't have time to shop. She didn't know if she should visit Edson again. What if the shop didn't make it with this time of being closed? She couldn't possibly keep Jeanette's money, and that meant they could not build in the spring.

"Well, now," Trace said, almost wanting to laugh—not at Cassidy but at the amazing number of things she could keep going in her head. He knew that Meg was like that as well, and sometimes Brad got into trouble for not keeping things straight.

"What did that mean?" Cassidy asked, her voice telling Trace she was not ready to be laughed at and that he'd best do some back-tracking.

"Okay, Cass, we're going to take today to cover the whole list. We'll talk about all of it. Not all at one time—that would be too much—but we're getting everything sorted out today."

Cassidy still wasn't sure she wasn't being laughed at. She looked over at Trace, who looked back.

"Will that work?" he asked in complete sincerity.

"Yes," Cassidy said, relieved to see the caring in his eyes. "That will work."

It was quiet for a moment, and Cassidy wanted to let it go but didn't. She asked, "Did you want to laugh?"

"Not at you," Trace replied honestly. "Just at the size of the list. Meg thinks like that too, and it always astounds me."

Cassidy had to smile at his tone. She was feeling too tender right now for her own good, and maybe a little laughter at her myriad thoughts was just what she needed.

⚜

Savanna's breathing rattled as she lay on her father's chest. She slept easier upright than in the cradle. Brad was going to ride out on the range today, but even this hour spent holding Savanna would give Meg a chance to catch up.

Brad was content to sit with her, thinking about things and praying, but heard the wagon out front and went to the window. He wasn't expecting Trace back so soon, but took it as a good sign. And Cassidy was with him. Brad smiled. He was ready to have Cassidy with them on a permanent basis. The next two weeks could not come fast enough for him.

⁂

"Why were you thinking we should postpone the wedding?" Trace covered that question first. Meg was working in the kitchen, and Brad had headed out. Trace had taken his niece onto his chest, his deep voice as familiar and comforting to her as her father's.

"It's two weeks away, Trace. We can't get married without Jeanette."

Trace nodded. He'd thought of that but just assumed she'd be well enough to be with them. She might not feel like doing much, but he thought she would be there.

"You're not saying what you're thinking."

"I'm thinking you're right. We can't get married without her, but I assumed she'd be on her feet."

"And if she's not?"

"We'll postpone."

"How do I make that work?"

"I don't want to make it sound like your planning is not important, but because we've always planned to keep this simple, changes won't be that hard."

"So I should keep making our clothing and going ahead with everything that still needs to be done until when?"

"I don't have the answer to that, but we know this: We won't be able to have the reception at Jeanette's. I'm sure Becky will say she still wants to make the cakes, but we can just enjoy those right at the church. There isn't much room, but we can make it work."

"What about my mother? She'll be expecting us around the twenty-third."

"Can you write to her about what's happened and tell her it might change things? Will she understand?"

"She'll understand completely. I was just looking forward to seeing her."

Trace squeezed her hand. "I was too."

They were still talking about the wedding when Meg joined them. They filled her in on their latest thoughts, and she actually laughed before saying, "I would be very surprised if Jeanette allowed you to change a thing."

⚜

"You can't be serious," Jeanette said when Brad visited on Sunday after the service and told her all the latest. "They can't postpone the wedding. I'll be there, and I expect the reception to be here, just as we planned."

"Can we be logical about this?" Brad asked.

"All right," Jeanette agreed, still tired but ready to talk.

"The wedding is in thirteen days. You are clearly healing fast, but I don't even know if you'll be navigating the stairs in thirteen days."

"And that means Trace and Cassie can't get married?"

"That's right."

His matter-of-fact voice stopped her. Before she could speak again, Brad went on. "They will not and should not get married without you. Not to mention what you're asking Timothy, Heather, and Becky to do. Not only might you still need full-time care, my mother's needs are ongoing. And then they will have to ready the house, food, and dishes for a party."

"Oh, Brad," Jeanette whispered, thinking this would hurt more than her wound. "Please find a way. Please don't let them put this off."

"Trace will be here pretty soon," Brad said, not wanting to promise but wanting to give her hope. "We'll put our heads together and see what we can do."

Cassidy made her way down the stairs, still in her bathrobe, to find Meg in the kitchen.

"I didn't think Trace was serious about not waking me up."

"You were a tired girl."

"I missed the service."

"Trace will tell you all about it. Do you want some breakfast or just to wait until dinner?"

"Maybe I could have a piece of toast." Cassidy sat at the table. "How is Savanna?"

"She had a better night last night, and she just fell back to sleep."

Cassidy thanked Meg when she put a cup of coffee in front of her but realized something needed to be said.

"I let you wait on me way too much when I'm here. I'll be living here very shortly, and you can't keep doing that."

"You make it sound as though you sit around and do nothing, and that's not true. I'm not the least worried about your taking advantage in any way, Cassie. We work well together, and the arrangement is temporary. We'll make it work just fine."

Cassidy nodded, thinking about the long discussion the four of them had had around the supper table the night before. She would feel terrible if the business fell through at this point, but the men knew their aunt well. Jeanette Fulbright would never return the money, even if it meant she took a loss.

"And besides," Meg continued, "both of us usually have much more energy. This house will probably be the cleanest it's ever been, the meals will seem like child's play with another pair of hands, and even with your clothing added in, laundry will never have been so easy."

Cassidy had to laugh. Meg was probably right, and even if it didn't turn out to be so rosy, Cassidy was looking forward to every minute. She took a sip of coffee and noticed one of the men had laid his chaps on a chair by the back door.

"Tell me something, Meg," Cassidy said, her voice thoughtful. "Do you like the way Brad looks when he goes out for work?"

"In his hat, you mean?"

"And chaps."

Meg had no choice but to smile when she asked, "I take it you like the way Trace looks in chaps?"

"Oh, my," was all Cassidy could manage, thinking her future husband the most handsome man alive. Meg would have argued the issue, choosing Brad's looks over his brother's, but considering how much the men looked alike, there would have been little point.

⁂

"Chandler came to me this morning," Rylan told Trace, Chandler also standing with them, "wanting to talk to you. I told him we had talked."

"This was never the plan," Chandler said when Trace's eyes swung his way. "I'm sorry."

"I don't think you have anything to apologize for, Chandler. I just hate to think of how the future will be for you."

"That's why I'm leaving Token Creek. I'm going to visit my family, and if I can find work, I'll come back and gather my things." He smiled just a little before adding, "I might come back and gather my things anyway."

Trace looked as pained as he felt, but he also could not think of any other way.

"When do you go?" Rylan asked.

"November nineteenth," Chandler said, and again Trace felt an ache inside. That was the day before the wedding. He knew it was for the best, but it didn't make it any easier. Trace put his hand out, and Chandler gripped it. Neither man could find words. Trace went on his way a moment later. Rylan, not wanting Chandler to be alone, invited him for more leftovers.

⚜

Trace, Brad, and Jeanette were still discussing their options when they found they were not alone. Becky and Heather had come to the door, neither looking too happy.

"Is something wrong?" Jeanette asked. She was growing weary but would not rest until the wedding day was settled.

"That's what we want to know," Heather started. "You're trying to move the reception to the hotel. We heard you."

"It's for your sakes," Brad started, but Becky, in an uncharacteristic move, put her hand up, and he stopped.

"We'll all be tired," the cook stated firmly. "It will be extra work, but that doesn't mean we don't want to do it. Jeanette has already asked two other women to help serve. We'll just have them come earlier and stay later. If they can't come, we'll find others."

"What about Jeanette?" Trace had to ask. "I'm not getting married if she can't be at the church."

"She will be," Heather spoke confidently, "and if she can't be on the day you've planned, then you can change the day, but the reception still stays here."

The brothers looked at Jeanette, but she only smiled and said, "The town thinks I'm a genius in business matters and time management. They don't know about these two."

Becky and Heather walked away, wide smiles on their faces, to the sound of Trace's and Brad's laughter.

⚜

Chas and Brad were in charge of Jeanette, getting her safely and comfortably to the church and into a front pew. Rylan was in charge of Trace, who woke up the morning of the twentieth so nervous he couldn't think straight. Miranda and Meg were seeing to Cassidy, who was remarkably calm.

Jeb would walk Cassidy down the aisle; Brad would stand with his brother; Meg would stand with her new sister-in-law; and Patience would see to Savanna, who was long over her cold.

Everything was in place at Jeanette's. Becky had done a great job, getting as much help as she and Heather needed, and the house was sparkling clean, the cakes perfect and ready to be enjoyed.

"Are you going to make it?" Rylan asked Trace, who had bathed and dressed in his new black suit at the parsonage.

"I think so. Why am I so nervous?"

"There's been a lot going on, and this day was touch-and-go until the middle of the week."

Trace nodded, thankful for Rylan's friendship. He needed his calm right now.

"Is it time yet?"

"Close enough. I think we could go to the church if you want."

Trace nodded, and Rylan laughed at him a little. Trace joined him, his heart easing a bit. He was going to be married today. The details didn't really matter.

⚜

"You look beautiful," Jeb told Cassidy, whose wedding dress was a dark blue, as he kissed her flushed cheek. "But then that's nothing new."

"Oh, Jeb," Cassidy smiled at him. "Thank you for being here."

"I wouldn't miss it for the world."

The two hugged before Cassidy asked, "How is Jeanette doing?"

"Just fine. She's sitting comfortably in a front pew, and it's almost time for us to make our entrance."

Cassidy laughed at his tone and face, and that was about all she had time for. The music was starting, and someone she loved was waiting for her.

"Ready?" Trace asked his bride.

"Very," Cassidy answered, settled on the buggy seat, blankets all around them.

The newly wed Mr. and Mrs. Holden had just laughed and visited for hours at Jeanette's house. The wedding and reception had been perfect, filled with precious friends, good wishes, and wonderful dessert. Trace had rented a buggy to make the trip to the ranch house. Brad and family would be staying over at Jeanette's. And now it was time to go.

The buggy set off, and for the first few minutes the couple was quiet. Cassidy thought about this night, wishing she could have talked with her mother or even questioned Meg a little more.

"Are you all right?" Trace asked, feeling her tensing up beside him.

"I think so. It's a silly time to admit this, but I don't know what I'm doing."

"We'll figure it out." Trace's voice was gentle, his head turned to catch her eyes. "The act isn't the important part—our relationship is."

"Oh, that was good. I need to think about that."

"Brad shared that with me just this week."

Cassidy sighed with contentment, all tension leaving her, and cuddled closer to her husband. Trace had been nervous about the wedding, and Cassidy worried over the wedding night, but everything was going to be fine.

The train pulled into the station at Billings, running a little behind schedule. Cassidy's eyes searched everything, not looking for her mother but taking in the sights of home. She disembarked, Trace and their bags right behind her, and then took her husband's arm.

"It's not far," she said.

"Excited?"

"Yes, and afraid I'm going to sob all over her."

"I think you've earned it," Trace said, and Cassidy went up on her toes to kiss his cheek before they started down the street.

Trace saw in a hurry that Cassidy was right. Just three short blocks from the train station, she stopped and stared at a compact house, neat but in need of some repair. Tears had already come to her eyes, and that was before the door opened. Suddenly a woman was running down the steps and toward them, an older version of Cassidy. A moment later her arms were holding her daughter tight.

"Oh, Cassie, my Cassie" was all Rhonda Sinclair could say. "My sweet, sweet Cassie."

"I missed you, Mama," Cassidy said, her voice thick with tears.

The two didn't break apart for several minutes, and when they did, Rhonda swiftly used her apron to dry her eyes.

"Look at me," she fussed, "having to meet my new son with a wet face."

"Mama," Cassidy announced, performing the honors, "this is Trace."

Trace had removed his hat and now bent to kiss his mother-in-law's cheek. Rhonda put her arms around him, and Trace returned the hug.

"Welcome to Billings, Trace."

"Thank you, Mrs. Sinclair. It's very good to meet you."

Rhonda studied him, thinking him handsome, certainly, but also liking his eyes. They were honest and forthright. She knew that if this man said he loved her daughter, it would be true.

"Come in," Rhonda invited. "Come in and make yourself at home."

Rhonda led the way as Cassidy slipped her arm back through her husband's.

"Thank you, Trace," Cassidy whispered. "Thank you for bringing me home."

Trace didn't answer but smiled into the eyes that looked into his so trustingly. Not for the first time Trace was convinced he'd married the sweetest woman in the world. And having her smile at him with all the trust of a child was all the thanks he ever needed.

Spring 1881

"WHERE ARE WE GOING?" Cassidy asked again, but Trace still would not tell her.

"Okay. Now right here," Trace told his blindfolded wife, "the ground dips down a little. Don't fall."

"Trace," Cassidy said on a laugh, "if you'll just tell me..."

"Soon," Trace said, "very soon."

Cassidy continued to walk with him, her hands held in both of his, not able to see a thing and completely disoriented. Trace had taken her around the house once and even around the barn until she was totally turned around in her mind.

"Okay," he said, sounding like a kid on Christmas morning. "We're almost there."

"Almost where?"

"Step up," Trace ordered, having stopped her with her toes against a board.

"Is it the house?" Cassidy asked, doing as she was told.

"Go on now," Trace ordered, keeping her moving. Not until she had both feet where he wanted them did his kerchief come off of her eyes.

"Oh, Trace!" Cassidy said, throwing her arms around him. She was standing on the far side of their new house. She had not asked for a big porch, but he'd given her one that covered two sides of the house. The far side was finished first and he'd been able to surprise her.

"You like it?"

Cassidy kissed him—then kissed him again, long and hard.

"Well, now," Trace said, his hands already reaching for her hair. "I'll take that as a yes." They kissed for a while, not noticing the cool spring temperatures or the cold wind that blew over them, before Cassidy began to look around.

"Two sides! I didn't know the porch would be on two sides."

"And right here," Trace directed her, "is another door into the living room."

Cassidy did not know how he'd hidden this extra door from her.

They had also planned on and built an extra bedroom with Rhonda Sinclair in mind. Edson was going to be in prison for a long time, and they wanted Cassidy's mother to have a place to live when she couldn't, or no longer wanted to, be on her own.

"How much longer before we can move in?" Cassidy asked, her eyes sparkling with excitement, her arms back around Trace's neck.

"I'd have to check with Chas to be certain. I'd guess a month, maybe a little less."

"I can hardly wait."

"Cass," Trace said, suddenly serious. "Let's commit to hospitality from the first moment. Let's share our home with others, so we never forget Who gave it to us."

"What a wonderful thing to remember right now," Cassidy said, "before we even move in."

"And to keep remembering for as long as we live in this house."

They stood for a long time in the living room, making plans

and talking about their dreams. They made a mental list of those they would invite over and ran out of time before it was finished. Cassidy needed to start supper soon, and Trace had chores in the barn. Not that it mattered. Their hearts were in the right place, in love with each other and not forgetting to honor God with what He had given them.

Walking back toward the house, Cassidy thought the only missing part was a baby, and that little person would arrive before the year was out. Meg was due again, and even though Cassidy hadn't told anyone, she was fairly certain she was expecting as well. A smile lit her face as she slipped through the kitchen door, looking forward to when and where she would tell Trace he was going to be a father.

READING GROUP QUESTIONS

1. Abi says she never read the Bible because "it's an old book, and I like new ones." Pastor Jarvik answers that "it's an old book, but not just any old book." What would you say to someone who feels the way Abi does about the Bible?

2. The love of members of the church family for one another plays a significant part in *Cassidy*. What examples of this speak most clearly?

3. Cassidy doesn't at first understand that losing her business doesn't automatically mean she'll have to leave Token Creek or lose relationship with her church. Is it possible to be honest about our pasts with each other today?

4. As a single woman with a business in a rough Montana environment, how does Cassidy deal with her own fears and struggles?

5. Was it a surprise when Edson and Neal returned to Token Creek? Could Cassidy have handled the situation differently? How?

6. Meg is happy that Brad will be home soon after the cattle

drive, but Cassidy is hurting because of her business, so Meg doesn't share her happiness. Should Meg have shared her happiness?

7. What course of action does Chandler take when he realizes he still has feelings for Cassidy? Was leaving town the answer? How do you think it would have affected Cassidy had she known what Chandler was feeling?

8. Sometimes we have to love people in spite of themselves. Abi's lack of social graces make it hard for people to embrace her, but Pastor Jarvik does. How would you have talked to her?

9. Theta Holden, Trace and Brad's mom, is largely unresponsive. Where does a person's value lie? What do the people around Theta learn from her?

10. How did Trace and Brad overcome a traumatic childhood?

11. Pastor Jarvik worked in the livery. The apostle Paul made tents. What strengths can pastors or elders draw from working outside the church?